AUTOBIOGRAPHY OF A BABY KILLER

DENNIS ELLEFLOT

Inquiries and Book Orders should be addressed to:

Great Writers Media
Email: info@greatwritersmedia.com
Phone: 877-600-5469

ISBN: 978-1-960605-72-6 (sc)
ISBN: 978-1-960605-74-0 (hc)
ISBN: 978-1-960605-73-3 (ebk)

Contents

I

"Hell, man, I know very well you didn't come to me only to want to become a writer, and after all what do I really know about it except you've got to stick to it with the energy of a benny addict."

—Jack Kerouac

I am the bastard son of Dorothy Goldman. I know nothing of my father. My earliest recollections are of living with an elderly black woman named Missus Miller and her adult son, Bill, on the bottom floor of their boarding house. Early each morning, while I slept comfortable in the big bed beside her, Bill rose and lit a fire in a cooking stove that dominated one wall of the kitchen. When the fire burned well, Missus Miller rose and woke me. I dressed and followed her to watch while she began her daily routine of cooking eggs, grits, toast, and coffee for all who lived there. When I grew bored, I'd go outside to the shed where Bill cut wood to keep the fire alive, and sit on the packed dirt floor waiting for him to tell a story. He'd put a large piece on the chopping block, snorted as he swung the ax, and continued to split it till the pieces would fit in the stove's firebox — with a final swing he buried the ax in the chopping block.

One morning, he says to me, "How ya doin', boy?"

"I'm hungry."

"Don' worry, we git our faces fed shortly." He squatted beside me, started a story, one I had heard before, but that didn't matter. "Picked cotton 'longside my folks soon'z I wuz big 'nough. Poo' Daddy, he pass young. Momma sez he work hisself ta death. Afta Daddy wuz laid ta rest, Momma sez, 'Livin' here ain't no kinda life.' Sez, 'I got a bit a money squirreled 'way. 'Nough fer a couple train fares 'cross da

1

country. We goin' west ta live wid Auntie Moe.' Gran' ol' lady Auntie Moe wuz. Live all by her self in dis place. When she pass, it come ta Momma. Dats how we come ta be here."

The backdoor screen squawked; Missus Miller called. "Come in da two a ya. Folks is waitin'—food gettin' cold."

We walked into a dining room filled with coffee smells. Six women sat around the table. After we sat, heads bowed for a quick mumbled Grace, and platters of food passed hand to hand.

Meal finished, women stayed a bit to yack about this and that while Missus Miller cleared the table. Bill and I went to the front porch, sat on the top step. He took fixings from his shirt pocket, rolled a cigarette, smoked it down to a nub.

I exhaled a sigh. He gave me a long look. "Ya troubled, boy?"

"Just wondering about my momma."

"She a busy womin fixin' up all dem hurt soljers."

I shook my head, concentrated on the sidewalk.

He put his hand on my shoulder. "Come on, boy. Let's take us a walk ta da park."

* * * * *

Two granite lions guarded the park's entrance. I scrambled onto the back of one, held tight the imaginary reins, rode it like a bucking bronco. "Whoopee. Whoopee." When I tired of it, Bill lifted me down. I stood in front of them, cracked my whip, became Clyde Beattie, World Famous Wild Animal Trainer. Bill laughed, took my hand, led me into the park. "Go on, boy. Have yoself some fun."

An older boy hung upside down by his knees on the monkey bars. I ran to them, climbed higher than I ever climbed before, looked down, got chills in my spine, sat on a bar, swung my legs hard, hung on tight, leaned back far back as I could stretch, felt danger, breathtaking danger, righted myself.

The boy climbed over to where I sat. "Whatch your name?"

"Thomas."

"Whatcha doin' here with that old nigger man?"

"Huh?"

He pointed toward Bill. "That old nigger man you came with."

"Bill?"

"That his name?"

"Yep."

"Your folks hire him to take care of you?"

"Don't know."

"Don't know? Whacha mean don't know?"

"I live with him and Missus Miller."

"She a nigger too?"

"What's a nigger?"

He laughed. "You don't know what a nigger is?"

"Nope."

"Look at his skin. Blacker than sin."

"So?"

"Makes him a nigger. You part nigger?"

I looked at my hands. "Don't think so."

"Why you live with 'em?"

"I guess because my momma's busy fixin' hurt soldiers."

"Boy—you're a special case."

"What's that?"

"Think you might be part nigger and don't know it. Can't be around you if you are."

"Why not?"

"'Cause my folks said so." He moved away, hung again by his knees.

Confused, I climbed down, walked over to Bill; hugged his legs. "Whuz a matter, boy? He say somethin' ta spoil ya fun?"

"He said you're a nigger."

He laughed. "A nigger, ya say."

"Uh-huh. Said I was part nigger because I live with you."

He laughed again. "Hell boy, ain' no bad thing if ya wuz, but ya ain't. Ya be lily white. Some folk jus' talk that a way. Seems dey got nothin' betta on dey minds. Don' know why. Maybe dey jus' ignorant. Life's too short to be worryin' 'bout such things. Come on, les's get on home. Soon be time fer lunch an' I'm gettin' hongry."

He scooped me up. Held me tight. As he walked I snuggled my face into his chest, listened to the raspy sound of his breathing, soon, fell to sleep.

* * * *

The last meal of the day finished. Missus Miller brought out coffee and pastry. We moved to the living room, sat on heavy horsehair stuffed davenports, listened to the Philco console radio as it played a transcribed program brought all the way to the west coast from New York City. It begin with the announcer saying:

"Ladies and gentlemen—from the Crystal Ball Room high atop the Winslow Hotel in the heart of beautiful downtown Manhattan— for your listening and dancing pleasure—it's Benny Goodman— THE KING OF SWING."

A sudden clarinet trilled against the background of a band. It swayed and swung and demanded action. Two women stood and began to dance; skirts swished as they showed off their steps. One grabbed my hand, pulled me up to join them. I tried hard to bounce my feet the way they did. Everybody laughed and clapped. Soon, my legs grew heavy, they squeezed me in tight hugs, gave me kisses, sat me down to another round of applause.

An announcer's voice interrupted the music with a jarring news flash:

"Earlier today, the most powerful bomb ever devised by man was dropped on the Japanese city of Hiroshima. Developed at the top-secret base in Alamogordo, New Mexico, it is called the Atom Bomb. Reports say the entire city was destroyed. The death count is astronomical. The end of the Pacific War may soon be at hand...."— and so on, and so forth.

Everybody sat in stony silence. Benny Goodman resumed and played on and on, but nobody heard. Silence broke. An orgy of talk began. Missus Miller picked me up carried me to the bedroom. "Time fer grownups ta talk 'bout things ya don' unnerstand, darlin'. Jus' git yerself comfortable. I'll be back when we done." As I lay in bed, she sat a moment petting my head. "Hope ya neva got ta fight no damn war, son. Hope ya never got ta." She kissed me on the cheek, left the room. I lay awake trying to make sense of words spoken just beyond the door, couldn't. After a time, boredom forced sleep upon me.

* * * * *

The iceman lugged in a block of ice, put it inside the bottom of the brass bound icebox. Spring had come. Missus Miller could no longer put perishables outside on the windowsill to keep. When he left, she brought out the laundry tub; sat it in the middle of the kitchen floor, filled it with warm water. I stripped off my clothes, got in and squirmed with pleasure as she scrubbed me pink from head to toe. Wrapped in a towel I ran to the bedroom, put on clean clothes, followed Bill to the woodshed, stood on my tiptoes to watch him sharpen his saw with a small triangular file.

Missus Miller's voice called from the back porch. "Son, yo momma here."

I folded my arms across my chest. Bill stopped working, wiped the back of a hand across his forehead. "Whuz up, boy?"

I shook my head.

He furled his brows. "Don' wan' ta see 'er?"

I shook my head again.

"Ya got ta, boy."

"No I don't. I can hide."

"Why ya wan' ta hide from yo momma?"

"'Cause I hate her."

Bill dropped to his hams, looked me eye to eye. I flushed—turned away. "She yo mama, boy. Ya got ta go ta 'er." He laid a hand atop my head. The solid weight of it felt good. I drew breath—let it out slow; saw sadness in his eyes. Why sadness, I wondered. He picked me up, held me tight. "Ya gotta go, boy. It be time an' ya jus' gotta go." He sighed, sat down on the chopping block, held me another minute, put me down, gave me an easy push away. "Git on in. Time ta be wit' yo momma." I left the woodshed, turned back as I climbed the porch steps, Bill sat, head hung as if burdened by some great weight.

In the living room, Mom stood beside a stranger—a man. She came to me, reached down to hug me, I pulled away. She came again, I twisted, met her with a shoulder, she bent and hugged me in an awkward way, pointed toward the man. "This is your new father."

I looked at the man with dislike, noticed his left arm ended just below the elbow in a shiny pucker of reddish skin. He rubbed it, gave a weak smile. It didn't placate me. He came close; I kicked at his leg. He moved aside, made me miss.

"Don't like him."

"You don't know him," said Mom. "With time you will."

"Nope. I won't." I glared. "I hate him."

He stood silent, looking somewhere past me, or perhaps through me.

"We have to get your belongings packed up so we can go." She moved to hurry things along.

"Go where?"

"To our new home."

"Away from here?"

"Yes."

"Nope."

"It's not up to you."

"But I live here."

"No, you don't live here. You only stayed here because I was busy with work and had no time for you."

Everything felt wrong. I needed Missus Miller's help. She stood at the far side of the room, head hanging, same as Bill's. I wanted her to protect me, to say: 'He's my son. You can't take my son.' She didn't.

Mom tried to hug me again. I broke away, ran to the bedroom, slammed the door, threw myself on the bed, burrowed into the blankets. "I won't go. I won't go. I won't go."

Missus Miller came in; sat beside me. "Come on, son. We jus' got ta git through it."

Enraged, I thrashed on the bed, twisted blankets, threw pillows against the wall, screamed till I grew horse. Why? Why? And I knew—I knew. Missus Miller knew. Bill knew. I hated them for knowing. I felt weak, sodden. Missus Miller lay down beside me, stroked my hair, whispered into my ear. "Goin' ta be fine, baby boy. Goin' ta be jus' fine." Her words relaxed me almost to the point of sleep. She sat me up. "We gots ta be strong, son. Both us jus' gots ta be strong."

All my belongings fit in a small pasteboard box. The man carried it under his good arm as we climbed down the steps. Mom tried to take my hand, I jerked away, counted the steps the way Bill taught me—one to nine. I always counted aloud with him. Did it in secret. Where was he? Why didn't he come? Didn't he like me anymore?

I fought tears. Felt an eerie feeling. It was as if I were not longer part of my body. I floated above it, watched Mom lifted the empty shell of me into the back seat of an old car and sat it down beside the pasteboard box. A steady drizzle fell. I rejoined myself, sat frozen; a painful constriction seized my throat, I couldn't swallow, my shoulders heaved, no tears came. Told myself, 'It's just a dream,' held onto that thought tight as I could. In spite of my effort to freeze time, the car's engine clattered to life, moved out onto the street—and everything—every important thing in my life disappeared in a cloud of blue exhaust smoke.

* * * * *

The car rode bumpy, tires chattered on uneven wood planks of a dock, brakes shrieked as the man stopped it behind a line of car and turned off the engine. Mom exchanged words with him; he looked straight ahead while she sat cocked, looking into his ear as if studying its convolutions. I made no effort to understand.

A huge boat bearing cars approached, bounced heavy against the dock end, jarred my head this way and that. Never having seen anything like it, curiosity mitigated my despair. We sat waiting till the last car drove off the boat. He clattered the car engine to life. It chugged with insistence as he moved it along the dock onto the boat.

I saw huge water—water so wide it seemed endless. It amplified my smallness, my unimportance; I nodded my head, acknowledged its greatness. Feeling returned; it started at the toes, crept up my body in silence. I inhaled normal breathes, sank back into the hard springs of the seat, felt strength; knew I would survive.

Crossing the water, noise from the boat's engine overpowered everything. That eased me more. The boat bounced its way into the sheltering arms of a similar dock on the other side of the water. We left with a clatter, again to move over uneven wood planks and onto a narrow paved road that curved through dense copses of evergreens and maples reminiscent of those in the park where Bill took me to play. Houses, spaced far apart, were set back from the road. Some had fenced fields where animals roamed. Others had large lawns and big flowerbeds. I pressed my forehead hard against the vibrating window as we passed berry fields where people worked in the drizzle. Dogs ran loose. One chased the car, growling—snapping at the spinning wheels. We crossed over a complaining wood bridge that spanned high above the delta of a wide creek; the hurky-jerky engine clacked my teeth as it pulled the car along at a faster pace. After a quarter hour we turned off the paved road onto a graveled one that climbed a steep hill. After a hard right turn near the top, the man pointed off through the wheezy sweep of windshield wipers. "There she is; the old homestead."

* * * * *

The kitchen smelled of fresh paint. Mom stood behind me. I allowed her to rest a hand on my shoulder. The man popped a stick match to life with his thumbnail; lit fire to wood already laid out in the stove. I sat down on one of four mismatched chairs at a large table, listened to cedar kindling crackle. Soon, beginnings of warmth radiated into the room.

"This is your new home, Thomas," said Mom.

I shook my head—said nothing,

"Come on, let's have a look at your bedroom." She led me from the kitchen, up twelve steps. At the top, three doors flanked a short hallway. She pointed to the one behind. "That's an unfinished bedroom." Opened the one on the left. "It's a storage room." I peered into its semi-darkness; dusty boxes and framed pictures were stacked on the floor in haphazard fashion. To the right, we entered a rectangular room with a smooth, unpainted plank floor. Two walls followed the steep slope of the roof to its peak, at the far wall; a naked brick chimney, flanked by two windows, rose through the floor and passed on. She put her hand against the chimney, gestured to me. "Here, touch it."

I did, felt warmth.

"It's heat from the stove downstairs. It'll keep your room toasty on cold nights." She sat on the bed, beckoned me. "See? It's a very nice room. You even have your own desk and reading lamp. You can keep all your toys here and play when the weather's bad."

"Do I have to sleep alone?"

"Yes."

"But I don't want to."

"Sweetheart, you're not a baby anymore. You have to start acting like a big boy."

"I don't want to be here. I hate it."

"You'll get used to it."

"Why do I have to get used to it? Why can't I go back to Missus Miller's?"

"Because you live here now."

"Hu-uh."

"Well, you do, and that's all there is to it."

I punched the bed, took a deep breath, punched it several more times.

"You stay here until you settle down. I have things to do."

She left the room. I heard her downstairs speaking to the man. I couldn't make out the words but heard a sigh of resignation in her voice. I felt victorious. Not wanting to waste time, I went down to the kitchen. She stood at the stove cooking.

"When am I going back?"

"We already talked about that. This is your new home. This is where we all live."

"I can't live here."

"You have to. You have no choice."

"I don't like it."

"You'll get used to it."

"You keep saying that, but I won't. I want to be with Missus Miller and Bill."

"Give it some time."

"I hate it here."

At mealtime, I refused to eat though my stomach churned with hunger. The man looked at me, shook his head. "Let him go without if that's what he wants."

"He has to eat something, Stosh."

"Nobody starves to death between supper and breakfast."

Thinking I had won, I stood intending to stomp away. He smacked the table with the flat of his hand. Mom flinched. So did I. "Where do you think you're going, Mister? Sit your butt down until the meal's done."

I sat down hard, stared at my knees, wished I were big enough to punch him, to destroy everything around me. Rage made my skin feel hot. He continued to eat as though nothing had happened. The smell of food knotted my stomach. I wanted it bad. Too late.

The meal finished; Mom led me upstairs, I didn't count the steps. "Are you sure about this? Are you sure you don't want to eat?"

I didn't answer. She tried to embrace me. I pulled away; flung myself on the bed. With a shrug she left. I lay awhile with no thoughts, got up, knelt beside the bed, recited the prayer Missus Miller taught me. Halfway through I choked up and couldn't finish. I curled in a tight ball on the floor, began a low mourning wail pining for Missus Miller, for the faint smell of lilac she carried, for the sound of her breathing as she slept beside me. A hard rain began to fall. It drummed the roof above my head in ferocious ways. I fell into imaginings hidden in the darkness of terrible hooded men, dangerous slinking shadows that moved like whispers, searching, probing the room, feeling their way toward me. Closer—closer they came. I quivered, disappeared somewhere in the depth of that dream.

* * * * *

Bright sunlight spilled into the room. It baffled me till I heard voices from below. I pulled blankets from the bed, wrapped them tight over my head, vowed to stay in that spot till they let me go back. Footfalls sounded, the door opened, blankets were tugged away. Mom smiled. "Come on. Breakfast is getting cold."

Driven by hunger, I forgot my vow and followed her to the kitchen. The man sat reading a newspaper. An awkward looking metal hook extended from his truncated arm; I couldn't look away from it; was he a pirate? When he moved his shoulders a certain way the hook opened into two curved fingers that clinked against his coffee mug as he picked it up. He looked at me, gave a smile. "You must be hungry." I turned away.

Mom sat me in the chair opposite him, dished up fried eggs and potatoes from a platter at the center of the table.

"Dig in," he said.

I tested the eggs with my fork. "Don't like them. They're gushy in the middle."

He looked over the paper. "Eat up. They'll grow hair on your chest."

It made me want to laugh. Had an uncomfortable thought, what if I liked him a little? Would it mean I had to stop liking Bill? What if I started liking Mom? Aloofness crumbled. I wolfed down the food, wiped my mouth with the back of a hand.

He smiled. "Good stuff, huh?"

"Guess so."

He finished reading the paper, put it aside, dawdled over his coffee, sighed, stood, gave Mom a solid kiss on the mouth and left. In spite of not wanting to like him, I did—just a bit.

"Where'd he go?"

"To work."

"Work?"

"To earn money so we have food on the table."

"Nobody went to work at Missus Miller's."

"They did, but in a different way."

"How's he work?"

"He works with a friend named Inky. They fix broken things."

"What things?"

"Things for boats."

"What kind of boats?"

"All kinds."

"Oh."

* * * * *

Grease smeared his right hand and forearm. He slipped off his shirt; hung it on a chair. Mom unbuckled the harness strapped around his chest and shoulders; laid it to the side so cables wouldn't tangle.

I wondered if he was part robot.

She pulled the hook assemblage off his truncated arm. He heaved a sigh. "Gawd, wearing that thing's damn near unbearable." At the sink, she helped him scrub clean. "Thomas," he said, "how about you and me walk down to the shop after we finish up lunch?"

I looked at Mom for the answer. "Go ahead. It's an interesting place."

* * * * *

We walked side by side down the graveled road. I kicked a stone. It skipped and ricocheted down the hill. Liking it, I tried again—missed. He laughed, kicked one himself. "Ain't done that in a while."

Near the bottom of the hill sat a one-engine firehouse with a huge siren atop a high pole. At the bottom, the road we walked butted against the blacktopped highway. Houses sat clustered around a building with a narrow sign atop its crenelated false front. Dad read the words aloud for me. "Harbor Merchantile. You can buy all kinds a stuff there if you got the mullah."

"What's mullah?"

"Money."

"Oh."

Five minutes more took us to the shop. The door complained as Dad opened it, machinery and workbenches filled its interior. A large window built from many panes of wavy glass covered most of the far wall and looked out over a harbor. A half dozen kitchen chairs lined the near wall. A man stood filing something shiny. Maybe he's sharpening it, I thought.

He wore a buttoned-up shirt and denim trousers slung low under a bowling-ball belly. Seeing me, he smiled, put down the file, wiped his hand with a rag, stuck it out to me to shake. "Welcome, kiddo. Been dying to meet you." He picked me up, stood me on a chair, gave me the once over. I did the same. Found his face, with its easy smile and pencil line mustache, pleasant. Liked the deep mellow sound of his voice. "Call me Inky. Your old man and me, we're a couple square heads. Come all the way from Norway with our folks when we was tads."

Wanted to ask what that meant, didn't.

He continued. "We fix boat stuff here." He lifted me down, took my hand, led me to the window, pointed out through the glass. "See them boats?" Beyond a short dock several swung at anchor. "Them's working boats. During the season they go up north to fish for crab and salmon. Sometimes stuff breaks, some of it you can't buy in a store no more, so they bring it here and we make it like brand new. Fix most anything made of metal. They bring it in, take a sit and chew the fat whilst we do the fixing."

He started to tap out a cigarette, noticed the pack empty, crumpled it, tossed it on the floor amidst piles of metal shavings. "Bought this place for a song when we come back from the war. Old man Bolin owned it. Spent most of his time bitching and moaning about wanting to retire. Jumped when me and your old man offered up cash." He looked at my new dad. "Been good partners ever since, ain't we, Stosh?"

"Good as gold."

Dad picked up a can of tuna fish, pinched it with his split hook, sawed the top open with a jackknife, sat it on the floor. A four-color-good-luck calico cat scooted out from under a Franklin stove, scarfed it down and bolted back to safety so quick I thought my eyes had tricked me.

The door squawked open. A thin man with stooped shoulders came in. Dad greeted him with throaty sounds I didn't understand. He responded in the same, took a seat. All three of them started making similar noises. The door opened again, two more men came in, twins, fair-haired with pale complexions. Soon they were all making noise and laughing.

Dad put his hand on my shoulder. "This is my son, Thomas."

I felt a swell in the pit of my stomach as each of them shook my hand.

One of the twins looked me over. "You speak the lingo?"

"What's lingo?"

"Language."

"I can talk."

"Yeah, but you got to learn the lingo."

I shook my head, still not understanding. Inky smiled. "Don't worry. Won't take no time 'tall."

"Think you can find your way back up the hill?" said Dad.

"Think so."

Inky dug a nickel from his pocket. "Here kiddo. Don't spend it all in one place."

I walked toward Harbor Merchantile, nickel hot in my pocket, strained to open the door, as it did, a small bell ting-a-linged, walked between selves filled with stuff I'd never seen before. Behind the front counter, a man wearing a shopkeeper's apron and a green-billed eyeshade tallied purchases with pencil and paper and rang them up on a huge brass bound cash register. He saw me idling, tossed a piece of bubble gum my way. "Scram kid, unless you've got business." I scooted out clutching the nickel. Tried kicking rocks as I walked up the hill, didn't work. When I opened the door, Mom said, "What did you think?"

"Pretty neat I guess, but everybody talks funny."

"They were speaking Norwegian."

"Oh, I thought it was square head."

* * * * *

A full moon cast shadows from an apple tree onto the wall of my room. I thought about the nickel, determined I would spend it the next day, fell to sleep, woke to sunlight. Dad's empty coffee cup sat on the table; Mom came in carrying an armload of cut wood. "Okay if I go to the shop?"

She laid the wood beside the stove. "You know the way?"

"Uh-huh. Remember, I walked home yesterday?"

"Guess it'll be alright. You have to be very careful though. Stay on the edge of the road and mind the cars. Promise?"

"Promise."

"Let me fix you some breakfast before you go."

"Not hungry."

"Sit down. It'll only take a few minutes."

* * * * *

I walked down the hill kicking rocks; threw one at a telephone pole, it hit with a satisfying smack, threw another, missed, caressed the nickel in my pocket. "Yahoo," I shouted to the empty road. "Yahoo." My shouts stirred a dog. It ran down a long driveway barking. I picked up a rock, cocked my arm; it shied away, threw it anyway, took in a breath. "Yahoo."

At the bottom of the hill, I pushed open the door of Harbor Merchantile with a grunt, the bell ting-a-linged, I presented myself to the storekeeper, nickel in hand. "What can I buy with this?"

He scrutinized the nickel, broke a smile. "You're new to me, son. What's your name?"

"Thomas."

"Folks call you Tommy?"

"Nope."

"My name is Halverson. Folks call me Mister Halverson. Now let's get down to business." He pointed at the candy with a gnarled finger. "All the stuff on that side's a penny. You get five pieces for your nickel. The stuff next it costs a nickel. You get one. The rest costs ten cents. You need ten pennies, two nickels or one thin dime to buy those. So—what'll it be?"

I studied the possibilities. The doorbell ting-a-linged. A woman, heavyset, entered. He gave her the same cash register smile he had given me. "Morning, Martha." He looked back at me. "Decided?"

I pointed to a five-cent candy bar, laid the coin on the counter.

"Good choice." He put it in front of me, tossed in a penny bubble gum. "Got to keep you big spenders coming back."

I ate the candy as I walked along a sidewalk fronting the store in the direction opposite the machine shop; passed a one-chair barbershop with a rotating electric bloodletting pole like the one Bill told me about when he took me for my first haircut. The barber snoozed in his chrome and leather chair. Beyond the shop stood an out of place building with two front doors that resembled a tiny Roman temple. I climbed the steps to the portico; peeped inside the left door, saw a one-window post office. The other door opened onto a room filled with books. A woman sat at a desk. How pretty she looked. She beckoned me. I entered.

"Hello, my name is Miss Brammer. I'm the librarian. I don't recognize you."

"Just came here a little while ago."

"Well, no wonder." She smiled, increasing my discomfort. "Tell me your name."

"Thomas."

"Where do you live, Thomas?"

"Up on the hill."

"Do you like to read?"

"Yep."

"What kind of stories do you like?"

"Comic book stories, because I can look at the pictures and figure them out."

"If you like, I can teach you to read the words."

"Got to ask my mom."

"Of course. If you have time now, I can read you a story. Do you think that will be all right?"

"Think so."

She walked me to the kid's section. "What kind of story do you like?"

"Any kind."

* * * * *

Pungent hot metal singed my nose when I entered the shop. Dad worked on an odd shaped piece of metal with a file. Seeing me he beckoned, took a drag from his cigarette, exhaled through his nose. "What's up?"

"Mom wants me to get some bread."

Inky stopped clanging with a ball peen hammer. "That's a long walk you had, kiddo. Have yourself a little sit."

Dad took the last drag from his cigarette; dropped the butt to the floor. "Need money?"

"Got a quarter."

"That's plenty. Get it and come on back. We'll walk up at lunchtime."

* * * * *

Dad and I headed up the hill. I fell behind. He beckoned me to catch up. I fell behind again. "Come on, you got to do better. No time to dawdle." Muscles in my legs burned as I struggled to keep up with him. Further on, he eyeballed me. "Be careful, damnit. You're squashing the bread,"

* * * * *

Mom stood at the counter making sandwiches from the deformed bread. Dad sat massaging the stump of his arm. "Boy's weak, Dorothy. I won't allow him to grow up like that."

"Give him time, Stosh. He's going through a big change."

Dad shook his head. Gave me a questioning look.

"You going to be able to hack it?"

"It's hard."

"Most things are."

* * * * *

Dad shook me awake. "Rise and shine. You're coming with me."

"Where?"

"The shop. Hustle up."

I heard his voice below as I pulled on my jeans, tried to make out the words, couldn't.

He sat in his chair, grimaced as Mom slid the hook's socket over his stump, didn't read the newspaper or dally over coffee like usual.

As we walked, the sun broke in a glare over distant eastern mountains casting elongated shadows behind. Halfway down the hill he broke silence. "You're going to be helping me and Inky."

"How?"

"Cleaning up things before the day's work comes in. Don't worry, I'll show you the ropes. Only take a half-hour or so. After, times your own. You need to start learning responsibility. Time to start growing up."

A flatbed truck loaded with metal cages scattered gravel as it rattled down the hill; the rust-streaked pickup that followed skidded to a stop beside us. Its broken muffler coughed fits and spurts. The driver poked his wind worn face out the side window. "Hey Stosh, who's that you got there with you?"

"My son, Thomas."

The man extended his hand to be shaken. It felt hard, like wrecked leather. "Name's Martin. Martin Larson." He turned his attention back to Dad. "What's your old lady think about you going?"

"She don't know yet. Telling her tonight."

"Christ, you're kidding. What's the hold up? Got to get it done."

"Been waiting for the right time. Don't think she's going to like it."

"Hell no she ain't. 'Specially you putting it off to the last minute. See you at the harbor."

Dad nodded, the truck rolled away, we walked on in silence, arrived at the shop just as Inky came out the door of his bachelor bungalow. He waved and stepped into the skinny outhouse that served both places. Martin Larson's pickup sat parked near the edge of the bulkhead. The flatbed sat there too along with two other loaded pickups.

"That's all gear and chow for his crabbing boat," Dad said. "He calls it Montezuma's Revenge."

"What's that mean?"

"I'll tell you another time."

* * * * *

Dad found two foxtail brushes, handed me one, pointed to the workbenches. "Careful when you brush. Easy to get filings in your eyes if you do it too hard." We went on to the lathe. "Shavings are razor sharp. They'll chop your fingers up bad, so don't pick them up; sweep them into the pan nice and easy. Same at the drill press."

Inky came in carrying two mugs of coffee, he handed one to Dad. "Morning, kiddo. You the new cleaning lady?" I grinned. He snapped a salute. "Got some work to do outside so you two carry on."

I finished with the foxtail, Dad inspected, found a couple places that needed more work, pointed them out between pulls of coffee. "Got to watch for stuff stuck in-between. Can't let it go." With everything done to his satisfaction, I swept the shavings into a pile on the floor and onto a dustpan. We took it outside to the edge of the bulkhead, tossed them into the water. I hung back a moment, looked at the water's chop, inhaled its essence, held it in my lungs long as I could.

Dad worked with a file on the same hunk of metal he worked the day before. Inky came in, started a cigarette on fire; bumped me with his hip, slipped a nickel in my pocket, gave me a Don't-Tell-Your-Old-Man look. "Have yourself a sit. If you got nothing on your dance card, I got a casting to finish up in a minute. Might be interesting to watch."

"What's casting?"

"It's when we make something brand new out of something old."

"Oh."

Dad stopped filing, shook out a cigarette, lit it, took a drag, and another. "Got myself in a pickle, Inky. Got to figure how to tell Dorothy I'm going."

"Christ, you ain't said nothing yet? You're plumb out of time. Should of done it way back."

"Suppose so."

Inky sighed as he walked to the door. "You ain't thinking right, Stosh. Ain't no damn good springing it on her."

* * * * *

Under an attached lean-to, Inky pointed with his chin to a small furnace built of brick. "That there's for melting metal. Tin shed over there's where we keep frames and clean sand for making molds." He pointed to a wood frame filled with sand on the ground. "This here's the piece I'm working on."

I gave him a worried look.

"Don't worry, kiddo. Ain't going be no test."

I sat on the ground, knees pulled up, leaned back against the wall of the shop. He tapped a small circle of metal that showed at the top of the mold with a fingernail. Shook his head. "Still too hot. Got to wait some more. Poured this thing a little while ago, afore you come in." He shook out a cigarette, lit it. "Me and your pop's been friends since we was tads. Met up when he first come here. Hell, he didn't even know the lingo yet. Old country's what tied us together."

"What's old country?"

"Norway. Where we come from."

"Oh."

"We hit it right off like two peas in a pod." He scoffed, shook his head. "His folks was hell on wheels. Old man was a hard-nosed drunk, old lady, some kind of religious nut. Thought all that wasn't her kind was going to burn in hell's fire. Things got real bad for your pop sometimes. When they did, he'd come to our place and stay a bit. My folks treated him like kin. Tried to talk to him about things, but he was shut up tighter than a clam." He finished his cigarette, shook out another, lit it from the butt, blew smoke out his nose.

"What's hell's fire?"

"Where bad people go when they croak."

"What happens there?"

"They burn in a hot fire forever and ever."

I shuttered. "Really?"

"Nah, it's just made up stuff."

I thought about the prayer Missus Miller taught me, wondered if Inky was right about hell's fire, thought maybe I should start saying it again—just in case he wasn't.

"Your pop's old man was a feisty SOB. Made trouble all the damn time. Met his maker in front of the tavern spatting with some young buck who ended up poking him up under the ribs with a pocketknife. Old man laid down on the brand new concrete sidewalk and bled to death. Young buck said he was sorry as hell, didn't mean to hurt him bad, just got scared's all. Old lady said, 'Don't worry about it too much. We all got to go sometime.' Sheriff Holkie said it was self-defense. That ended it."

He tapped the circle of metal again. Unsatisfied, he resumed. "Stosh was twelve or so when it happened. Quit school. Went to work at the sawmill up to Center. Two—three years later, the old lady started getting chest pains. Doc looked her over—found a bad cancer. She went pretty quick. Soon's she was in the ground, Stosh disappeared. Just dropped off the edge of the earth like he never was. Didn't even lock up the house. Nobody knowed nothing about him till he come back end of the war and took up like he never left."

We sat quiet a while. Inky reached out, tapped the metal again. Satisfied, he split the mold open. "I'll tell you more another time. Metal's cooled enough. Got to get it out the door soon's I can."

* * * * *

Supper finished. Dad lit a cigarette. Mom cleared the table, sat back down, lit a cigarette herself.

"Guess I'll come right out with it," said Dad.

"Come out with what, Stosh?"

"Going north with Martin."

"Going north? What do you mean going north?"

"Going on his crab boat, work for a share of the catch."

Mom ground out her cigarette. "When?"

"Day after tomorrow."

"What? Stosh, you can't be serious."

"Been planning it a while."

"Why am I only hearing about it now? What am I supposed to do while you're gone?"

"There's money in the sugar bowl. Inky'll be around."

"Money in the sugar bowl? Inky will be around? That's it? That's your plan for us?"

Dad drew in a harsh breath. "I knew this was going to be trouble." He drummed his fingers on the tabletop, stopped, turned his eyes on me. I scrunched down much as I could. "Time to hit the hay, buster."

"It's still early."

"Shut your yap and get your butt upstairs—now."

I bolted from the table and up the stairs. Standing at the top I paused, pulled in a breath. Dizzy thoughts swirled in my head. I sat down on a step, hunched my shoulders, dug elbows hard into my thighs, came to a sudden understanding: Dad kept secrets. Bill told me keeping secrets was the same as keeping lies. They shut doors; made you dirty inside, made you not think right.

Downstairs plates clattered. I flinched. Dad resumed talking. "Didn't want to give you too much time to think. Knew if I did you'd try to talk me out of it."

"Of course I would."

"Listen—not much work comes in after the boats go. Not enough to live decent. Inky does fine because he's got but one mouth to feed. I did too before you come along." He paused. "It's the only way to make ends meet."

"Fishing's dangerous, Stosh."

His voice raised a notch. "Dangerous? Christ, you think I'm simple minded? I survived combat. I'll goddamn sure survive this."

"Yes, you did survive combat, but look what it got you."

"Enough. I won't hear no more." Silence followed. The shock of Dad's voice came from bottom of the stairs. "What the hell you doing skulking around up there? You was told to get to bed. Move it, mister. Don't make me come up. Be hell to pay if I do."

* * * * *

Heard the barking cough of Martin Larson's truck before full light. After a pause, it rattled off. I got up, dressed, went downstairs. Mom sat at the table, looked at me, tapped the ash off her cigarette. "You must be hungry,"

"Hu-uh. Kind of feel sick."

She pulled me toward her, put her palm against my forehead. "You're not feverish."

"Not that kind of sick."

"Tummy ache?"

"Hu-uh."

"What then?"

"Headache."

"Oh?"

"It's my fault."

"What's your fault?"

"Everything."

"Everything? What do you mean everything?"

"I'm not supposed to be here."

"No, no, no. You can't think like that. There are just things you don't understand."

I stomped my foot. "You're going to tell me I'm not old enough. I know lots of grown up stuff. More than you think."

"I want you to be a child. To play. To have fun."

"Why?"

"Because that's what you're supposed to do."

"I hate being a kid. I want to be grownup."

"Sit down, let me fix you a nice breakfast. It'll make you feel better. After, you can go pick up some aspirin."

"Can I go see Inky?"

"Not today."

I finished eating, she handed me a dollar bill. "Come straight home. Bring back all the change."

I wished Dad would stay gone forever. Felt guilty for wishing it. Probably be my fault if he did. I kicked at a rock, missed, picked it up, threw it hard at a telephone pole, it hit, ricocheted back, landed at my feet, I kicked at it with hatred. Tears welled. Maybe with the dollar I could run away. Run away? Where? I recited the prayer Missus Miller taught me a couple times. It didn't help.

Mister Perkin's drug store sat across the intersection from Harbor Merchantile opposite the gas station. It occupied half the building, the other taken up by Matt Morrissey's Meat Market. Inside, Mister Perkins sat on a tall stool behind a counter. "What can I do for you, Thomas?"

"Got a headache. Mom wants me to get some aspirin."

"Fix you right up." He reached for a bottle on the shelf behind. "I'll get a cup of water so you can take one now."

Took a pill. Drank the water. It washed away the bitter taste.

"Your dad left this morning, didn't he?"

"Yep."

"Tell your mom she can run a tab if need be."

"What's a tab?"

"She'll know what I mean."

"Please, can you tell me?"

"Sure. That's where people buy things now and pay for them later."

"How come they do that?"

"Sometimes they don't have the money to pay right away."

I left the store, walked back up the hill, pill bottle rattled in the small paper bag I carried, change jingled in my pocket. Took my time because Mister Perkins made me feel a little grown up, and I wanted to enjoy it.

* * * * *

I sat at the table still cluttered with breakfast dishes, the day hot, muggy. Mom lit her second cigarette, shook out the match. Sounds of a car engine broke the quiet. I looked through the open door; saw

Inky climb out of his Plymouth, he gave a quick wave, came in. Dad's chair creaked when he sat. Mom got another mug from the cabinet, filled it with coffee. He took a big slurp, smiled. "Nectar of the god's, Dort. Nectar of the god's." He cleared his throat, pointed at me with his chin. "Ain't seen hide nor hair of you, kiddo. Been doing my own titivating. Seems you're falling down on the job."

"We've been getting used to being alone," said Mom.

"Being alone." He snorted. "That's what I come for. Want to leave a couple bucks to tide you over."

"Oh Inky, you don't have to do that. We're fine."

"Sure you are. I know that. But Stosh and me's partners, and partners is partners. Doing so fine myself I got cash coming out my ears. Need to spread it round to keep my luck going." He took a worn wallet from his back pocket, dug out a twenty-dollar bill, laid it on the table, sat Mom's coffee mug on top of it. "Don't say nothing, Dort. It'll just embarrass me."

That night, Mom let me stay up late. She fixed hot chocolate and we listened to Yours Truly—Johnny Dollar on the radio. When my eyes grew heavy, she switched it off and I went to bed.

* * * * *

Mom sorted groceries delivered by Harbor Mercantile. Hungry for lunch, I lurked close by, willed her to hurry. A car horn beeped. Mom looked out the window. "It's Oscar. He has a letter for us. Run out and get it."

When I reached the mailman's car, he handed me a long white envelope. "For your mum, Tommie-boy. From the school board."

Mom put aside her sorting to read the letter. "Damnit. Damnit." Remembering me, she changed the tone of her voice. "Sorry. I'm just so angry. You won't be starting school this year. There are so many new students they had to change the birth requirements. You're ten days too young. The letter says there'll be no exceptions. Seems unfair. Must be a big disappointment for you. I'm so sorry."

I didn't feel disappointed, but remained silent and organized my face into the proper expression in case I should. Turned out to be the right thing because she smiled big.

"Because of that," she said, "I'm going to fix you a special lunch."

"After, can I go to the shop?"

"Of course."

While I ate, a weatherman on the radio said it would cloud up in the afternoon with rain by nightfall.

As I left, Mom said, "Don't stay too long. I don't want you bothering Inky all day, and I don't want you walking home in the rain."

"I don't bother him. He likes me."

"I know he does, but he can't spend all his time entertaining you."

"I work too."

"I bet you do."

"He tells good stories."

"About what?"

"About when him and Dad were kids. Most fun is when he tells me about fighting the Japs."

"Japanese, Tommy. It's disrespectful to call them Japs."

"He calls them Japs."

"I can't do anything about him, but I can about you. I don't want to hear that word anymore, understood?"

"Yeah."

"Yeah what?"

"Yeah, understood…"

"I don't think it's a good idea for him to tell you those kind of stories."

"Why?"

"Because they put bad words in your head."

"I heard Dad say Jap, too."

She frowned. "Go. Be home by supper time."

* * * * *

As I passed the window of Matt Morrissey's Meat Market he tapped it, beckoned me. The huge man wore his usual outfit, a green blood spattered apron that bulged around his jouncing belly, baggy tweed trousers, brown oxfords that never saw a lick of polish. "Got something for you." He reached into the meat case, pulled out the butt end of a bologna log, handed it to me. "Meat lollipop."

"Thanks."

He made a sweeping bow. "De nada."

"Huh?"

He scoffed. "It's nothing."

"Oh."

I gnawed on it the rest of the way, threw the remains in a trash bin outside the shop. Surprised to find the door padlocked, I walked to Inky's bungalow, knocked, he answered, coffee mug in hand.

"Howdy, kiddo."

"Wondering if you got some work to do."

"Come on in. Have a cup-a-joe. We'll talk it over."

"Cup-a-jove?"

"Cup-a-joe—coffee. Nectar from God hisself."

I stepped into the small kitchen. It had a Franklin stove like the one in the shop. He sat his mug down on the table next to an open pack of cigarettes, among the butts stumped out in the ashtray one still smoldered.

"Have a sit, kiddo." He got another mug. "How do you take it?"

"Don't know."

"Don't know? Still a virgin?"

"What's that?"

"Somebody who ain't never tasted the nectar hisself."

"I snuck a sip of Bill's once."

"By golly, you're qualified. We'll get you fixed up. Us tough old coots drink it black as coal. Don't melt the spoon, it ain't strong enough. You'll like it that way too when you're a coot. For now we'll mix it up blond and sweet same way you're going to like your girl friends."

He filled the mug halfway from an enameled pot. "Milk's in the fridge. Got no sugar. We'll use honey to sweeten her up."

First slurp burned my tongue, bitter taste overpowered honey's sweetness, felt grown up as I took more cautious sips.

He ground out his cigarette. "Take your time drinking. Don't want you getting no whips and jangles."

"What're those?"

"Nothing to worry about till you're a hard drinking man." He paused, shook out a cigarette, pasted it to his lip, lit it, cleared his throat as he exhaled smoke. "Decided to take me a day off because ain't much going on. Slept in a little. Chowed down on a big breakfast. Been relaxing, enjoying the day. Didn't know I was going to have the pleasure of your company. What say we drink our joe and have us a little bull session."

"What'll we talk about?"

"Oh, I don't know. Must be something two good looking fellas like us can find to talk about."

"How about the war?"

He gave me an earnest look, raised his eyebrows. "Got any girl friends?"

I shook my head. "Don't like them."

He chuckled. "Okay. Okay. Let's find something else. What's your old man talk to you about?"

"Nothing much, except when he's mad."

"Well, that's damn a shame. He's got a bunch of good stories. Maybe he figures you ain't growed up enough."

"Don't think he likes me much."

His eyes widened. "Oh, he likes you fine. Wouldn't of took you in otherwise. Just don't know how to show it. Still lots of old country in him. Lots of marine, too. Too damn much maybe. Most of all he don't like flim-flam. Don't like it at all."

"Know when he's coming back?"

"Oh, be three-four months, anyway. Depends on the ice. They fish till the sea's all froze up and they can't go out no more."

He stood, tossed the last of his coffee down the sink. "Getting cold. No good that-a-way." At the stove, he refilled his mug. "Had lunch?"

"Hot dogs."

He smiled. "Good old All-American chow. Going to rustle up a little something more for myself. Got a taste for breakfast again. I'll throw on some extra bacon case you want to gnaw on it."

Finished with cooking, he sat down, slid the plate bacon toward me. "Help yourself, kiddo." He ate with gusto, wiped his mouth clean with a paper napkin, tapped the mug in front of me. "Going to spoil pretty quick if you don't drink it down."

I took a sip. "Why'd we fight the Japs?"

"Already told you some."

"Tell me again. Please…"

"Seems they got mad at us. Decided to drop some bombs on Hawaii."

"What's Hawaii?"

"Bunch of little islands off in the middle of the ocean. Anyhow, they picked a fight thinking we was soft round the gills and they could whip us easy. Weren't the case."

"Was it back in the olden days?"

"Olden days?" He scoffed. "Olden days? Is that what they was? Seems like they was yesterday." He shook his head, paused, looked away. Chills ran down my spine, seconds passed, his eyes came back to me, he smiled, tapped the ash off his cigarette. "Liking that coffee, ain't you?"

"Yep."

"Good, it'll grow hair on your chest."

I nodded.

He took a drag from the cigarette, stubbed it out. "Plane I flew in was called Dauntless. She was a good bird. When we was airborne, I curled up back aft in the turret tight as a ball and shot hell outta the thirty caliber to keep the Japs off our tail. Sometimes I saw pieces fly off their planes so I knowed I hit them, but never knowed if I downed one. Japs was good shots, so I spent a lot of time patching up bullet holes."

"You scared sometimes?"

He took a long pull from his coffee. "Scared spitless every damn minute."

"Really? Thought nobody was scared."

"Anybody tell you that's either a damn liar or too dumb to know better. Sensible folks was all scared."

"What about heroes?"

"What about them?"

"They weren't scared."

"They was probably most scared of all. But they was more scared for others than for themselves. That's how come they done what they done."

"You a hero?"

"Come on kiddo, I just done my job like most."

"Ever get shot?"

"Nope."

"Any bad stuff happen?"

"It was all bad stuff, kiddo. Nothing good comes from war. Not nothing." He stopped talking, drew in a breath, whistled it out through his teeth. "Sure you want to hear more? Your momma might not like it."

"Bill told me all about the blood and stuff when he was fighting the Bosh. Even told how he almost got killed when he was buried under lots of dirt because of the big explosions and how his friends got killed in bad ways. Always talked grownup to me, same as Missus Miller. I don't like being a kid. There's nothing good about it."

He blew out a breath, leaned back, looked past me. "There was a couple times. Once, we run out of gas because a kamikaze hit our ship and the deck was afire. You know what a kamikaze is?"

I nodded. "Saw about them in Life Magazine."

"Other ships didn't have room for us, so we landed in the water. Pilot brought it in smooth as silk. Plane didn't sink, so we climbed out and sat on a wing. Watched the action like it was a picture show till things simmered down enough for the ship to send out a Boston Whaler for us.

"Next battle we was hit by Jap ack-ack. Took off part of the tail, put us in the drink again. Plane was tore up bad. Sunk almost afore we got out. Miracle nobody got hurt. So we was floating along in our May Wests waiting again. Waiting's hard. Damn hard. After a while, sharks come twisting through the water. Showed dorsal fins so we knowed exactly where they was. Water stirred up round the pilot's chest. He got a big open-mouthed look on his face—something like I never see'd afore. Got jerked this way and that like a rag doll. Got flung clean up out of the water. Seemed like it went on damn near forever. When it finished, he rolled over on his side like a top-heavy log, nothing left below his waist. Nothin t'all" He paused, drew a deep breath. "Sounds crappy to say, but it seemed to me his problems was over. Nothing left for him to worry about no more. Different for us two. Things was just getting started. We was helpless, floating along like baby ducks with nothing left to do except think and think while we was waiting our turn to die." Inky gave a deep sigh. "That's enough story telling for today. Drink up. Got to make a pilgrimage to the old outhouse to have me a sit on the throne. After, I'm going to fill the gas tank and take a drive uptown. Want to tag along?"

"Sure."

"Finish up. I'll meet you outside."

* * * * *

The gas station, a dilapidated building, sat across the highway from Matt Morrissey's Meat Market. It had two gas pumps under a narrow overhang and a service bay filled with indiscriminate clutter. Toby, the owner, a hollow-chested man with a bald head and flaring white side whiskers, viewed the world through milky cataracts and spent his hours sitting on a creaky weatherworn chair leaned back against the front wall. He treated business like an unwelcome guest. Customers pumped their own gas and made their own change inside at an open cash drawer. Teenage boys with stripped-down hopped-up jalopies stopped often to squat in front of him and yack about carburetors and camshafts. They sat at the feet of a master, so well did he know his stuff.

Inky stopped next to a gas pump, got out, clunked the gas nozzle into the car's filler, started pumping. In a rare display of mobility, Toby rose, walked to my side of the car, leaned through the window. "Ol' man's gone fishin', huh?"

"Yep."

"Hard life. Told you some 'bout my own fishin' days, didn't I?"

I nodded.

"Ever tell you 'bout the Swede with the glass eyeballs?"

"Nope."

"Ol' fool called hisself Sven. Mean streak a mile wide. Got his eyeball thumbed out in a fracas up Sitka way. Had a whole bunch a glass ones made up—all different. They was red and blue and green. Hell, they was damn near every color you can imagine. Had hisself a jack-a-spades. Even had a volcano and a naked lady. Changed 'em whenever he took a fancy. Sometimes he'd get snockered up, pop it outta the socket, put it on yer shoulder, and say, 'I got a eye on you buddy—I got a eye on you.' An' oh boy, he'd jus' laugh his dumb ass off, an' if you didn't laugh too he'd bust you one right on the snoot."

Inky finished pumping gas, went inside to pay, came back out. "Hell, Toby, you got nothing but copper in there."

"Well, since you're headin' uptown anyways hows 'bout I give you some foldin' money an' you bring back silver?"

"Suppose I can. I'll pay up then."

We drove off. Inky shifted up through the gears. Wind blew through the open window. It felt good on my face. We climbed Morgan Hill. On the downhill side Inky slipped the shifter into neutral and coasted. "Mexican overdrive."

I laughed.

"Shame on me for that."

As we passed near the high school, the road leveled. A scattering of businesses bordered the highway till we reached town, biggest on the island.

Inky parked in front of Kimmel's Market, gave me a wink. "Better prices here than what that ol' fuddy-duddy at the Merchantile. Big magazine rack too. Go have yourself a look. Chose a comic or two if you want whilst I take care of business. Got to pick up a couple things across the road at the hardware store too. After we stop at the bank maybe we'll go on to the Alibi for a milkshake. How's that sound?"

I smiled ear to ear.

* * * * *

Toby closed up shop in his own particular way; leaving everything unlocked and the cash drawer open should anybody come by needing gas. We headed for the harbor. There, he threw his fishing gear into a small, flat-bowed dinghy, sloshed the accumulated water out with a coffee can, and started pushing it down the boat ramp. I stood by and watched with interest till he stopped and gave me a hard look. "Well don't jus' stand about playing with your piccolo. This sucker's heavy."

Soon as the dinghy floated he scrambled aboard and extended a hand to help me. The waters had a slight chop that splashed against the boat and caused it to shudder and shake. Sitting on the stern seat, I hung on both gunwales with white knuckles while Toby rowed toward the center of the harbor. Only us and a single yellow sea plane owned by the Long family populated the waters. Their vacation house sat on the opposite shore. They spent only a little time there. Inky called them Weekend Warriors.

"Ever rode in a plane?"

"Long time ago. Back afore you was a glint in somebody's eye."

"Was it fun?"

"Humph. Don't know if I remember fer sure. Seems like it was."

I freed one hand, made it into an airplane, flew it through twists and rolls. "Got to be fun. Got to be the funnest thing ever." The boat lurched; I grabbed hold again.

Near the center of the harbor Toby pulled in the oars and let the boat drift. I held my breath feeling a thrill inside my chest, laid my hand on top of the water; it soothed me, words that always scrabbled in my head slowed. I looked at Toby. He gave me a smile like he understood.

With both lines in the water, Toby tongued a tobacco wad to the front of his mouth; spat it out with a hacking sound. It smacked the water and spread out into an ugly brown stain. "Stay far away from this stuff." He dug a round tin from his hip pocket. "No damn good. Once you start, you can't stop." He ran his tongue around the inside of his mouth, spat again, took a pinch from the tin, settled it inside his cheek.

"Why'd you start?"

"Used to smoke cigarettes back when I was hoboin'. Kept runnin' outta matches so I started suckin' this stuff. Better don't start. Keep away from them damn cigarettes too."

Time passed. Nothing happened. I grew restless. "You in the war?"

"Nope. Too young fer the first, too old fer the second."

"What'd you do?"

"Worked a job or two. Mostly just bummed 'round the countryside ridin' the rails an' such. Even made it down to Old Mexico once or twice. Liked them Mexican folks. They was a friendly lot, but all of 'em only talked the Spanish lingo. Had to use our hands to say what we wanted. Sometimes I got lonesome so I stayed in hobo camps. Ate Mulligan Stew outta tin cans. Drank Sneaky Pete wine. Slept by the fire. Made buddies. Lotsa good uns on the bum back then. Different now. Too damn many of um'd steal the bread outta yer mouth. Do miss them ol' timers."

Toby pulled in his line to check the bait. It looked fresh, so he dropped it back in. "Better peek to yours." He spat a stream of brown saliva. "Moved up here 'cause a yer pa. Met 'im on the road. He was hoboin' too, tryin' hard to get over a real bad time. Couple weeks afore couple a men dragged 'im off in the bushes an' buggered 'im."

"What's that mean?"

"Means they throwed him down an' done mean nasty things."

"They hurt him?"

"Hurt 'im bad. Bad enough he was thinkin' 'bout killin' hisself. He thought somethin' must be wrong with him attractin' that kind a thing. We talked about it lots. Might a helped a bit. Anyways, we become good friends an' bummed together a while. Ended up somewheres in Oregon, I think. Yeah, Oregon. On the coast, 'cause he said it reminded 'im of here. We was in some podunk ville with a recruitin' place in the post office. He wanted to join up. Had to lie 'bout 'is age, so I stood by an' helped out. Told them recruitin' folks I was his uncle or some such."

We fell silent. Pristine blue sky caused the eastern mountains to feel close. In my imagination I reached out and touched their snowy peaks.

"Come here 'cause your pa said it was so beautiful. Started ridin' workin' boats. Fishin' like he is now. Made damn good money. End a each season I come back an' lived the life a Riley till it was time ta go again. Did it fer years. Finally got tired, called it quits, collected up my money an' bought me the station. Soon got married to a Canuk gal. She quick decided she didn't love me no more, an' run off. Soon's we was separated, she quick fell in love again, an' quick as a wink we hooked up again. In the end, she run off back to Caneeda. Lookin' for somethin' more excitin', I figure. Decided that weren't no kinda life fer me. Started learnin' cars. Learnt 'em like I never learnt wimmin. Got me a good life now. Don't want fer nothin'."

* * * * *

I stood in front of the Roman Temple, saw a small stack of books near the library door, heard footfalls behind, turned; saw Miss Brammer approaching, dashed up the steps, picked up the books.

She gave me a smile as she unlocked the door. "Why aren't you in school?"

"Not old enough."

She furled her brows. "Not old enough? You're five aren't you?"

"Almost, but my birthday's too late."

"Oh, that's a pity."

"Can you teach me how to read?"

"If you want to learn I can."

"My mom reads all the time. Says it's better than listening to the radio."

"You bet it is. You can travel the whole universe by reading."

"What's the universe?"

"It's something you'll learn about through reading."

A waft of perfume followed her as she guided me to a chair, my face flushed; I didn't know why. She sat, opened a drawer, took out a pasteboard card with scribbles on it, laid it in front of me. "This is the alphabet. The ABCs. They're the first things you must learn. All words are made from them."

"Thought I was going to learn to read books."

She smiled; I flushed again, squirmed a little, she smiled bigger. "You are, dear. This is the first step. After you learn the sound of each letter I'll teach you to sound out words. After that, you'll be on your way. With time, you'll be able to read any book in here. The sky's the limit."

"Can I really do that? Can I really read everything?"

"With time, but to do it you're going to have to work very hard. Are you willing to work hard?"

I smiled. "Yep."

"Let's get started."

We went through the letters on the card. Together, we said their names over and over to stick them in my mind. The door opened. A woman returned a book and went to the bookshelves to search for another.

"I think we've done enough today, Thomas. You did well. Take the card home with you. Practice the sounds. Memorize the shapes of all the letters. Ask your mother for help if need be. The more you practice the easier it will become. When you have done that you can start reading."

"When can I come back?"

"You're welcome anytime."

I kept the alphabet card secret. While night's shadows danced on the wall, I said the ABCs aloud, and sang the song Miss Brammer taught me over and over till I fell to sleep.

* * * * *

I sat impatient, no appetite for breakfast. Mom stood at the stove cooking. "What's the matter? Got ants in your pants?"

"Got to go."

"Where?"

I pulled the crumpled ABC card from my pocket, laid it on the table, smoothed it out best I could, gave Mom my biggest smile. "The library. Miss Brammer's teaching me how to read. She said I can go back anytime I want."

"Of course, Tommy, but it's too early. The library isn't open yet."

"Then, can I visit Inky?"

"Okay, but you're going to have breakfast first."

Walked down the hill quick as I could, sat inside the shop staring at the electric clock as time dawdled by. Inky gave me a glance, poked me in the ribs with a finger. "What's going on? Things so serious?"

"Huh?"

"You been studying that ol' clock like you don't want to miss something."

"When's the library open up?"

"About ten more minutes. Why? Got something special there?"

"Learning to read."

"Learning to read, huh? Never done it proper myself. Who's teaching you?"

"Miss Brammer."

"Oh my, ain't she the pretty one."

I flushed.

He guffawed. "So, you want to scoot bad, huh? Here's a hot nickel to take with you. Ought to spend it buying her a flower. Hell's bells, I'd court her myself if I weren't such a cranky old fart."

* * * * *

I ran from the shop, past the butcher's, past the pharmacy, gave a quick wave to Toby, ran on before he could say anything, climbed steps to the library, reached for the door handle, breathed in deep, remembered the widow who lived on the second floor at Missus Miller's, a retired school teacher from the deep south, who sometimes invited me into her room to sit while she read stories in her beautiful voice about Merrie Olde England or about riding down the Mississippi River on a raft with your best friend. I wanted to own all those wonderful adventures.

Inside, Miss Brammer attended to a woman. She left carrying several books. "So, you've come back for more?"

"Yep. Want to learn bad."

She nodded, took another moment finishing up paperwork; rose, walked me over to the place where children's books resided. We sat. "Can you recite your ABC's?"

I said them aloud without mistake.

"Remarkable. Today I'll teach you to sound out words." She ran her fingers tips over book spines, picked one. "We'll start with this. It's titled Timothy The Little Brown Bear. When we finish our practice today you may check it out and take it home for two weeks."

As we sat, she moved her finger along the text teaching me the sound of each syllable and how to say them as a word. I left filled with confidence.

* * * * *

Inky sat in the shop smoking a cigarette. "What you got there, kiddo? Give me a squint."

I handed him the book.

"Gawd-a-mighty. You reading this?"

I nodded. "It's real hard though."

"Hell yes it's hard. Shoot, and you ain't even to school yet." He shook his head. "Stosh's going to be mighty proud when he gets back. Can you say a bit for me?"

* * * * *

Three beeps of a car horn sounded. Mom looked through the kitchen window. "It's Oscar. Go see what he has."

The former Brit handed a letter through the car window. "From your father, Tommy-boy."

Mom slit open the envelope with a paring knife, took out a short note and a money order. "Your dad's fine. He's working hard and they're catching lots of crabs." She waved the money order. "And guess what? We're having pork chops tonight."

"Pork chops? Whoopee. My favorite."

"Finish your lunch and we'll go shopping."

* * * * *

Mom hurried me along. I picked up a rock to throw; she grabbed my shirt, yanked. "Don't even think about it, mister." Chastened I dropped the rock, sent it rattling down the hill with a kick. "Is that what you do when you're by yourself?"

"Sometimes."

She scoffed. "Not any more you don't."

Thoughts of pork chops filled my mouth with saliva. We stopped at the Post Office where she cashed the money order and went on to the butcher shop.

"Afternoon, Missus," said Matt Morrissey. "What can I do for you?"

"Pork chops," I said. "Pork chops."

"Two thick ones," said Mom.

"On your tab?"

"No, I have cash."

"First paying customer I've had all day. Fix you right up." He dug into the refrigerated meat case; lifted out a large loin, smacked it down on top of a scarred chopping block. "Thick, you say? How thick?"

"Inch and a half or a bit more if you can."

"Double cut." He rolled the loin over so Mom could see the bones; drew an imaginary line with his finger. "How's that look?"

Mom looked, nodded. "That'll be fine, Matt."

He began carving. "Got a story for you, Missus. Not a dirty one, but still a ripsnorter. Farmer wrote Sears Roebuck saying, 'I would like to order ten thousand corncobs, Cash-On-Delivery. Yours truly, A. Farmer.' Well, they wrote back saying 'Dear Mr. Farmer, If you had our latest catalog you would see we do not stock corncobs. Thank you in advance for your future patronage. Yours truly, Sears Roebuck'. Farmer got mad as hell, took up pencil and paper again, wrote, 'Don't know nothing about that patronage stuff, but fact is if I had your latest catalog I would not need corn cobs'."

Mom laughed. Matt Morrissey started his own guffaw. I stood, feeling left out.

I asked Mom about it as we walked home. "Don't worry. Someday it'll come to you."

I thought and thought, grew frustrated because it didn't come to me. I picked up a rock, cocked my arm.

"No, you don't. Put it down."

I threw the rock hard into the ditch and in spite of the hard look she gave, felt better.

* * * * *

Mom stirred up the coals in the stove, added cut wood to make the fire hot, placed a large frying pan over the firebox, put in the chunk of lard the butcher wrapped with the chops. I stood close by, watched it melt into oil. She dipped the chops in buttermilk; turned them over and over in seasoned flour, when the melted fat sizzled and spat, put them in to fry. A delicious odor emanated. We sat, she turned on the radio, twisted the dial till she found what she wanted. Through the speaker a man's voice said, "Gun Smoke." We ate with little talk between us.

* * * * *

Missus Meyer tapped on the kitchen door. Mom looked up from her sewing, gestured for her to come in.

"Dorothy, I'm so sorry to tell you, but I just received a call from Inky. There's been an accident. Stosh was injured."

Mom dropped her work. "Oh my god. How serious is it?"

"I don't know. Come, have coffee with me. He may call back."

We hustled across the road and up the long grassy pathway to the Meyers' house, entered. I stood, mouth agape, at the sight of a television set in the far corner of the living room.

"Make yourself at home, Thomas," she said.

I started to sit on a couch, but before I could, Mom said, "Are your clothes clean?" I nodded, locked my eyes on the television again.

"Let's see if we can find something to keep you occupied," said Missus Meyer. She switched on the set.

I watched as it hissed static and come to life. Shadowy gray figures flickered across the screen. Missus Meyer turned a knob, thunk—thunk—thunk, waited as the picture squiggled and settled into images of children cheering a puppet and a man wearing a cowboy suit. Music played. The world around me evaporated. I could not comprehend the miracle.

In the background I heard Missus Meyer say, "Come to the kitchen, Dorothy. I'll put on a pot of coffee. We can chat awhile."

I watched the television while they drank coffee deep into the afternoon. No call came. My concentration broke when Mom said, "I don't know what to do, Ruth. I just don't know what to do."

"I can drive you down to the shop if you wish."

"Oh yes, please."

I stood as they prepared to leave. "I'm hungry, Mom."

"Run home. There's leftover chicken in the refrigerator."

"Thomas is welcome to stay," said Missus Meyer. "There's milk in the fridge and cookies in the jar on the counter. He can help himself."

Mom pursed her lips, bled them colorless, worry lines surrounded her eyes. "Will you be okay, Thomas?"

"Yeah, I'll be okay. Promise."

They left; I went back to watching television. A new program had started. A man appeared. He yacked on and on about a doe-eyed dog he called Slo-Mo-Shun that lay in a basket at his feet and seemed too lazy to breathe. After a few minutes, he turned on an imaginary switch and something he called a cartoon appeared. I shook my head in wonderment as the picture book moved and talked. Before it finished they returned.

"Inky wasn't there," said Mom. "Let's go back to the house. Missus Meyer will let us know if calls again."

* * * * *

Mom fixed a late lunch. I gobbled down the sandwich. She ate half hers, pushed it away, fetched Dad's whiskey bottle from the cabinet, filled part of a glass, drank down with a gasp. I fought the urge to squirm, heard a car pull into the driveway, ran out to greet Inky. He grabbed me; dutch rubbed my scalp. Mom waited in the doorway as we approached.

"I called the cannery up north, but my friend there knowed nothing more. Don't think things is too bad. If they was we'd of heard more."

We sat at the table; he eyeballed the bottle. "A short snort might help settle us a bit." Mom got second glass, poured slugs for both of them; they drank them down quick. "Got to hit the road, kiddo," he said. "Take care of your momma. Time to be man of the house. I'll swing by *mañana if I hear something.*"

Mom and I stayed up late listening to radio dramas. Finally, she said, "Time for you to hit the hay, buster."

Climbing the stairs, I heard the bottle clink against a glass.

* * * * *

Inky sat leaned back in a chair, feet propped up on another.

"Mom's worried a lot. Think she smoked a couple packs of cigarettes."

"Well—I'm guessing things is pretty much okie-dokie."

"Don't think he's hurt?"

"Oh, he's hurt alright. Just ain't so serious. If he was in the hospital or something I'd of got another call. Probably pulled in, patched him up and went back to fishing. How about you? How you doing with it?"

Felt my face flush. "Don't know. Feels funny."

He shook out a cigarette, lit it, waved away the smoke. "How so?"

"Don't like him very much."

He furled his brows. "Why's that?"

I looked at the floor. "Doesn't feel like he's my dad. I like you better. Wish he could be like you."

He scoffed. "Well, you don't got to like your old man, but you do got to respect him."

I picked up a foxtail.

"Don't bother. Nothing going on today. Titivating can wait." He flipped me a nickel. "Go get yourself a soda and come on back.

We'll sit and shoot the breeze a while. Maybe we can think up something to do."

I left the shop thinking soda—soda, already tasting the fizzy tang of it. As I ran across the highway a horn blared, tires squealed, a driver shook his fist.

Toby snapped awake. "Damn, Tommy, ya damn near give me a heart attack."

I showed him the coin. "Need a soda."

He got up, walked to the battered machine, cranked open the door. "Have yer pick." I selected one, handed him the coin—he returned it. "Gittin' kinda lonesome here all by myself. Stay an' jaw awhile."

"Can't. Inky's waiting for me."

"Then gimme back yer nickel." He snatched it from my hand, grinned at my dismay, handed it back. "Go on, keep it. I wuz just funnin' ya." I started to walk away; he called me. "Heard you wuz readin'. Next time ya wander down this away bring a book. Gimme pleasure to hear ya tell a smidge aloud."

I returned to the shop, saw the open door of Inky's bungalow. He stood at the stove filling a mug with coffee, tossed me a church key, I popped off the cap, fizz ran down the sides of the bottle, I took a quick, burning gulp, burped. "How old do I have to be before I can smoke?"

"Christ-a-mighty, don't ever start. Hell, I could of bought me a working boat for the money I spent."

"I want to be grown up."

"Smoking sure as hell ain't going do it for you. Anyways, what's your hurry? Take your time. Once you ain't a kid no more you can't never bring it back."

"I want to be in the navy. Shoot guns like you."

"Don't worry about it kiddo. You'll get your chance. Happens every damn generation. Time comes some son-of-a-bitch'll give you a war." He blew smoke; crushed out a cigarette. "Never fails. Not never."

* * * * *

Mom opened the door, Inky entered, waved a telegram. "Got news, Dort. Martin's bringing the boat back. Stosh's too bunged up to work. Maybe got a broke rib or two. Ain't so bad he needs hospitaling but he's bearing considerable pain. Plus, Martin's got mechanical troubles. Has to make it on one engine. Damn shame. Money'll be short, but that's a fishermen's life."

Mom sighed. "Coffee's fresh. Have a cup." Inky sat. She lit a cigarette. "Any idea when they'll be back?"

"Running on one engine it'll three weeks, four weeks." He nodded. "Maybe longer. Depends on the weather"

We sat quiet; Inky took a final sip of coffee, punched at my shoulder. "Got errands to run, kiddo. Want to tag along?"

I looked at Mom. She nodded. I walked with him to his car. "Is Dad really okay?"

"Yeah, he's fine. Going to need time to heal. He's a tough ol' buzzard. He'll make it fine."

* * * * *

I lay in bed, rolled left right, left right trying to rock myself to sleep. Outside, wind stirred naked branches of the apple tree; a full moon cast shadows on the wall. Their shimmying movement reminded me of the earthquake that came while I lived with Missus Miller and Bill. Everything jarred and jolted under my feet, plaster chunks fell from the ceiling; I cried out. Missus Miller scooped me up, held me tight to her wizened breast, crooned, "All's fine, baby boy. Everything be jus' fine. Gonna be gone soon. Be gone like it never was. Be gone like it never was." Wished all my thoughts would be gone like that; gone like they never was.

* * * * *

I sat at my desk reading. The chugging bark of Martin Larson's truck broke my concentration. Went downstairs, watched through the open door as Mom and Martin helped Dad out of the truck, led him to the bedroom, laid him down while he squirmed and made involuntary grunts. Martin reached into his back pocket, retrieved a flat brown bottle, broke the seal with a thumbnail, took off the cap. Dad took it, drank several long snorts. Mom put her dormant nursing skills to work and began undressing him.

"Let me know what you need, Dorothy," said Martin. "I'm good for it." He left the house.

Mom stroked Dad's forehead. "I'm going across the road to call Doc Osborne."

He grunted, squinched his eyes. "Don't want that high priced saw-bones poking around." He pointed to the bottle with his chin, grunted again, "Got all I need right here."

Mom shook her head. "I'm not going to argue, Stosh."

An hour later, Doc Osborne arrived. Over Dad's objections, he poked and prodded. "Did you get this looked at in Alaska?"

"Nope. Weather was bad. Couldn't get in. Best Martin could do was get off a radio messages telling the problem. Soon after an engine broke and we headed home."

"You must like living with pain. You have at least one broken rib I can hear with my stethoscope. You may have a bruised liver too. I want to put you in the hospital on the mainland for x-rays and a couple days of observation."

"Ain't happening. Bottle's better. That's my prescription. Write me up another and get out."

"Stosh, you can drink until the cows come home but it's not going to help with the situation."

"I been cramped up on a boat with seven other foul smelling souls damn near forever. Got no intention of going anywhere right now. I can lay around here good as I can in the damn hospital. You're done; Doc. Give Martin a call, he'll cover damages."

Mom saw Doc Osborne to the door. "We need to keep a close eye on this," he said. "Any change for the worse, call me immediately. I'll stop by and have another look tomorrow afternoon." He walked to his car muttering something about stupidity.

* * * * *

I snuck out, followed the pull of gravity, sent stones ricocheting ahead, felt guilty for it all. At the bottom of the hill, I walked across the highway onto the jutting peninsula that sheltered one side of the harbor. A blast from Franklin Freeman's motorcycle roused me from my ruminations. With no time to run or hide, I stood at the edge of the road—frozen. Believed him to be a cannibal. Believed if he ever got hold of me he'd put me on a spit, cook me over a fire, and eat me like roast chicken. The small, wiry man lived a reclusive life in a one-room squatter's shack thrown together from this and that with no electricity or running water. Spent summers laboring in berry fields like many of the island's down-and-outers. He pulled the machine to a stop beside me, shut off the engine, pushed up his aviator goggles. "Where you off to?"

I croaked an answer. "No place particular."

"You're Stosh's boy, right?"

"Uh-huh."

"Climb on, I'll give you a ride. We'll look for it together."

I choked back fear, swung a leg over the rear fender, scooched up tight against him, pressed my cheek hard against the back of his fatigue jacket. He kicked the starter pedal twice; the machine's engine barked to life. He cranked on the throttle, rear wheel stuttered, chewed through loose gravel down to the road's hard surface and sling-shotted us forward. I sat precarious on the slick fender as he flew around the perimeter road of the peninsula kicking up stones and dust. Wind teared my eyes, tore at my clothes—vibration chattered my teeth. In the thrill of it, I almost peed my pants.

Back at the beginning of the circle he blasted back toward Harbor Mercantile and turned onto the highway. Saw Toby sprawled comfortable in his leaned back chair as we passed. Franklin zoomed the motorcycle along the curved edge of the harbor, past the elementary school, over Judd Creek Bridge. When we reached the Y at the base of Morgan Hill, he turned left onto the narrow, unpaved road. An eerie feeling teased the pit of my stomach as we passed by the cemetery. After several miles and several turns, he took another onto an unfamiliar road that led us back to the highway and back to the ville. Saw Toby again. In a gutsy move I let go with one hand and gave a wave. He grinned, waved back. Franklin turned up the hill, made the climb that ended up in front of the house. I slid off. My whole body quaked. Without a word he goosed the throttle, dropped the clutch, thumped down around the corner and out of sight leaving a rooster tail of dust.

* * * * *

Doc Osborne came again; looked Dad over, left. Inky came, talked to Dad in private. After, he drove Mom and me to Kimmel's Market. "Going up the street for a beer while you're shopping. Come get me when you're ready."

While she shopped, I stayed at the magazine rack, flipped pages, scrutinized glossy pictures of everything imaginable, found one of particular interest, concealed it behind me, slipped it down the back of my pants, covered it with my shirt.

She put the groceries in the trunk of Inky's car. "Wait while I go get him." Driving home the magazine rubbed against bare skin. At the house, I went straight to my bedroom, buried it deep under the mattress among others hidden there.

* * * * *

It surprised me to see Dad sitting at the table smoking a cigarette. For the previous week he had hardly moved from bed. "Morning," he said. I nodded. Mom placed a platter of food on the table. Dad ground out his cigarette, winced as he dished up his plate. Seemed every move made him grunt. My appetite waned; I doodled with my food. He studied my face; I met his eyes, looked away.

"Eat up," he said.

Finished eating, he smoked another cigarette, rose with care, and with Mom at his side, returned to the bedroom.

She returned, poured a fresh cup of coffee, reached across the table, tousled my hair. "Time to get your ears lowered." She dug a quarter from her coin purse. "Be sure and tell the barber to give you white sidewalls so it'll last a while."

* * * * *

I left the house with a burst of energy, ran at top speed, kicked rocks ahead. Oscar drove by on his mail route, gave me a wave. I waved back, stumbled; almost fell, slowed to a walk. I liked the barbershop, liked sitting in the big chair while the barber sizzed my scalp with electric clippers, liked it most on busy Saturdays with all the benches taken by men and their unending burble of conversation.

I entered a quiet shop; a man I didn't know sat in the chair. The barber, a New Jersey immigrant named Gioachino Rossini, mixed lather in a shaving cup. "Be with you in a minute, Thomas." I sat on a bench next to the table laden with worn and torn magazines, dug till I found a comic.

Gio pulled the striped apron away from the man with a flourish, shook cut hair to the floor, dusted his neck with talcum powder. The man handed over three quarters and left without a word. Gio swept loose hair into a pile, collected it with a long-handled dustpan. "Unfriendly sort. Unhappy, I think."

"How come?"

"Bad kids. Bad wife. Money troubles. Who knows? Could be he's just lazy. Takes work to be happy."

I stood; he sized me up. "By god, you're growing like a weed. Don't think you need the kiddie board anymore. Have a seat. Let's take a look." I climbed into the chair, he stood back, studied me the way an artist studies a model. "You're just fine. Going be tall when you grow up. Going to be a heartthrob too."

"What's a heartthrob?"

"You'll know when you need to."

I scoffed. "I always hear stuff like that, you know—about being a kid and all, like I'm not smart enough."

"Forget about it. You're a smart cookie all right. Just saying when you grow up, you're going have the ladies falling at your feet."

Still didn't understand, but I let it pass.

* * * * *

Mom woke me. "Rise and shine. First day of school."

I dressed in a new-button up shirt, corduroy trousers with legs too long and clodhoppers a size too big. While I buttoned the fly of the trousers, Mom rolled cuffs at the bottoms. "You'll grow into them." Downstairs waited a breakfast of steaming hot chocolate, toast slathered with peanut butter and an apple cut in quarters.

Trembling excitement grew inside me as we stood at the edge of the road waiting for the bus. Reading, I thought. I can read all the time now.

Mom worried that I had no friends. I always responded the same, 'I have friends. Inky and Toby and Miss Brammer.' 'I mean kid friends. You shouldn't be hanging around grownups all the time.' 'Why not? I like them a lot.'

I only wanted to think about reading. I had worked hard reading the children's edition of Moby Dick. Miss Brammer told me there were important things to learn from the story, things about people and life. When I returned it, we talked a long time about it. "I'm so very proud of you, Thomas," she said.

The bus arrived. I pulled away from Mom's embrace; got on, found an empty seat. It drove over unfamiliar roads, stopped often to pick up kids, all strangers to me. They chatted and laughed together as the bus traveled on and came to a final stop in a semicircular driveway behind other busses and in front of a long, low building with several doors. The driver opened the door, beckoned us off.

Kids filled a grassy playground, some, with sleep still in their eyes, wandered dreamlike. Others, wide-awake, rambunctious, formed and reformed into noisy, chaotic clusters.

As I stepped down, a woman clanged the brass bell she held. "Good morning, students. My name is Missus DeHope. I'm the kindergarten teacher. I will call names. If you hear yours called go to the classroom behind me."

* * * * *

My belly ached—I had to pee. I squirmed in my chair while Missus DeHope read aloud from a book, her words a blur to me. At last, she looked at the wall clock and put the book aside. "Time for recess. Go play. I'll ring my bell when it's time to return to the classroom."

I ran for the small building that housed the Boy's and Girl's room, entered the wrong door, screaming girls scattered and ran. I ran too. Missus DeHope came charging from the classroom, caught me by an ear, towed me inside, a horde of curious children followed. She sat me down in a chair. "Don't dare move, mister." She got a bright-stripped ribbon from her desk drawer, wrapped it around my head, tied it into a big bow that flopped over my forehead. "This is what happens to boys who do nasty things."

Given no chance to explain, my mind blurred as I attempted to shut out the sound of children's laughter. The ache in my belly became unbearable. When I could stand it no longer, I relaxed, spent the rest of the day wearing the bright striped ribbon and urine soaked trousers, a pariah, banished from childhood forever.

The bus pulled to a grinding stop in front of the house, I clambered down. As it pulled away, a trailing dust cloud caught up and engulfed me. I stood motionless, hidden within it, hoping it would stay forever and somehow erase all that happened. Instead, it settled, the air cleared. Nothing had been erased. Not one single thing.

Mom stripped off my clothes; bathed me with warm water. "It's okay, Thomas, accidents happen. By tomorrow everyone will have forgotten." I hadn't told her all of it. For shame, I could not.

That night I fell into a despairing dream. Inside the dream I sat frozen to my chair at the front of the classroom stark naked, flushed with humiliation. Desperate to feel normal, I tried to cover myself but felt very much the nasty boy. I seemed to be the only one aware of my nakedness, others took no notice; the business of schooling went on. I woke to Mom's urgings. Her voice smiled, "Time to start a new day."

No. I thought, not for me. For me, there will never be a new a day. All will be a continuation of the one before with nothing forgotten, nothing forgiven, but I didn't breathe a word of it.

* * * * *

I sat sullen and silent under the baleful watch of Missus DeHope. During recess, she followed me place to place. To get away, I went into the Boy's room, sat on a toilet, waited to hear the bell calling us back to class. A safe refuge I thought till I heard her call. "Thomas, what are you doing? No one takes that long to do their business. You come out right this minute."

Some days in the classroom, we smeared paint on paper with our fingers while she ooo'd and ahh'd as if we were doing something brilliant. In the afternoons, she read stories that bored me. I wondered when we would have our own chance to read.

I had read part of a book given me by Miss Brammer. I can take it to school, I thought; let Missus DeHope see it. I did—she took it away. "I'll return it at the end of class today. Don't ever bring anything like this again."

* * * * *

I decided to sneak away during recess, to walk home, didn't care how far it was. Nothing at that school mattered to me. During recess I left the noisy gaggle of kids, crossed the highway, walked its graveled edge. A car pulled to a stop beside me, Missus Knutson, a fisherman's wife, rolled down the window. "What are you doing out of class, Thomas?"

"Going to see Inky"

She reached across and opened the car door on my side. "Get in. We need to get you back to school."

"Not going back."

"You have to. Your teacher will be worried to death. Get in."

"No." I scrambled away from her car, ran deep into bushes that lined the road. She called several times. Finally, I heard the car door close, and she drove away. Stayed hidden till I felt safe, went back to the road, continued walking. Several cars passed. I felt invisible; that felt good. My feet began to hurt. I wondered how much further I had to go, decided to sit a while on the dirt bank that edged the highway, felt instant relief. A car slowed, pulled to the shoulder, stopped. The driver, a man wearing a white shirt and necktie got out. "Do you have a problem, son?"

"Nope."

"Where are you going?"

"The harbor."

"What are you going to do at the harbor?"

"My dad works there. I have to find him."

"You still have a long ways to go. Come on. I'll give you a lift."

"Okay."

He tossed a suit coat into the back seat to make room. "What's your dad's name?"

"Stosh."

"Oh, I know of him. He owns the machine shop."

"Yeah, I guess."

"Will he be there?"

"Nope. He's fishing in the Straits this week. Inky's my dad till he comes back."

"Oh, I see."

When we arrived, he found Inky, "You know this young man?"

"Yep, sure do. Don't know why he's out of school though."

"I'll leave him with you to sort things out."

* * * * *

Inky tore open a fresh pack of cigarettes, tapped one out, took his time lighting it. "So kiddo, what's the deal?"

"I hate school."

"Why's that?"

"Everybody hates me—even the teacher."

"Come on, that ain't so."

"Yeah it is. Besides, everything's dumb. Nobody can read yet. Can't even say their ABCs."

"Nothing going on here. Let's go over to the shack and have us a sit. I'll brew up some joe, and we'll talk it all over."

"Okay."

Inky fussed around making coffee. I sat silent. "Still taking it blond and sweet?" I nodded. "Well hell… You ain't no coot yet." I nodded again. "Now—what's going on?"

Tears pushed at the back of my eyes. "Don't know what else to tell you. I just hate it, that's all."

"Something bad happen?"

"Can't tell."

"Can't tell me, you can't tell nobody."

"Everybody laughs at me."

"Why's that?"

"Because of the first day."

"What happened?"

"Teacher made me wear a big ribbon on my head."

"A ribbon? What for?"

"I accidently went in the Girl's Room."

He guffawed. "Oh my god, hell's froze over for sure. You snuck in the little girl's room, and she made you wear a ribbon for it?"

"I didn't sneak in. Honest, it was a real accident."

"Real accidental, huh. Don't you see how funny that is?"

"Funny?"

"Yep. Funny as can be. I'd of laughed my ass off—her making me wear some damn ribbon. I'd of asked her to let me wear it home so I could show off."

I snorted coffee through my nose.

Inky laughed again. "Was you shamed by it?

"Uh-huh. Couldn't even tell Mom."

"Well, you don't got to tell her if you don't want. Anybody else says something; laugh your ass off at them. As for the rest of them pathetic souls in that school, ain't none of them's read no books like you done. None of them's got one damn thing to laugh at you about."

* * * * *

Missus DeHope looked at the clock "Class dismissed for recess." Everbody scattered for the door. As I left my desk, she called to me. "I need to speak with you, Thomas."

I walked to the front of her desk, stood tight as I could so as not to tremble, looked down, studied patterns in the linoleum floor, waited.

After eternity, she spoke. "I'm worried about you, Thomas. Your attitude is very bad. You're disruptive, and you show little interest in class. That has to change."

Trembling over took me. I forced tears to stay behind my eyes.

"Why are you creating so much difficulty?"

I chewed my lip.

"Answer me."

I flicked my eyes up to hers. "Because it's stupid."

"Stupid? Stupid? You're so smart it's all stupid?"

I couldn't hold her glare.

"Who do you think you are, young man? There are forty-two children in this class, all well behaved. You're my only problem."

I heard 'young man.' It didn't feel good like I thought it should. I shut my mouth tight the way I did when Dad yelled at me.

"Is there something wrong with you? I notice you eyes have a peculiar shape. Do you have difficultly seeing?"

"No."

"Are you sure there's nothing wrong with your eyes? They're almost slanted. Why is that?"

"My real dad's a Chinaman."

"What?"

"My real dad's a Chinaman."

"You're lying to me."

"Honest."

"Your name's not Chinese."

"I got my mom's name because she doesn't know his."

I looked up. She averted my eyes, drew a breath. "Go play."

I pivoted on my heel, ran from the room, felt exultant because I tricked her.

* * * * *

I studied the shelf bearing ammunition, shielded what I saw from Mister Halverson with my body. With care, I picked up a box of thirty-thirty cartridges, slipped it inside the waistband of my trousers. The box rattled, my heart thumped, I looked around, two people waited at the counter, nobody paid attention to me. I ambled toward the door, reached for the handle, Mister Halverson called my name, my knees almost buckled; when I glanced up, he tossed me a piece of penny candy. "Got to keep you big spenders coming back."

The door ting-a-linged shut, a thrill rippled down my back; across the highway, Toby beckoned; I responded with a quick wave and started running. Part way up the hill, I slowed, inhaled deep, blew out hard, wiped away perspiration from my brow with the back of my hand, took the box out, slid it open, the bullets were bigger than I expected. I closed the box, stuck it in my pocket, every step caused a rattle; murmurs of guilt crept into my mind but were overpowered by excitement. Heard a car coming, Oscar pulled to a stop beside me. "Hey Tommy-boy, needing a lift?

I forced a smile. "Nah. Want to walk."

"Well cheerio, my little friend."

I sat on a bank at the edge of the road; stared down into a gulley and the sun dappled creek that ran at its bottom. What to do with them? What could I do? Thought about ways to explode them. The danger of it thrilled me. I took them home, hid them under my mattress.

* * * * *

Dad came home from a week of fishing with a good paycheck. I ate crisped bacon while he talked about our future. "Want to get started on the fence soon's possible." He looked at me. "We'll step off the field so I can figure what's needed. Finish up so we can get to it."

Outside, Dad stepped off ten paces, measured the distance he covered with a tape measure; calculated the length of each stride, did the whole process twice more to check his accuracy. Satisfied, we set off walking the perimeter of the field intended for pasture through knee high, dew wet grass. He took a pen from his pocket, handed it to me. "Every ten steps I take, make a mark on your wrist. Got to be right with it, mistakes'll cost time and money." We circled the field once counterclockwise and once clockwise. He counted the marks had made, divided them by two. "Okay, let's go figure it out."

At the table, Dad set to calculating. "Watch careful what I do. I'm going to figure how many fence posts we need. I watched him work. There were so many numbers, so many processes; it baffled me. He finished, looked at me. "Think you can do it?"

I shook my head.

"You got to learn. Numbers're more important than the reading. Don't learn them, you get taken for a ride on the business end of life."

The following week, a flatbed truck delivered a load of Cedar posts. We stacked them crossways on wood rails under the apple tree to sit till we were ready to start.

* * * * *

"Where'd these come from?" Dad held the box of cartridges pinched in his split hook. "Your momma found them when she changed sheets. Where'd they come from?"

My tongue seemed to swell; I couldn't speak.

"I'll ask once more. Where'd they come from?"

I hesitated.

It came as a blur, caught me high on the cheek, sprawled me against the wall, I banged my head; it dizzied me. He jerked me to my feet. Still holding the box, he pressed the curve of his hook into my chest, pinned me like an insect, backhanded me again. "You know what these'll do to a man? You got any idea? By god, I do. Seen it almost every goddamn day fighting japs." He doubled his fist, punched me in the belly, air whooshed out, I curled into a tight ball, rolled on the floor, tried to suck air in with all my might, frantic. He loomed over me. "That's nothing compared to what they'll do to a man. They'll rip his guts open. Steal his life. That's what they'll do." He threw the box on the floor; cartridges scattered.

I heard Mom's voice, a far distant echo. "Stop, Stosh. Stop. That's enough. You're going to hurt him. Stop. Please, stop."

A frantic eon passed before I could inhale, it came in shrieking intakes, gasps of bruising pain.

"On your feet, mister. You ain't hurt."

Mom reached out to help. He pushed her away. "On your goddamn feet—now."

I scrambled up, certain of another blow. Put my hands up as a shield. He batted them aside. "Get to your room. Stay there. We ain't finished."

Upstairs I laid on my bed, mind racing. When I heard him coming I went to a corner of the room, curled tight into it trying to disappear. He came in. "You hiding more stuff?"

I nodded.

"Where?"

I pointed to the bed.

He grabbed the mattress, flung it aside; exposed everything. "Where'd all this come from?"

"The store."

"What goddamn store?"

"Harbor Mercantile."

"All of it?"

"The bullets."

"What about the rest?"

"Kimmel's."

A vein pulsed in his forehead. I cowered. "Know where this is leading? Got any goddamn idea? The Big House, that's where. They got a bad one over in Walla Walla. Been past it a couple time. It's hell being locked up there. Pure goddamn hell." He pivoted on his heel, left the room. I heard his voice below. "That little shit's worthless. Don't want to do the things he's supposed to. Just lays around reading books. Try to teach him stuff, but he don't learn a goddamn thing. Now, he's a thief. What the hell am I supposed to do? Just what the hell am I supposed to do?"

"Stosh, he needs friends."

"Got no friends? That's his excuse? Got no goddamn friends?"

"He needs you, Stosh. He needs you to be his friend."

"Be his friend? I don't want to be his friend. He bores hell out of me. Christ, I don't even like him."

I stopped listening, made up my mind not to care, hoped he'd come back upstairs, finish what he started so there'd be no more me. No more nothing. Mom said he loved me. Told me how he put a roof over my head, food in my stomach. How that proved it. Maybe to her; not to me. I didn't believe any of it. I imagined leaving, living on my own, made up my mind, went downstairs. Dad saw me, his eyes flashed. "What're you doing down here?"

"Leaving."

"Leaving? Where you think you're going?"

"Anywhere."

"Fine and dandy. We'll pack you right up, get you on your way." He left the kitchen. I heard him climb the stairs. He came back with a dusty pasteboard box. Mom started to speak; he cut her off with a wave. "This is between me and him." He turned to me. "Get what you want. Pack it up."

Time froze. Terror burbled deep in my chest. I couldn't breathe. Too late. Too late to change my mind. I went to my room, packed what I thought important. Heard him holler from below, "Get your butt in gear, mister, I got better things to do."

I sat in the back seat as he drove south on the highway. The pasteboard box sat beside me with déjà vu familiarity. We traveled several miles; he pulled to the side of the road, stopped. "Get out." I stepped onto the running board, down onto the black top. "Get your stuff."

I stood at the edge of the road holding the box. The car disappeared in the distance. I sat down on the gravel, threw rocks into the bushes, everything turned numb. Rain began to fall. Time passed. The sound of a car engine came into my hearing, increased as it came closer. I wanted to not care, but glanced up anyway. Saw Inky's car coming toward me. My shoulders melted. He slowed, pulled onto the shoulder, stopped a few feet short, shut off the engine, stepped out. "Come on, kiddo. Stow your gear in the backseat afore everything gets soaked. Don't worry about your ol' man; he's off on a bender. It's just you and me. We got some important stuff to figure out. Got to get you back straight with this world."

The fabric of the front seat, soft and comfortable, made me feel sleepy, next I knew, we bumped onto the driveway at the machine shop.

"Gonna brew up a pot of poison so's we can have us a proper bull session." He busied himself at the stove. "Heard all about what you done. Bad thing. Bad way to start life." He got mugs, sat them on the table, the pot rattled as it came to a boil. "Think you can fix things up good, though. Think you can fix them up fine and dandy if you do it right. Got to be truthful. That's the solution. Got to 'fess up everything, and figure out how to make it right. Think you can work it off with ol' man Halverson. Go tell him what you done, ask what he's got you can do to make it up. Opening boxes maybe. Moving cans around. Who knows what he needs."

"Think he'll hit me?"

"Nah. Doubt he'll even be much upset if you tell him truthful. Truth always works. You got to remember that for your future."

I went to the refrigerator, got out milk, poured some in my mug, Inky poured in coffee. "Blond and sweet." He smiled. "You can do the same with Mister Kimmel. He's always looking for boys willing to help out."

"But that's far. How can I get there?"

"Kiddo, I got an answer for that too. Promise to do it proper and I'll drive you back and forth much as you need. But afore I help, you got to promise to do it right."

I sighed; I could do it. Knew I could. "Promise."

"What're you promising?"

"Promise to 'fess up for everything I did bad and do what they tell me to do."

"That's just fine. Good as gold to me."

We drove up the hill, he came inside the house with me, Mom sat smoking a cigarette, her eyes brightened; she crushed me in a hug. "Do you know where Stosh is, Inky?"

"Not for sure. Got a fair idea, though. Probably up to the tavern drowning his sorrows."

"There's no money for it. He spent all he brought home on fence posts and barbed wire."

"They'll run him a tab for him."

"That doesn't help. In the end we still have to pay."

Inky dug out his wallet. I pushed away from Mom. "I'll work in the shop, help fix things, and bring all the money home."

He smiled; laid a twenty-dollar bill on the table. "We'll consider it a loan against your work. I knowed you had a good side. Knowed it for sure, kiddo."

* * * * *

Next morning, Dad wasn't at the table, I went to school sullen, distracted, sat under the constant scrutiny of a teacher who knew none of it. Decided again not to care about anything. I absolutely would not care no matter what.

Dad didn't come home for Friday grocery shopping. Mom fretted and stewed, finished a cigarette, we walked down to the shop, found it closed; Inky gone from his bungalow, walked back up the hill, waited more.

She turned on the radio, twisted the dial searching for a program, changed her mind; turned it off. I sat knowing it would always be my fault, told Mom what I heard him say.

"Don't believe everything you hear. People say things they don't mean when they're angry. Besides—I know he loves you"

"You say that all the time."

"He puts a roof over your head and food in your stomach. That's what you need to remember."

"You always say that too. I don't believe you."

We ate a cold supper. I went to bed.

Morning, Dad sat at the table carrying a foul, unwashed stench. He ate a little, went to bed without washing. As he slept, I heard him thrashing, calling out to ghosts it seemed. I looked at Mom.

"He has bad nightmares, sweetheart."

"About what?"

"The war."

"How come?"

"His mind was injured."

"How'd that happen?"

"War damages people's minds."

"You mean like his arm?"

"Uh-huh, very much the same. I saw many like him when I worked in the hospital. I understand it a bit. That's the reason I'm so forgiving."

"Is that why he's mean to me?"

"Part of it, I'm sure. But he also wants you to grow up tough like him. He wants you to be able to face the world with strength. He feels that's the best way he can love you."

* * * * *

We started building the fence by pounding a row of stakes into the ground along one edge of the field, stretched twine from one to another to mark the fence line, dug the first hole, dropped in the post, shimmied it around in the hole till it was straight up and down, and touched the string, packed dirt tight around it, moved on to the next. Dad smiled a real smile as we continued on, had six more posts in the ground before darkness fell.

By spring, we were ready to pull the barbed wire. Dad made an idiot stick by cutting four notches into a beanpole—the height for each strand of wire. The work went fast.

* * * * *

With the four-strand barbed wire fence finished to Dad's vision of artistic perfection, he had the first two animals brought over from the mainland in a high-sided truck. It backed up to the open gate next to the barn and two squalling white faced steers shambled and skidded down a wooden ramp. "Both were castrated two weeks ago," said the driver. "They're in guaranteed good health. Won't be no problems with them." He got a clipboard full of papers from the cab of the truck, Dad signed, so did he. Finished, he tore off carbon copies for Dad to keep. They shook hands to finish business; he and his helper loaded up the ramp, drove the truck through wild grass out to the road and were gone.

The steers stood, skittish and bewildered, on the unfamiliar ground, but soon settled down and started grazing on the abundant grass and clover. Early next morning, they came up to the fence near the house to drink from the water barrel. Dad and I watched. He smiled. "We'll butcher one next year. Going to have a locker full of steaks and roasts packed away in Matt Morrissey's freezer."

When they finished drinking, we fed them grain from buckets; they took salt from the lick, sipped more water and returned to grazing.

* * * * *

I lay on my belly reading *Tarzan of the Apes*, heard Dad's footfalls on the steps, switched off the flashlight. He came into the room. "Still awake, huh?"

"Yep."

"Been reading?"

"Yep."

He sat on the edge of the bed. "Switch the light on. Show me the book." With the light on, I handed it to him. He looked at the title; flipped through some pages. "You're reading this?"

"Uh huh."

He shook his head, scoffed. "Well, put it away for now, get some sleep. There's so much work in the shop Inky'n I got to work through the weekend. Going to need your help."

* * * * *

Sleepy eyed, I pulled on a shirt. Dad sat reading the newspaper. Mom put a platter of food on the table. We ate in silence.

He and I climbed into the car; he stepped on the starter, the engine grunted but didn't turn over. "She's sat too long. Battery's dead. We need to give her some help. Hop out. Give me a hand pushing her out to the road."

We pushed it out, started it rolling down the hill, Dad hollered, "Jump in." I scrambled up into the seat, he put the car in gear, popped the clutch, the car bucked and bolted, rear tires skidded, caught the road, engine coughed; fired, clattered to life, we drove down the hill, brakes squealed as if under torture.

Dad spoke loud, to be heard over the engine. "Got no love for college boys. Educated idiots is what they are. Man's nothing if he don't do skilled labor. You got to work a trade if you want to amount to anything. Them that wears suits and ties ain't worth a pinch of shit."

* * * * *

Inky stood eyeballing the measurements for a piece that needed to be trimmed. The stoop-shouldered man sat nipping from a bottle, he handed it to Dad who took a nip, he handed it toward Inky.

"Give me a minute, Stosh. Got to get this thing doped out."

Two men I didn't know entered. One carried a complicated piece of metal broken in two pieces. "Glad you're open," one said.

Dad took metal pieces, eyeballed them; shook his head. "Don't think we can make it right. Probably need to take it to the mainland."

One of them gave a disappointed grunt. The other said, "Can you give it a try? If it don't work, it don't work. If it does, it'll save us a trip."

"Can't make no guarantees."

"Understood. We'll take the chance. Shops over there charge just to have a look."

Dad handed the pieces to Inky. "What do you think?"

Inky turned them over in his hand. "We'll be happy to give it shot. Take maybe a week with what we got going right now. Going to cost you either way. We got to get paid for our time."

They nodded.

Inky picked up the bottle from the chair where Dad set it, took a swig, offered it to the men; they declined. After handshakes, they left. Inky put the pieces on a bench. Scrutinized them with care. "Think we might be able to pull it off, Stosh. It's worth a good chunk of change if we do."

Dad pointed at me with his chin. "You know the drill. Hop-to."

I busied myself with a foxtail cleaning bench tops, swept the floor, gathered it up, tossed it in the water. Dad inspected; found everything satisfactory. "Rest of the day's yours. Tell your momma I won't be up for lunch."

Inky, in his sly way, slipped a nickel into my pocket. I left the shop with a real smile on my face, thinking about how to spend the nickel. Toby gave me a big wave as I passed by.

"Where ya off ta?"

"Library."

"Oh? Got a sweetheart there, I reckon."

I fled down the sidewalk, heard Toby call, "She's a purdy un fer sure."

* * * * *

Mom sat at the table smoking, eyes focused on an unopened letter under the heel of her hand. She looked up from her reverie as if surprised to see me, pointed to the letter. "It's from Daddy."

"From Dad?"

"No, from my Daddy." She shook her head. "Don't know how he found me."

"Were you hiding?"

"Not hiding, just…" She shook her head again, took drag from the cigarette, crushed it out.

"You going to read it?"

"I'm not sure."

I shifted my weight, looked at her face, her expression distant, unfocused. "I can read it if you want."

She shook out a new cigarette, studied it; dropped it on the table. "Well—what the hell." She slit the envelope open, unfolded the letter; began to read. I saw the writing, tiny script written with pencil in neat, straight lines. After reading part of it, she stopped, sighed. I waited for her to say something, she didn't; instead, she picked up the cigarette, lit it, smoked it halfway down, resumed reading. I counted the pages as she finished each. Five altogether.

"He sent his telephone number. Wants me to call him collect. God—after all this time he wants to talk to me."

"What about?"

"My stepmother died. He's all alone." I raised my eyebrows. "My real momma died when I was a little girl. Daddy remarried a German immigrant. I didn't like her. We fought all the time." She drew a breath; I squirmed a little, feeling her discomfort. "When I got pregnant she threw me out."

"Because you fought?"

"No, because of you."

"Was I bad?"

She scoffed. "No. You couldn't have been bad. You were still inside my tummy."

"Then how come?"

"Because you were illegitimate."

"What's that mean?"

"It means I wasn't married."

"What about Dad?"

"He's not your real dad."

"What is he?"

"He's your stepdad."

"Did my real dad die like your mom?"

"No."

"I don't get it."

"You will one day."

I furrowed my brow. "I hate it when you say that. I'm not dumb, you know." Decided to leave. As I walked out the door, she called to me. I didn't respond.

* * * * *

Inky raised his brows. Smoke from a cigarette curled up and dissolved into the air as he tapped off the ash. "Illegitimate, huh. Who said that?"

"Mom. But she won't explain."

"How come?"

"Said I'm not old enough."

"Well—probably I shouldn't say nothing."

"Please. I got to know." I tried a sip of coffee. It burned my lip.

Inky tapped the ash off his cigarette again, breathed in; studied my face. Snorted. "Yeah. You got a right to know. Fella needs to know stuff like that. Ain't right keeping it secret. All got to do with who's your old man."

"Kind of figured. She said she had a step mom and I've got a stepdad. Means he's not real, huh?"

"Oh—he's real alright. Just he ain't the one that made you."

"Made me?"

"Yep. Takes a man and woman together to make a baby."

"How come?"

Inky drew in a deep breath, breathed it out. "Well—what the hell. A man's got special juice he puts in a woman's private parts and that grows a baby."

"Where's he get it?"

"Comes natural from his own private parts."

"Have I got it?"

"Nope. Not yet. But you will when you're older."

"Do you?"

"Far as I know. But I ain't shot my pistol for so long I ain't really sure no more."

"Shot your pistol?"

"That's something your going to have to wait to find out. I can't explain it because I don't know how."

"Because I'm too young?"

"Yeah—partly. But I ain't talking down to you. Just ain't possible till you got the juice your own self."

"When'll that be?"

"Maybe when you're twelve—thirteen. Something round then."

"So Dad didn't put his juice in Mom's private parts to make me?"

Inky nodded his head, stubbed out his cigarette.

"Who did?"

"Don't know."

"So—that's what makes me illegitimate?"

"No, that's what makes it that your mom weren't married. That's what all does it."

"Being not married?"

"Yep."

"That bad?"

"Some folks say so."

"How about you?"

"Me? Kiddo, me and you's buddies now and forever. Ain't nothing bad about you in my book."

"Still don't understand it much."

"Well—you'll figure it out someday. Just don't never let nobody talk down to you about it. Not never."

* * * * *

I kicked a rock as Mom and I walked. She hummed a bit. Her eyes held a distant expression. She blinked several times, looked down at me. "Your grandpa's coming for a visit in a couple days. That's why I want to get this shopping done. You'll like him. He was an army man when he was young. A Master Sergeant."

I half listened as she droned on thinking how fun it would be to smash a glass telephone insulator with a rock. I took two quick steps; skidded my feet sideways in loose gravel at the edge of the road. Mom lit a cigarette. "Hey wisenheimer, knock it off. You're going to bust your butt." Chastened, I dropped behind. She stopped, turned toward me. "Keep up. I don't want to waste the whole day with this."

"Can I go to the shop?"

"No."

I used my whiny voice. "But I want to."

"No."

"How come?"

"Because I said so, young man."

I kicked at another rock. It rattled straight ahead. When it stopped, I kicked it again. "How come you call me a young man, but you treat me like a baby?"

She reached down, tousled my hair. "When do I treat you like a baby?"

I kicked another rock. "Most of the time. I like going to the shop. Please, can I go?"

"I need help carrying groceries. I don't have enough to pay for them to be delivered."

"How about a tab?"

"Huh-uh. I don't like living beyond my means."

"What's means?"

"Means is money. I don't like living with money I don't have."

I kicked the rock again, a feeble effort. "Inky likes me a lot. I want to be like him when I grow up. You know, fly planes, shoot guns, stuff like that."

"So, you want to be a tough guy?"

"Nope, a good guy."

Mom started singing. The sweetness of her voice bounced with each step she took. It rang down the hill, paused, and echoed back. "Che gelda manina—se la lasci riscaldar—cercar che giova? Al buio non si trava—ma per foruna e una notte di luna—e qui la luna l'abbiamo viccina…" She stopped; fondled my hair again. "Daddy loves opera. His favorite singer was Caruso. He actually heard him sing while patrolling the streets of San Francisco for looters after the Great Earthquake."

I sighed.

"Am I boring you?"

"Yeah, I guess. Mostly I don't know what you're talking about."

"Okay. That's enough. You'll have plenty of time to listen to his stories when he comes."

* * * * *

At the train station, Mom greeted a man. tall—rawboned, with a brief, silent hug. "Come on. We can catch the next bus if we hurry."

"Nah. No worry. I brought plenty of cash. We'll catch a taxi." He looked down at me, tousled my hair. I wondered why everybody wanted to do that. "So this is the squirt, huh?"

* * * * *

I rode in the front seat next to the cabbie, watched with interest as the meter ticked and the numbers changed. Heard Mom speak. "Our neighbor, Missus Meyer, is going to meet us at the ferry dock."

The man 'uh hummed,' leaned forward, laid a big knuckled hand on my shoulder. "Hey squirt, I hear I'm your grandpa." His voice ambled in a sweet accented way. "Think I'm going to like getting to know you."

I put on a weak smile, turned, gave it to him. The corners of his eyes crinkled when he smiled back. Aboard the ferry, he swung me up off my feet, hugged me hard to his chest, rubbed a whiskered cheek against mine like we had known each other forever.

* * * * *

Dad fished the straights. Grandpa, Mom, and I sat at the table. Mom drank coffee, a full cup sat idle in front of Grandpa; words were sparse. I felt the pressure of it. Grandpa let out a sigh. "Look, Dorothy, I've got so much to make up for, so let me get started. Turning my back on you is the worst thing I ever did. I came here hoping to mend the fence."

Mom said nothing. I squirmed in my chair. No one noticed. I squirmed more, caught Grandpa's eye. "Might be better just the two of us. Why not let the squirt run along?"

Mom pointed her chin toward the door. I left, decided to go to the shop, ask Inky about it. I picked up a rock, side armed it hard at a glass insulator, it thudded against the pole, picked up another, saw a car coming up the hill, hid it behind my back, threw it after the car passed, hit nothing. Clouds gathered in the north and swept south at a steady pace. I hurried my steps. By the time I reached the shop, fat raindrops smacked the earth. Inky stood at the bench studying an odd shaped piece of metal.

"What's that?"

"Motor mount from the Long's speed boat." He picked up a second piece from the bench, held it out for me to examine. "Broke somehow. Think I can weld it up and save them some cash."

"They don't care. There're rich."

"Yeah, they are. Got that way by not wasting their muhla. I see you got trouble on your face, kiddo. Come on, have a sit." He picked up a rag, rubbed some of the grease off his hands. "Let's us have a bull session and figure out what's up."

"I got a grampa."

"Uh-huh. That ain't uncommon."

"He's here."

"Heard he was coming."

"Don't know if I like him."

Inky took a crumpled cigarette pack from his shirt pocket, felt around inside with a finger, found none. "Dead soldier." He tossed it on the floor. "Leave it for the cleaning lady. Let's go to the shack and have us some joe."

* * * * *

I blew into the coffee cup, took a careful slurp. Too hot, I put it down. "I'm kind of scared of him."

"Did he talk mean to you?"

"No."

"Did he talk mean to your mama?"

"Don't know. Kind of feels like it."

"What'd he say?"

"Can't remember exactly. Something about fixing a fence."

"Mending a fence?"

"Uh-huh."

Inky rolled his head back and laughed. "Ain't no bad thing, kiddo. Means he wants to fix up things between them. Come on. Let's carry this joe over to the shop. I'll give you a nickel if you sweep up."

"How about a dime?"

"Damn kiddo, you're getting too smart for your britches."

70

* * * * *

Asleep on the couch, I woke to Grandpa coming down the stairs, sat up, rubbed my eyes, looked out the window into the still dark morning.

"Go back to sleep, squirt. It's too early for decent folk to be up."

"What are you going to do?"

"Shave."

"Can I watch?"

"Sure."

Grandpa stropped his razor, the same way Gio did, and shaved his face. Finished, he stirred up more lather, painted it on his scalp; shaved it clean too.

"How come you do that, Grandpa?"

"It's the old army way. Keeps everything clean and tidy so you don't get lice.

"What're lice?"

"Itty-bitty bugs about the size of a grain of sand that like the taste of your blood."

"Oh."

Grandpa wiped his face and head dry with a towel, bent down, took my hand, rubbed it against his cheek. "See? Clean as a whistle." I laughed.

Dad, home from fishing, sat at the table when we came out of the bathroom. Mom finished cooking, sat the platter on the table. When the coffee pot rattled, Grandpa took it from the stove, filled the cups. "You a coffee drinker, Squirt?"

"Sometimes."

Mom looked at me. "When have you ever had coffee?"

"With Inky."

"Figures," she said.

Grandpa got another mug. "How do you like it?"

"Blond and sweet."

Mom snorted.

Grandpa filled the cup. "Get your own fixings, squirt. I like mine dark as night."

I smiled. "Same like Inky. He says if it doesn't melt the spoon it isn't strong enough."

Finished with the meal, Grandpa leaned back in his chair till it creaked; dug a package of Red Man Chewing Tobacco from his shirt pocket. I eyeballed it with interest.

"Want a chew?"

"Really?"

"Sure. Reach in and get yourself a good pinch."

Mom started to say something, Dad gestured. I got a pinch; Grandpa did the same. "Now watch close, squirt." He poked it deep inside his cheek.

I followed suit. "Now what?"

"Give it a minute."

A torrent of caustic saliva filled my mouth, my eyes teared. "Now what Grampa? Now what?"

"Oh—just swallow it down."

I gagged down what I could, my belly cringed, I scatted for the bathroom, puked it up, guzzled water from the sink's spigot, heard them laughing, heard Grandpa say, "Now you don't have to worry about him sneaking it."

* * * * *

"Hungry?" said Grandpa.

I nodded.

"Like peanut butter and jelly?"

"It's the best."

"I see you're my kind of man."

He opened the bread drawer, took out a new baked loaf, sawed slices. "Got a dog at home I call Ninnyhammer. She's a grand ol' bitch. Sharp as a tack. Neighbor's keeping an eye on her. Wish I could of brought her along."

"Wish I had a dog."

"Maybe your pop'll let you get one if you ask. Let's wrap up these sandwiches and go for a walk."

"I used to go for walks with Bill. Sometimes we'd go to the park."

"Who's Bill?"

"The nigger I lived with before I came here."

"Nigger?"

"Uh-huh."

"Not a good word, squirt. Nope. Polite word is Negro. That's what decent people say."

"Oh."

* * * * *

We walked down the hill under near cloudless sky. I fought to keep up with his long legged stride. He saw my struggle, slowed his pace, wrapped an arm around my shoulder, made me feel like I had nothing under my feet but air. We came to an area wooded with alder and fir.

"Ever wander back there?"

"Couple times."

"Not much in the way of woods where I live now. Mostly flat, open country. Place here reminds me of where I grew up in the Ozarks. What say we have a look?"

A few paces in he stopped, shushed me, pointed. A doe and her fawn stood in front of us, startled; they vanished into the underbrush as if by magic. Further on, we encountered the long creek that welled up from some hidden place deep underground and almost bisected the island as it sang its way through fir and cedar and wild berry bushes ending in a sandy delta where it entered the sound. He squatted on his hams, brushed back loose pine needles. "Those're coon tracks. Come back some morning before light, you can spy on them."

We sat, knees drawn up, backs resting against the mossy creek bank, ate the sandwiches. "I was raised up with an older brother named Jackson, after the Great Stonewall. Don't know exactly how old I am by a year or so. Births weren't recorded well back then. Lived in a two-room cabin my great granddaddy built from logs. Had a roof that sometimes leaked a bit when it stormed hard, a stinky outhouse in the back, and a sweet water well in front."

We finished the sandwiches, I belched, Grandpa rolled on his belly, drank from the stream, wiped his mouth with the back of his hand, sat back next to me.

"Ma grew spuds and carrots and other such stuff on a rocky patch she tilled nearby. I learnt to hunt when I was still a tadpole. Poor old Jack—he was walleyed. Never could quite decide which way he was looking. Couldn't shoot worth a hoot. I had a sweet little twenty-two handed down to me. Got to where I could shoot the eye out of a squirrel. Shot other varmints, too. Long as it had legs and a face and could be brought down with a .22 rifle, it went in the cooking pot and got et."

He stood, brushed pine needles off the butt of his pants. I rose, too. We started back to the road. "I was told we were Jews somewhere way back. Didn't matter. I never saw any of it. Mostly, it was a happy place. Pa drank a little. Sometimes when he had a snoot full, he'd get frisky and start kissing on Ma on the neck, but she wasn't having any of it. Said she didn't want to bring any more of his kind into the world. If he pushed too far, she got a stick of wood and wailed on him until he lost his urges."

We reached the road, started our climb back up the hill. A dog barked at us from a long driveway. Cumulus clouds scudded the western horizon.

* * * * *

I sat on a log in the woodshed while Grandpa chopped wood. "After I joined the army, I was posted at the old Spanish fort in San Francisco called Presidio. When war came, my regiment packed, formed up, and marched down Lombard Street like we were already heroes. Loaded on a steamship called City of Peking. Biggest damn thing I ever saw. Bigger than most buildings. Had two giant smoke stacks and four tall masts." He grunted as he swung the axe. "Soon as we loaded and steam was up, we set off through the Golden Gate and out into the Pacific headed for the Philippine Islands to fight the Spaniards. First time I ever heard of such a place." He put the axe down, took his tobacco pouch out, offered it in my direction. I shook my head. He grinned.

"Was a miserable damn trip. Took the hero right out of me. None of us ever been to sea. Chow was so bad it couldn't hardly be et. Didn't matter because most all of us were green around the gills. Sailors got a big hoot out of it.

"Traveled clear on the other side of the world. Took over a month to get there. By that time, I was skinnier than a fence rail. Arrived end of June. Hotter than perdition. Admiral Dewey had already sunk their fleet, so we fought for the city of Manila. Wasn't a real battle; Spaniards didn't have anymore fight in them, but they couldn't give up the place without a skirmish. Agreements were struck. We whooped and shot off our guns, they whooped and shot off theirs, and nobody got bad hurt. By afternoon our flag was flapping over the old walled city called Intramuros. Folks there were happy as clams to have the papists booted out, but President McKinley ruined everything by beating his gums. Said it was time to civilize them Filipinos. Time to Christianize them too. Called them: 'White Man's Burden.' That's when the real fighting started."

He hawked and spat, wiped his jowls with the back of his hand. I stood, picked up the axe, stuck it in the chopping block, Grandpa smiled. "You're going to grow up to be a bull, by golly."

"What's White Man's Burden?"

"Kind of complicated. Some think white folks are the smartest folks. Smarter than all the dark skinned folks."

"How come they think that?"

He shook his head. "Don't know. Most thought that way where I grew up. To Ma and Pa color made no difference. They wouldn't put up with those prejudiced kind. Wouldn't even let them draw a drink from the well on a hot day. Caused trouble sometimes, but they were strong headed. Had no back down in them. None at all."

* * * * *

Grandpa pulled his coat collar up around his ears as we walked across the yard. "Brrr. Feels like snow's coming." When we got to the road, he pointed the direction opposite the hill. "Ever been that-a-way?"

"Uh-huh."

"Where's it go?"

"Other side of the island."

"Long walk?"

"Kind of."

"Much interesting?"

"Some farms and cows and things. You can see the Olympic Mountains from there."

"Never seen them. Want to walk it?"

"Sure. I know the way."

As we walked, he put a pinch of tobacco in his cheek; only sounds were of gravel roiling under our feet. I breathed in through my mouth; the air tasted good.

Grandpa spat toward the edge of the road. "Foul stuff."

"How come you chew it?"

"Habit from my soldiering days."

He spat again. I picked up a rock; side armed it at a glass insulator. Missed, reached for another.

"Break them often?"

"Sometimes."

"Bad idea, squirt. They're telephone wires. Folks need them to talk. Break the glass and the line's busted. Telephone company's got to fix it so people can talk again."

I dropped the rock, sighed.

"Best to do no harm when you can."

I looked up at him. Nodded.

"Guess I was fifteen—sixteen when I become a professional soldier. Army recruiter passed through one day dressed up all spiffy, knocking at doors. Told Jack and me we could make a fine career for ourselves till he saw ol' Jack's eyes. Shook his head, said nope, sorry, they couldn't use him but they'd be happy to take me. Ma fussed, but Pa got firm with the idea.

"I was illiterate. Couldn't read nor write except for one thing. Before he died, Grandpa taught me to sign my name. Told me only ignorant men make a mark. Taught me a fancy signature—all loops and curlicues. I was damn proud of it. Signed that old army contract with a flourish."

I liked the way he said his words. They sounded like they were wrapped up in his nose before they came out his mouth. Nobody I knew said them like that. Remembered listening to Bill speak. His words rumbled like they were coming from an empty barrel.

We walked on, quiet again. Ahead, the road intersected with another. I pointed left. "Got to go that way."

A mile down the new road, two abrupt hills stood like the backs of Asian camels I saw in Life Magazine. At the bottom of the second hill, a small house set back from the road. In front of it, a woman worked cutting rose bushes. Apple trees lined the edge of the road. Grandpa called out to the woman. "Mind if we pick us a couple, Missus?"

She straightened up, pressed her hands into the small of her back, smiled. "Help yourself. Most are going to fall and rot. Can't eat them all myself."

"You alone, are you?"

"My husband passed three years ago."

"Sorry to know that."

"Hard to keep up with things on my own."

"Need a little help? We can both dig."

"Thank you, no. Work helps pass the time."

Grandpa cleaned the wad of tobacco from his mouth with a finger, spat twice. "If it's not too much trouble, Missus, we could use a little drink of water."

She smiled again. "Well's in back, tin cup hanging from the pump handle."

We had a drink and resumed our walk. Grandpa gave the woman a wave. "Thank you, Missus. Nice talking to you."

She waved, turned back to her bushes.

* * * * *

77

We climbed a final hill, a vista of snow-crowned mountains opened before us. Grandpa dropped to his hams, shook his head. "The beauty of it all. The beauty of it all. I could stay right here middle of the road and just look, cars be damned."

Squatted, his face sat level with mine. I rolled my eyes hard to the side to look at him in secret, studied the gray of his eyes, the shape of his cheekbones, the deep cleft in his chin. Touched my own face, ran fingertips over it, found similarity.

Grandpa swooped me, held me tight, grinned big, rubbed his nose against my cheek. "You're a chip off the old block all right. Can't be any doubt about that."

I flushed.

"Don't have to feel shy, squirt. What say we head back? Going to be lunchtime soon."

As we walked back down the hill, I took quick steps and stopped my feet, skidded in the loose gravel. Did it a couple more times before we reached the bottom. Grandpa laughed. "Easy to forget what it was to be a kid."

We passed the house with the apple trees. Didn't see the woman. I wanted Grandpa to talk more. "Inky told me lots of stories about the war."

"He's the fella works with your pop?"

"Yep. Flew planes and shot guns and lived on a ship in the war. That's what I want to do more than anything. Think he's a hero or something."

"Not everybody fights a war is a hero, squirt. Most did what they had to do to make it through."

"Inky shot Jap planes."

"Humph, that's not something everybody did. Would of scared the pants off me."

"You fight the Japs?"

"Oh no, no. My fight was long before that."

"Like Bill? He's kind of old—like you."

He scoffed. "Old like me?" He scoffed again. "Ever see him anymore?"

"Nope. They live on the mainland."

"Miss them?"

I fell silent.

"So—you pretty much cared for him, huh?"

I nodded.

"Mad when your momma stole you away?"

"Got mad as hell, Grandpa."

"I bet. Ever tell her?"

"Nope."

"Why not?"

"Don't want to be mean."

"We'll keep it a secret between us. How's that?"

I nodded.

"Come on, squirt, let's get down the road."

"Bill fought in France, wherever that was. Told me he lived in a muddy holes most a the time."

"He was probably telling you about World War One—about fighting the Bosh."

"Yeah, that's what he called them."

He took out his pouch, settled the tobacco in his cheek. "I've told you most of what's worth telling."

I looked up. The air seemed glow around him. I felt its warmth.

We walked on; our pace slowed a bit. He reached down, chucked my chin. "That cleft you got's an heirloom, squirt. Been in the family for generations." He spat, drew in for a minute. "Real fighting started after the papist left. Didn't look to the Filipinos like we were going to leave, so the patriots declared war on us. That upset most, especially the old timers that fought the Indian Wars and believed the only good one was a dead one."

We reached the intersection, turned onto the final stretch of road. Grandpa cleaned his cheek of tobacco. "No place to get a drink, I suppose."

"Don't know anybody here."

He looked around. "Maybe we can spot a faucet outside. Doubt they'll mind me taking a sip." He pointed. "There's one over there, outside that brick house. I'll sneak a drink. If I'm lucky, I won't get a butt load of rock salt." He had his drink; we walked on.

"You were with real Indian fighters?"

"Yep. Some bore scars from where they'd been shot by arrows."

I remembered seeing a western with shooting and the shriek of bugles on the Meyer's television.

"One of our generals said, 'Kill everybody over the age of ten.' Ol' timers said, 'Let's civilize them all with our spandy new Krag rifles.' Slaughtering commenced. Went on till the Filipinos give up. Come away not knowing the right or wrong of it. Told myself I was a soldier doing my duty, but it wasn't that simple. That wasn't enough to explain it away. Still think about it sometimes and wonder. Anyway, after that, I came back to San Francisco. Couple years later the great earthquake turned most everything to ashes and dust." He drew a breath. "Your momma's got to be worrying by now, squirt. Let's hustle up. I'll tell you the rest of the tale some other time."

* * * * *

Dad's chair squawked as Grandpa sat. Mom poured coffee. "Any plans today, Thomas?"

"Nope."

"It's Saturday, the weathers fine, you should go out."

"I want to stay with Grandpa."

"Better if you give Grandpa and me a little time alone. We have lots to talk about before he leaves."

I looked at Grandpa. He gave a smile, nodded. I took a breath. "Okay."

* * * * *

Started down the hill, morning's chill hung. Heard them talking before I slept. Grandpa would leave the next day. I picked up a rock, flung it at a glass insulator, missed, frowned, stopped, squatted on my haunches, squinched my eyes. A voice interrupted my reverie. "Tommy-boy? Tommy-boy, are ye okay?"

I looked up. Oscar stood at my side. "Are ye okay?"

"I miss him."

"Who do ye miss?"

"Grandpa."

"Something happen?"

"No."

"Well come on lad. I'll drive ye home."

He stood me up, brushed gravel from my pants. "Hop in the car."

I broke away, sprinted down the hill, grew breathless, slowed to a walk, came a hollow feeling, an emptiness that stretched on forever, dug in my pocket, found a squirreled away nickel, thought it might be the answer, crossed the highway, changed my mind, headed for the shop, maybe Inky had work.

He sat, leaned back in a chair. "Long time no see, kiddo."

"Been with my grandpa."

"How is it?"

"He's leaving."

"Oh. Feeling bad, huh."

"Yep."

* * * * *

The night after Grandpa left, I slept with gabbled voices rambling inside my head. Saw myself walking down an unfamiliar road. I trembled. Picked up a rock to fling. It weighed heavy. Too heavy to throw. When I dropped it the heaviness stayed in my arm and spread through my whole body. I sat down at the edge of the road. A car passed by, and another. Neither regarded me. I followed them with my eyes, till they disappeared in the swirl of fog that lay on the road ahead.

As the dream continued to play itself out, I saw Bill some distance away—his back to me. Around him, fog swirled and swirled. I called. He did not answer. I called again. He started to walk away. I ran after him, but his long legs opened the gap further. I called—louder—louder—felt vibrations from my voice inside my head as though the sound never left my mouth. As time passed, the fog became denser, and poof—he was gone.

* * * * *

Old Man Hartvickson stopped by the house; took a chair, Mom poured coffee. "Got work for the boy if he wants it. Sold my chickens. Truck's coming from the mainland Tuesday. Got four night's work. Ten bucks total. Your boy interested?"

Dad looked at me.

I nodded. "How come we do it at night, Mister Hartvickson?"

"Chickens can't see in the dark. Makes them easy pickings."

* * * * *

I stood outside with five boys shivering in the night air while the truck driver and his helper unloaded a mountain of wooden cages from a flatbed truck. Old man Hartvickson waited with us. "Birds go fourteen to a cage. No more, no less. Catch them seven at a time. Reach under, grab them by one leg until you've got three or four in one hand, catch the rest with the other. Have to work sneaky. Make too much noise; they start bunching up in the corners, climbing on top of each other. If they get piled up the ones underneath smother. Can't sell dead birds."

One boy, tall, wiry, with crossed eyes, approached me. "Never saw you before. What's your name?"

"Thomas."

"My name's Jon. Done this before?"

"Nope."

"It's not so bad. I've done worse. Got gloves?"

"Nope."

"Me neither. It's going to hurt like hell. Going to rub you raw."

I showed my hands. "I've got calluses."

"Yeah, so do I, but that not where it rubs. You'll see."

Inside the coop, red lights were so dim they cast no shadows; stench engulfed me; a thousand or so chickens murmured in their sleep as we prepared to become their worst nightmare. All the excitement left me when the first one I grabbed shit on my hand. Within twenty minutes, the skin of both my hands between thumb and forefinger wore into raw sores and began to bleed. When I stopped to nurse them Old Man Hartvickson said, "Get back to work. We have to finish loading the truck before sunup."

My arms tired, chickens began to slip from my grasp, had to catch them over and over. At the first edge of daylight, the old man said, "That's it for tonight, boys. Come on to the house. Wash up, have some cookies and milk. After, I'll drive you home."

* * * * *

I walked through the door. Dad sat reading the newspaper. "Looks like you been ridden hard and put away wet."

"Don't know what that means."

"Go look in the mirror."

"Too tired."

"Guess you expect us to clean up our own mess at the shop today, huh."

"Do I have to?"

"Nope. Not while you're doing this job you don't."

"Sit down and have something to eat," said Mom.

"Not hungry."

She looked surprised. "You should be starved."

"Just want to go to bed. Already washed up and everything."

"Go ahead," said Dad.

I crawled into bed, slept like a stone.

* * * * *

Jon lived in the second floor apartment of a dilapidated building on the peninsula built last century for some forgotten purpose. From his apartment, we climbed two flights to the attic where he kept his hot rod magazines stashed inside a steamer trunk. "Like it up here. Got privacy from my sisters." We sat cross-legged amid a hundred years of left behinds, looked at pictures as he flipped pages. He pointed to a picture of the reddest car I'd ever seen. "That's it. That's what I want. A '36 Ford coupe with a flat head V8 and a four-barrel, all chromed.

Got it all planned in my head how I'm going do it. It'll sound like the hounds from hell. Been talking to Toby. He says I can probably find one at Buster Stoltz's junkyard for thirty-forty bucks. Got more than that saved up." He picked up an oil can from inside the trunk. "Almost full. Every cent I make goes in here. Toby says before I buy it, I have to be careful of rust. Too much and it's not worth beans. Said he'll even kick in a little cash here and there when I'm short. We're going to make a frigging masterpiece. They'll hear it clear to the mainland when I punch the gas. " We spent another half hour looking at the magazines. "I'm tired of this," said Jon. "Let's go do something."

"What?"

"Let's look for empty bottles to cash in."

"Nah."

"Then, let's go look at the Model A Donny's fixing up."

"Don't care about it. We got one."

"Well, everybody's gone. We can sneak one of my ol' man's beers. He keeps it hid under the kitchen sink."

"You've done it before?"

"Lots of times.

I made the long walk home with a foul taste I couldn't spit out. Wondered why anybody would drink that stuff. No more for me. Not again. Not ever.

* * * * *

Mom hummed a tune as she prepared sandwiches. She placed one in front of Dad, bent, and kissed him hard on the mouth.

"To what do I owe the pleasure?"

"I'm late."

"Late?"

"Yes, late."

Dad looked puzzled. "You mean…?"

"Exactly."

He stubbed out his cigarette, cracked an ear-to-ear smile, reached out for her—lost his smile. "Going to be expensive."

"It'll be fine, Stosh. We'll figure out a way. There's always a way. Think about it. You're going to have one of your own."

He refound his smile, kissed her on the mouth in a way that made me blush.

"What's it mean?" I said.

"It means you're going to have a little brother or sister," said Mom.

"Wow, really?"

Dad turned his face to me. "Yep, that's what it means alright." He looked back at Mom. "What do you think it'll be, Dorothy?"

"There's no way of knowing."

"Yes there is. If a man overwhelms his woman, it'll be a girl. If a woman overwhelms her man, it'll be a boy. It's going to be a boy for sure." They kissed again.

He and I walked in silence. Sometimes I looked up at his face. He had an expression new to me. At the shop, he pushed open the door. The three fisherman sat inside, one held a bottle. "I'm going be a father," he said.

* * * * *

Wind blustered. Jon and I meandered through a jumble of seaweed-encrusted driftwood looking for penny beer bottles.

He called from a distance, "Hey, look what I found."

I scrambled to where he stood. He pointed to a bird lying motionless on the rocks. "Looks dead."

"Yeah." I bent to pick it up. It burst into a fury of motion. I lost my balance; fell. "It's alive, but it's hurt bad. What'll we do?"

"Let's take it to Mister Edson. He'll know."

Jon took off his jacket, covered the bird, picked it up.

Mister Edson's studio neighbored the gas station. Toby sat on his usual perch. "What ya fella's carryin'?"

"Got a hurt bird," said Jon. "Taking it to Mister Edson to see if he can fix it up."

"He'll do 'er."

Mister Edson sat at his drafting table applying pigments to one of his black and white prints. The master photographer had white hair and a beardless Santa Clause face. In the studio with him lived a gray owl named Stieglitz. It had a flat, silver face, and often twisted its head to see things from a backward point of view.

"Think it's a Tern," said Jon.

"Right you are," said Mister Edson.

Stieglitz, unimpressed, regurgitated a waxy hairball and resumed watching.

"It has a broken wing," said Mister Edson. "I'll splint it up and keep it here until it's ready to fly."

Finished with splinting the bird's wing, we all went outside for a photo shoot. Jon christened us The Burton Bird Watchers.

* * * * *

Old Man Hartvickson slaughtered a hundred chickens. Dad bought twenty. We spent the day plucking and gutting them. Dad took them to the butcher shop to have them wrapped and stored in a rented locker in Matt Morrissey big freezer.

* * * * *

Rain fell. "I'm going to drive this morning," said Dad. "Don't want to come back up the hill more than once. Don't trust the car's going to hold up much longer if I do it too often. Want to squeeze as much out of her as I can before we think about getting something newer."

"I'll fix you a lunch," said Mom.

"That'll be fine. Boy'll have to walk back when he finishes. Shop's too crowded with work for him to hang around all day."

"I think it's better to keep him home until it clears up."

"Not likely to happen soon."

"I don't want him down sick, Stosh"

"Idle hands are the devil's workshop."

Mom tied it up his lunch in a towel. "I know, but I don't want him sick."

"Well—can't do nothing about the damn weather."

He took up his lunch, gave Mom a quick kiss, ran for the car. I heard the starter grind, grind again, on the third effort the engine clattered to life. He backed out onto the road and went his way.

* * * * *

Mom's belly grew. Memories of the pregnant woman at Missus Miller's came to mind, remembrances of how she nestled me close so I could hear the gurgling sounds of new life.

She came out of the bathroom. "Stosh, I'm bleeding."

I studied her, looked for cuts.

"Sit down," said Dad. "I'll run across the road and give Doc Osborne a call."

"Where are you bleeding from, Mom?"

"My private parts. I may be losing the baby."

"How'd that happen?"

"I can't explain."

"How come?"

She shook her head. "Because I don't know."

Dad returned. "Doc's on his way." He helped her stand, gave her a shoulder, walked her to the bedroom.

Doc Osborne arrived. I stood outside the closed bedroom door listening. "I don't hear the fetus. It may no longer be viable. We need to get her to the hospital immediately."

"I got no money for it."

"Money or not, she has to go."

Dad carried her to Doc Osborne's car, placed her in the back seat, stood staring into the rain as they drove away.

* * * * *

The phone rang, Inky picked up the receiver, talked, handed it to Dad who talked a long time about things I didn't understand, he hung up, stood silent, eyes cast downward, shook his head.

Inky put down the tool he held. "What's going on, Stosh?"

Dad drew a breath, breathed it out audibly, shook out a cigarette, lit it. "Goddamnit, how's this kind of shit happen?"

I made myself invisible.

Dad shook his head. "Baby's dead. Dorothy's got a bad infection that's spread to her kidneys. Says he's got her on strong antibiotics. Thinks he's might have to remove one. Said he's hoping for the best with the other. Things ain't looking good. She might not make it."

After a dismal evening, I knelt beside my bed, said Missus Miller's pray twice, stayed on my knees till they hurt, got into bed, lay awake a long time.

* * * * *

Dad stood at the stove heating leftover spaghetti. "Going see your mama tomorrow, maybe bring her home."

"Really?"

"Yep. I'm just hoping the old jalopy'll make it up Morgan Hill. She's getting pretty damn feeble. Have to get something newer pretty soon."

"What happens if it doesn't make it?"

"If she don't, I'll swing by Ink's and borrow his."

"How come you don't do that first?"

Dad scoffed. "What made you think of that?"

"Donno."

"That's a pretty damn good idea."

He served up spaghetti, turned on the radio. "What's you and your momma listen to?"

I looked at the clock. "Five minutes Gun Smoke's on KIRO."

"KIRO it is."

We ate without talk. I washed the dishes; Dad lit a smoke, when the dishes were done, I started for my room; he waved me back. "Come on, sit. We'll finish up the program."

The program ended, Dad turned off the radio, sighed, looked at me. "I grew up in this house. No love in it. None at all. Like living in a damn desert." He paused. "Hard to explain. Guess you got to be there to get it. After my folks were gone I packed what I needed and left intending never to come back. Tramped a long time. Learnt to be damn tough because that's what you got to be when you're hoboing. Never learnt much else. Sixteen, I joined the corps. Being tough worked good there. I was a damn fine marine. Anyhow…" He fell quiet for a moment. "Anyhow, that's all history. Now here I am, father to a boy, husband to a real sick lady wondering what the hell to do. Makes no sense for me. Know I ain't good at being neither. Figured that out sometime back. Probably a big mistake getting married in the first place. Should of stayed a bachelor. Would've been the smart thing. Ain't much fun being grown up with all that responsibility. Just ain't no fun."

"Isn't fun being a kid, either."

He nodded. "I know about that for sure."

We fell silent. The Kit-Kat-Klock rolled its eyes and wagged its tail—impatient—as if expecting more. None came.

* * * * *

Mom came home a ghost. Dad fell into despair. Every night, as I lay in bed, I heard them talking about money they didn't have and bills they did. One night Mom asked, "If there's no money to pay bills, how is it there's always money for liquor?" I shut my ears.

* * * * *

We sat eating breakfast. Summer rain fell. "Going north again, Dorothy."

Mom dropped her fork. "Oh Stosh, you can't do that."

"Already took an advance from Martin."

"Christ, don't you ever think about us?"

He scoffed. "Think about you's all I do. Why you think I took the advance. You know money's short when the working boats go; and I want to finish this place."

"I just think about the danger, Stosh. I don't want to lose you."

"Ain't going to happen. I live a charmed life."

Mom soured her face. "No, you don't. No one does. I saw many just like you at the hospital, all chewed up and ruined. I'll bet before they were wounded every damn one of them thought he lived a charmed life. So no, Stosh, I don't want you to go. Give Martin his money back. We'll get by without it."

"Chances of something happening again are a million in one."

"You're still suffering pain from the last trip. How are you going to be able to do the work?"

"Same as I always do. Mind over matter. I don't mind, and it don't matter."

"Well, it does matter to me. I don't want a crippled husband."

"Hell, you already got one—or didn't you notice?"

Mom lit a cigarette, blew smoke at the ceiling, I sat silent; the Kit-Kat-Klock scrutinized the scene. Mom took another drag from her cigarette, crushed it out; looked at me as if I were a stranger.

* * * * *

I lay in bed. A single car passed on the road below, it showed a brief flicker of light against the dark, its sound muffled by rain. Maybe he'll stay gone forever. Didn't mind if he did, not one bit.

Tried to like him. Maybe he tried too. None of it mattered. I had grown to enjoy my aloneness, living with thoughts, imaginings. They took me wherever I wanted to go. I could be safe beside Missus Miller, or play at the park under the loving eye of Bill. So easy—all of it. I had only to think, to imagine, nobody knew but me.

In the morning, I went downstairs. Mom sat smoking a cigarette, a half full ashtray sat in front of her. She looked up at me, shook her head. "Your Dad didn't come home last night."

"Where'd he go?"

"I have no idea."

"Is he coming back?"

"I don't know that either."

I slumped into my chair.

She tried to erase her anger, to look tender, but didn't succeed. "Are you hungry?"

"Not so much. Feel kind of sad."

"Why is that?"

"Because last night I wished he'd stay gone forever."

* * * * *

Dad came through the door, staggered straight to bed, slept till the next noon, rose, sat walled-up and wordless. Mom queried him till he slapped the tabletop. "I went to the mainland, goddamnit."

I left the room. Upstairs I read with intense concentration, trying to shut out things being said below; heard anyway.

"What did you go to the mainland for?"

"To get away."

"To get away from what, Stosh? From me? From your son?"

"From all of it."

"How much did you spend?"

"Don't know."

"Did you spend the whole advance?"

"Said I don't know, goddamnit."

"I need to know because there's almost no food in the house."

"Get off my back. What's done is done."

"So—we're broke?"

"That's none of your damn business."

"It is, goddamnit. I'm your wife, not some floozy you picked up off the street. I have a right to know. I want an answer. How am I supposed to put food on the table? How do you expect me to do that? Run a tab like you do at the tavern? Hock my wedding ring? Should I do that, Stosh? Hock my wedding ring? Doesn't seem to mean much to you. Seems like all I am is chief cook and bottle washer. Is that what I mean to you?"

Something shattered, a door slammed, the car started, gears clashed, it drove away. I stayed sealed up in my room. Hunger cramped my belly. No food in the house, I thought. Maybe it will be that way forever. Wondered if I should get Dad's rifle, go into the woods, kill a deer as I sometimes did in my imaginings, skin it, carve it up so Mom could cook it, be man of the house, but I had never shot a gun before.

*****

I walked the road kicking rocks. Came to Bart's house.

"Hey Thomas, where you headed?"

"To get a chicken for Mom."

"I'll tag along."

"Okay."

We shuffled our way down the hill searching ditches for bottles to trade for pennies. Found none. Inside the freezer, Bart said, "Bet you won't touch your whanger to the wall."

"How much?"

"Don't know."

"Got to be something."

He dug a quarter from his pocket. "How's this?"

"Okay."

I unbuttoned my fly; touched it to the wall, held it there for a long minute to prove myself, pulled away—the wall didn't let go. The slightest movement brought shocks of pain.

Bart laughed. "Knew that'd happen."

"Why'd you tell me to do it, then?"

"Thought it'd be funny."

Time passed. Chills spread through my body. I stood glued to the wall on the verge of panic, Matt Morrissey came in to check on us, saw the situation, choked with laughter, face and jowls suffused bright scarlet, he clutched his chest, took a tin from his pocket, slipped a tablet under his tongue, paused till it had it's affect. "Don't worry kid, I'll get you fixed up." He left, returned with a cup of warm water. Still chortling, he poured it down the wall, everything detached. "Think you ought to keep that little pecker of yours locked up in those trousers from now on. That's my advice to you, sonny boy."

We left. I walked ahead of Bart so I didn't have to see his face. When I got home, Mom said, "Where's the chicken?"

"Chicken?"

* * * * *

The Alibi jukebox played a song sung by some guy with a mournful voice, Inky and I sat chewing our food. "How's your mama doing since she got back?"

"Okay, I guess."

"She getting around okay?"

"Think so."

"Any problems?" I stopped chewing, cast my eyes down. Inky cocked his head. "Any?"

"Dad says I'm not supposed to talk about it."

Inky wrinkled his chin, nodded. "Okay kiddo let it go. Eat up, we got more running around to do."

We walked down the sidewalk, past the tavern to Kimmel's Market. "Go get yourself a funny book whilst I pick up some chow for the sugar shack."

*****

I found ways to earn money. In early summer I picked strawberries for a Japanese farmer named Toku whose fields were near the north end of the island. It paid fifty cents a flat, which was considered decent.

I hauled hay for Gus Greene whose real first name was really Giuseppe, part time farmer and full time musician with a firm politician's handshake. He hired me, and Jon and an unnamed old man who wore faded bib overalls who carried a flat pint bottle of Four Roses Whiskey in a brown paper sack in his back pocket and drove the flatbed truck while Jon and I humped the bales. Gus paid a nickel apiece for each bale hauled and stacked in the loft of his barn. That sounded pretty good till I found out it got split three ways. When he paid up at the end of each day his count was always seemed short so we haggled and fumed till he agreed to split the difference. I always walked away feeling cheated.

There were other things I did. I caught chickens, dug ditches for Bill Beymer, and so on and so forth.

That passed the years.

II

We did so much with so little for so long Pretty soon We could do everything with nothing

—Franklin Freeman

My fourteenth birthday. I finished the deal with a whiskered cadger in front of the tavern, carried a bottle of fortified wine under my shirt to the alleyway behind Kimmel's Market, sat between groddy trash cans, unscrewed the cap, took a swallow, spewed it through my nose, felt disappointment, my hopes for an eighty-eight cent romance dashed. Tried again, kept most of it down. A few minutes later, I chucked the empty bottle into the tall grass across the alleyway, waited—waited. In cool night air I began to sweat, felt it under my arms, felt it rolling down my back, thought I would vomit, didn't. On the verge of disappointment, it happened—all the bad shit swirled away, all the fears—the voices—gone. Quietude—as if I were submerged in deep water. Stood, tried to walk, staggered across the alleyway to the tall grass, laid down on my back, watched stars swirl, watched the whole fucking universe swirl, didn't care—not about that—not about a single goddamn thing. Kept saying, "Fuck it-Fuck-it-Fuck it." Fell into twining sleep. Oblivion. Woke to a jarring thump at my foot—ignored it—it came again—persistent—annoying. Squirmed, squinted, saw Franklin Freeman, a slur of my drunken dream, I thought, closed back my eyes, came a harder kick.

"Come on kid. On your feet. What kind of soldier are you laying there in your own puke?" He grabbed a wrist, pulled me to my feet,

94

a lightning bolt ricocheted inside my skull. "It's late. Your folks'll be worried."

"They don't give a shit."

"Can you sit on the bike?"

"I guess."

"I guess isn't good enough. Can you do it? Yes or no?"

"Yes."

I climbed onto the rear fender, hung on in desperation as he gunned the engine, flew down the alley onto the highway and eventually onto the gravel road that led to his shack. Inside, he lit a kerosene lamp. Its dim flicker shadowed a back wall with piles of books. In a far corner stood an army surplus cot made up neat and tight. Beside it, on a wooden box, sat another lantern. "I have a couple extra blankets. You can curl up in the corner. Do your best to get some sleep."

* * * * *

The smell of cooked eggs woke me. Franklin sat in a folding chair eating with gusto. "Hungry?"

I shook my head with care.

He finished eating. "Come on outside. We'll get you cleaned up." There, a small cooking fire seethed near the wellhead. "Put you head under the spout." He worked the handle. An icy spew hit me. I tried to jump away; he grabbed my shirt collar, held me fast. When he stopped pumping, water dribbled down to nothing. Like a fool, I shook my head, thunder roared, felt overwhelming thirst; said nothing. He led me back inside, tossed me a towel.

"Don't know what I'm going tell my dad."

"Tell him only what you have to. Nothing more."

"How will I know?"

He scoffed. "You won't."

* * * * *

95

Dad stood on the porch, I slid off the rear fender, Franklin goosed the throttle, went his way.

"Where the hell you been?"

"Spent the night at Franklin's. Sorry I wasn't here to start the fire."

"Never mind that. You done a bad thing. Your momma's been worried sick. Scared you was laying in a ditch somewhere. Wanted me to drive all over hell looking. And what the hell you doing spending a night at his place? He's a goddamn queer, you know. Same's that longhaired fruit living down at the beach. Hang around him, he's going to turn you queer too."

I knew who Dad was talking about. Everybody knew of him, but nobody seemed to know his name. He was just The Queer At The Beach. Nothing more. Tall and skinny in a near emaciated way with high sharp cheek bones and deep eye sockets below carefully groomed eyebrows, he wore his coal black hair long, oiled heavy, and tied with a single colored ribbon so it laid in a solid mass between his prominent shoulder blades, wore brown Mexican huaraches on his feet and had a gait that was limber and slack and exaggerated by the loose clothes he wore.

The way he lived seemed regular enough. Commuted daily to the mainland, and in the evenings, if I passed by his house I would see him sitting in his lighted living room reading or listening a jazz recording being played on his record player. The sound of the music spilled out through the walls of the house. During warm months he sat on the beach in the company of another man wearing a swimming suit and no shirt exposing his body to the sun, and it was all bony ribs and vertebrae with a small dense tuft of hair between his nipples, and skin, pale like his face that never tanned. Together with the other man he sat on a large blanket with a wine bottle half buried upright in the sand next to them. They drank from long stemmed crystal glasses and chatted in friendly ways. Others kept their distance always, isolating him to his own little island on the beach within the island on the sound and he spent his time alone among many.

* * * * *

"Yer pa come knockin' yesternight. Said yer momma wuz worried spitless 'cause ya went missin'."

I squatted on my hams, drank a swig of soda, belched, sat the bottle down next to me. "I was out late."

"Figured ya wuz hell raisin'."

I nodded with care, thunder still banging. "You think Franklin's queer?"

"Dunno. Don' care. Pays fer his gas, same's all."

"Dad says he is. Said if I hung around him he'd turn me queer too."

"Yeah?"

"Could he?"

Toby leaned forward till all four legs touched the ground, leveled his eyes with mine. "Son, ain't nobody can change ya from whacha are ta whacha ain't."

"How do you know?"

"'Cause I don' jus' listen ta what folks say. I read 'bout stuff, do my own figurin', think it all through so's I know fer sure. Don' need nobody else ta do it fer me. Prob'ly ya need to start doin' that yer own self. That way nobody can bullshit ya inta wrong thinkin'."

"Think Dad's bullshitting?"

"Nope."

"What do you think, then?"

"Think he's a true believer."

I scooted my legs out, sat down. "What's a true believer?"

"Somebody that don' ask no questions. Somebody that might call somebody else a nigger er a faggot."

"I lived with colored folks when I was young."

"How wuz it?"

"They treated me fine—like their own son."

"That good, huh?"

I sighed, nodded my head.

"So negroes is okay in yer book?"

I nodded again.

"Well then maybe ya oughta think 'bout makin' homos okay too."

I sat silent. Toby nudged my leg with the tip of his shoe. "Yer thinkin' 'bout it too hard. Won't come thata way."

I took a final swig of soda. "So how do I figure it out?"

"Nothin' ta figure really. Nothin' ta do but open the door an' let it in."

"Think I'm going to town, maybe have coffee or something."

"Good idee. Jus' think 'bout walkin'. Don' let nothin' else trouble ya. Got foldin' money?"

"Nope."

"Get some inside."

* * * * *

As I walked up Morgan Hill, a car slowed to offer a ride, I waved it on. Aloneness felt good. Pushed my steps hard, reached the crown sweating, out of breath—passed down through Center, past the Co-Op up the last slow grade to Vashon. Saw Franklin's motorcycle parked on the street near the Alibi. Inside, he sat in a booth alone. I scooted into the seat opposite, waved for a waitress. She came. "What can I get you, Hun?"

"Coffee for me, and a slice of apple pie for both of us."

"Coming up."

Franklin scoffed. "Poker winnings?"

"Nope. Struck gold. Got three bucks." I paused, thought about what I wanted to say, sighed. "Dad says you're queer."

He snorted, shook his head, gave me a full on grin. "Funny he'd say that. We've known each other several years. Even drink beer together at the tavern sometimes."

"Are you? It's okay if you are."

"No, I'm not."

"Why's Dad think so?"

"Don't know—maybe because of the way I live. I live by my own rules. Don't live like others."

"Because you're broke?"

He laughed. "No, because it's what I want to do."

Pie came. Waitress sat it down along with a coffee cup, filled it, topped off his; gave a professional smile, moved on.

"I don't get it."

"I was twenty-two, ready to start law school when the war came." He paused, took a bite of pie, chewed slow, swallowed. "My father had me all set up to follow in his footsteps, big career with his law firm, big money, big house, fancy car, trophy wife, my whole future planned down to a gnat's ass."

One of my classmates came in, saw me; smirked as he passed.

"He knew big shots who could keep me out of the military. It was fine for a while. I had a snooty girlfriend with plans to marry and raise a batch of snotty brats, but the war started me thinking about my prefab life. Started me wondering if what he wanted was right, if that was what I wanted." He shook his head. Scoffed. Sipped some coffee. "First time I ever did that."

Bud Bath, owner of the Alibi, came by. "You fellows doing okay?"

"Everything's good," I said.

"Where's your dad? I haven't seen him in a while."

"Not much work in the shop, so he's been going out on a local boat. Sometimes he's gone three-four days."

"How's your mom?"

I shook my head. "Don't think she'll ever heal up."

"That's a shame." He patted my shoulder, moved on.

Two more classmates passed by without regarding me. Franklin continued. "Next day I went to the recruiting office, joined the army. That evening, I told my father his high priced son was off to war. He went into a rage. Called me an idiot. My mother became hysterical. I left the house with only the clothes on my back. That's the last time I saw either of them."

He drank down the last of his coffee, raised the cup over his head to signal for more. "When I finished basic, the army wanted to make me a ninety-day-wonder. Told them I wasn't interested. Told them all I wanted to do was jump from airplanes. They thought that was just fine. Served in the Pacific. Did insane things. I remember one of the guys saying; 'We fly on silk wings into hell itself with twenty pounds of TNT strapped to each leg.' It was near the truth. We started calling ourselves Hell's Angels. Every time someone got killed, I put on another stripe. In the end, I wore a silver bar. If the war had lasted longer, I'd probably be wearing stars." He took a sip of coffee, grimaced. "Think I'm coffeed out, and this place is getting crowded. What say we take a walk?"

The sun sat to the west. We ambled along the concreted sidewalk. Franklin drew in a deep breath, sighed. "The war ended. Army cut me loose. I had a good amount of money banked. Stayed with a friend for a while thinking about what I was going to do. Could have looked for work or gone back to school, I suppose. Could have done about anything, but I had ants in my pants. When you've lived on the razor's edge as long as I did you can't settle down. Can't go back to anything that's called normal. I bought a war surplus Harley and took off with no destination in mind."

We came to the end of the street. "Well, now what?" he said.

"Let's walk up by the bank."

We turned, faced into the sun; walked on. "So, I bought the bike and took off. Along the way, I figured out how easy it is to survive if you don't need much. Bought a surplus tent and sleeping bag. Tied them to my rear fender. Wore my fatigues until they fell apart. Worked small jobs here and there to keep gas in the bike, food in my belly. Sometimes, I'd meet up with someone like me—another airborne bum on a bike. We'd spend a day or two running country roads fast as we could, raising dust, scaring chickens, pissing off farmers, then part company with a handshake feeling like we'd lived a little of the old life." He sighed. "A necessary thing. An absolutely necessary thing."

We passed the bank, kept walking. "Slept in the open when weather was good. Quiet nights except for a dog or two barking off in the distance. Gave me room to think. Made me realize I could never go home.

"Spent time in libraries when I hit towns. Read until they closed. Then, I'd ride on. Thought about what Plato said regarding the unexamined life and how it's not worth living. Self-examination became my *raison d'être*."

I shook my head.

He smiled. "My reason for being. Figured in my whole life, at most, I'd probably do only two or three important things. You know, things that really actually made a difference. Figured they'd probably be small things—like maybe a smile given to the right person at the right time, things I wouldn't even remember. Perhaps things I'd already done. How would I know? Move your elbow and you change the periphery of the universe. Anyway—in the end I drifted back to the west coast. That's pretty much the whole story."

We came to the end of the concrete sidewalk. I drew a breath. "Can we talk again sometime?"

"I've got an empty dance card for the next week or so. I'll pencil you in."

"What'll we talk about?"

"Think about it."

"Okay."

"Come on. I'll give you a ride home."

I sighed. "Rather walk."

"Suit yourself."

* * * * *

Jon and I walked to Toku's strawberry field. "School's starting pretty soon," I said.

"Not going back."

"How come?"

"Joining the army."

"What?"

"Yeah. Ten more days, I'll be seventeen. Old man said he'd sign the papers. Glad to get rid of me, I think."

"But—what about school?"

"Fuck school." I stopped walking. Jon took two more steps, stopped, turned. "Got to get off this podunk island. Got no chance for anything here. Staying'll be like pounding my pud."

"What the hell am I supposed to do?"

"What are you, sixteen?"

"Almost."

"Do your time and get the hell off."

"Do my time? Sounds like a prison sentence."

"Isn't it?"

We walked on in silence. A line of raggedy cars edged the field, all old smoky Fords and Chevrolets with cracked windshields and rusted rocker panels driven by Indians who migrated down from British Columbia to harvest fruit. Franklin's motorcycle was parked in the shade of the outhouse. Everybody worked under the careful watch of Toku; a short, stocky Japanese-American with dangerous eyes who had served in the Army's 442nd and carried a fierce reputation for killing Nazis. He indicated the rows we were to pick. We sat to our task.

Day wore on. I grew thirsty. Walking to the water bucket, I twisted my ankle in the soft dirt; fell hard. Franklin came, squatted beside me; I winced as he removed my clodhopper, he pressed here and there with his thumb, shook his head. "Nothing broken. Wear the shoe loose, go easy on it, you'll be fine."

End of the day, Franklin stood behind me in line with his punched ticket waiting to be paid. "Come on, I'll give you a ride home." He dipped a bandana into the water bucket, squeezed out the excess, tied it around his neck, gave me a shoulder, straddled the motorcycle, kicked the starter pedal. The engine thundered. I climbed onto the rear fender. A rooster tail of dust followed the machine as it chewed down the road.

Franklin stopped in front of the house. "Imagine you'll still be hobbling in the morning. Be ready to go at six sharp. I'll be by." I slid off the fender. He goosed the throttle, dropped the clutch, rumbled off.

I rode to and fro with him the rest of picking season. At the end, the *sturm und drang* of his motorcycle disappeared from the roads and the island lacked the weight of his soul. Nobody else seemed to notice. His last words to me were, "Don't ever own anything you can't walk away from in thirty seconds." The rest of summer I worked at other this-and-that jobs. In fall, I went back to the unhappiness of school. Without Franklin and Jon, Inky and Toby became my only friends.

III

Two Hundred Years Of Tradition Unhampered By Progress

—Chief Joseph J. Joe

Dad sat at the table reading.

"Joining the navy," I said.

He looked up with no change of expression. "Told your momma?"

"Not yet."

"Got to be done."

* * * * *

Rain fell, pregnant clouds hung low. First car I thumbed pulled to a stop, drove me to within an easy downhill walk to the ferry dock. Fog lay on the water. As the ferry moved into it, air became chilled, unpleasant. On the mainland, I rode a city bus down 1st Avenue to Pike Street, got off, walked past flophouse hotels, dime porno peep shows, and under the garish marquee of the Green Parrot Theater. At Pine Street I turned, walked three blocks uphill to the Fourth Avenue recruiter's office. A negro Chief Petty Officer with equatorial black skin greeted me as if I were a rich uncle, took me by the shoulder, led me to the chair in front of his desk.

Tall, slender built, and glamorous, he wore smart dress blues, left sleeve loaded with salty gold hash marks. On his chest, rode a scramble of fruit salad topped by a set of golden aircrew wings. He wore his hair in the fashion marines call high and tight, spoke in a deep southern way. We jawed about this and that, then got down to business.

"Tell me about yourself," he said.

I told him about Inky and his stories, about how I wanted that life and would do anything to have it.

"If you enlist, I will personally see to it you get all that and more. Before the end of your first year you'll be wearing wings like mine."

I left stuffed to the eyeballs with prattle, a fist full of documents, and scheduled for a physical examination.

Back on the island, I walked straight to Franklin's shack, peered through the window, saw everything as I remembered it, missed him, wondered if he would find stars that night.

* * * * *

"Honestly, kiddo, your life here ain't been no smashing success story," said Inky. We sat on the edge of the bulkhead dangling our feet. I fixed my vision on a small sailboat at the far side of the harbor. "I believe you're far better than you've shown. Most here don't think that way. They think you'll fall flat on your ass. It's yours to show different. Don't worry about your momma; I'll look in on her. You'll be one less bother, and you'll make her damn proud. Make me damn proud, too."

* * * * *

The evening before I left, Dad brought out his dress uniform from the closet. With Mom's help, he put it on. It fit as though made for him yesterday. When he moved, his medals chimed like medieval church bells. Tears formed at the corners of his eyes. Late in the night he came into my room; sat on the edge of the bed. In the darkness, I could only make out vague edges of his face. "I loved you best I could," he said. "You got to make your own way from here on. Hope you get your dream."

* * * * *

I stood in the starboard catwalk forward of Elevator One alongside my shipmate Dirty Bob and watched the world set ablaze by a new day's sun. At the far distance, towering swells of cumulus clouds paraded the curved edge of the earth. Close by, Vietnamese fishermen went about their business as though we didn't exist, tending nets from small reed boats shaped like teacups with missing handles. Their junk rode a short kilometer away. If I listened hard, I could hear their voices over the steady rumble of the ship's turbines as they called to one another across the featureless waters of the Tonkin Gulf.

Dirty Bob, a cogitator, a ruminator, a philosopher of the highest order, carried a righteous and forced sense of optimism the way most men carry a loaded gun. Everything for him became fodder, to be worried, chewed, swallowed, and later, belched up to be chewed again. He held immutable opinions about such important and diverse things as Detroit Diesels, Johnny Apple Seed, and the Continental Divide. As usual, he stood, brows furrowed, deep inside himself searching for his day's mojo. After a minute, he slapped the rail with both hands, heaved away, climbed five steel steps to the flight deck, hunched low to pass under a wing of the Alert-Five-Phantom, and walked aft. "Another fine navy day," he said to nobody particular.

The Alert Five Phantom sat manned up and tied down with six chains on Number One Catapult, bridle and holdback laid out beside it, everything in readiness to turn engines, hook up, and launch within the allotted time. Green Shirted catapult crew and Shit-Shirted plane captains lay curled up on the steel deck trying to catch a little shuteye. The pilot slumbered in the front seat of the aircraft, head cocked back at an uncomfortable angle, while the Radar-Intercept-Officer sat in the seat behind reading a Superman comic—his helmet, well decorated with multicolored reflective tape that spelled out LEO THE RIO, sat balanced on the edge of the cockpit.

Air Boss sounded off in his morning voice. He warmed it up like a world-class tenor; his voice, amplified through bullhorns of the 5MC speakers that lined the deck edge, covered us like fine mist. He spent his day sitting in his armored perch three decks up behind thick glass sucking down coffee while moving his eyes over every square inch of the deck. A maestro, he conducted us like a world-class orchestra through a symphony written harsh and dissonant. One that only ended on tonic if men and machines came through unscathed. No guaranteed thing.

Jets formed two angled rows along the deck edges aft of the island, tails hung over water. On the centerline, spotted fore and aft, sat staggered rows of A-1 Spads with dangerous propellers that reached near the butt end of their folded wings and spun like invisible axes. Every plane filled to the gills with volatile fuel and armed to the teeth with pyrotechnics.

Engines began to turn—one, two, uncountable many—planes moved nose to tail under the direction of Yellow Shirts as they made their way forward to the steam powered Catapults that boomed and shuttered the entire ship's hull when their shuttles hit the end of the stroke and snapped the aircraft into the air. A poisonous cloud exhaust fumes that scorched my lungs hung heavy over the deck, flecks of razor sharp non-skid broke loose and nicked exposed skin. Plane after plane was flung airborne as if mere toys. Jets gone, Spads cranked their engines to full power, and one by one, started slow acceleration toward the end of the angle deck, lifted their noses and lumbered into the air. Finished, the deck became quiescent, a temporary lull to be shattered when the second launch began.

Midday, Bob and I broke for chow. We joined the long queue for the mess deck in Hanger Bay 2, and wended our way aft to a hatch, down a steep ladder where we squeezed our way between a half dozen garbage cans filled to the brim with fermenting slop waiting to be dumped overboard when the Fan Tail opened.

We ate amid the clatter of forks and spoons on tin trays. In our midst, BB-Stackers sweated and stewed trying to make sense of the jumble of pyrotechnics coming up from the magazine faster than they could handle. Milling bodies searched for places to sit.

"Make a hole. Make a fuckin hole," the Ordies bellowed, as they moved skid loads of assembled bombs, rockets and flares to the ordnance elevator and up to the flight deck to be parked on the narrow space outboard the island called the Bomb Farm.

Brig Rats marched through nuts-to-butts, stomping cadence at a half step, lead rat bellowing, "Sir! Gangway, sir! Prisoners, sir!" Jar Head Chasers, posted fore and aft, moved along with them carrying riot guns at port arms. The Rats, an unhappy bunch, marched with eyes fixed on the shaved head inches in front of their nose, wore torn, sweat soaked dungarees with a P stenciled on the back of their shirts, were up from chipping rust in the deepest, foulest voids of the ship, the nautical equivalent of making small ones out of big ones. Bob and I forced our way through that crowd, found two empty seats, ate food, plain but substantial. 'Makes a turd,' we said.

We were half finished when Woody showed up. "How's it hangin'?"

Bob said, "How's it feel to be a motherfucking two digit midget?"

"Ninety-eight and a wake up and you all can blow me."

"Got plans?"

"Bet your ass I do. Going back to the real world, find me a hippie chick with a rich daddy and fuck myself into a coma."

Back on deck, things ground on launch after launch, recovery after recovery till the sun dipped below the horizon and stippled the sky in pastel colors. My feet were tired and swollen, boot seams cut into the flesh, few thoughts rattled inside my head. Just one more recovery and it would finish. Just one more recovery and I could drag my cruddy ass to bed.

With abruptness, it ended. I walked aft slow, nursing my feet, savoring the relative quiet as the last plane engine spun to a stop and it became possible again to hear human voices. In spite of pain and fatigue, I felt exultant. Got to the Round Down, sat, dangled my feet; watched the ship's turbulent wake. A cool breeze soothed my back, dried the sweat from my hair, and I remembered, as always, it was small things that pleasured most.

* * * * *

The berthing compartment smelled of unwashed clothes and rancid sweat. Air hung still—damp. I began to sweat again. Dim red light filled the compartment's corners leaving the rest in bloody twilight.

At a table near one bulkhead, McQuinn sat with Freddy Flitter and two others under a clot of cigarette smoke playing catch-me-fuck-me Pinochle. The game had been in continuous play since we left the real world; the scrawl of score filled the pages of several yellow legal pads, but didn't matter because nobody paid real attention. With the passing hours and days, players came and players went. Only the game had a continuous nature.

I sat down on the deck beside McQuinn's chair, leaned back against the rack behind, watched. He nodded to me, took a drag off the butt glued to the corner of his mouth, squinted as exhaled smoke smarted his eyes, turned back to the game. We were surrounded by wet sounds of sleeping men and by the easy swimming motion of the ship. I let out an audible sigh feeling pretty damn good about the world I lived in. Directly above, on the flight deck, diesel sounds of tractor engines made their way through to me, but they were soft, muffled, pleasant to the ear. Occasionally, somebody dropped a set of aircraft chains that sounded like a handful of nuts and bolts poured into an empty coffee can. Behind all of it, the steady rumble of the ship's turbines. All familiar. All comforting. I felt exhaustion seep into my body.

Dirty Bob burst into the compartment full of his usual piss and vinegar, looked me eye to eye, started singing some cutesy made-up song in falsetto, something like: *'I wanna lick your ear—I wanna lick you all over…'* and so on and so forth. He grinned, bent down, gave me a great smacking kiss on the lips. I didn't relish it, but he was my good and great friend, so I let it pass. That he was a crazy fuck nobody doubted. He himself knew that to be true but didn't give a fat rat's ass.

The complexities of knowing Bob pushed some away. Under his mirth lived a cynical misanthrope. Booze lubricated his life. It allowed his internal machinery to run the proper way. "Keeps me honest," he said. "Takes away my illusions. Allows me to see the absurdity of life." He seldom smiled when drinking and had bloodied my face more than once as I steered him back to the ship so drunk he couldn't have slapped his ass with either hand. He'd say, "Fight, fuck, or go for your gun," and pop me in the kisser. One time it pissed me off. I put him hard on the ground, held him tight with an elbow, cocked my fist. He looked me in the eye, gave me his best shit-eating grin. "Goldie—Goldie—I think I just saw God." Without hesitation I would have laid down my life for him as would any of us, even those put off. That was the nature of relationships in that place. Nobody died alone.

Bob got hurt a week before standing on the steps of a plane as he leaned around the strapped in hot to go pilot working a radio problem to save the sortie. The plane had taxied forward, and sat positioned directly behind the Jet Blast Deflector next in line for the Cat. A Phantom, hooked up, ready to shoot, cranked on afterburner and created a fulminating maelstrom of seething air that rumbled aft and plastered Bob against the side of the plane. It twisted and lifted his jersey and fricasseed his back for a long dicey minute. Only after the Phantom snapped off the bow could Bob drop to the deck. McQuinn tried to get him below, but he would not go till his plane launched. PJ finally got him to Sick Bay. There, Mac-the-Quack took one look, called for the Flight Surgeon who treated him, gave him a fistful of dope pills, and put on him light duty.

I remembered sitting with him one morning at the bar in the scuzzy little Hole In The Wall Bar. We were feeling sorry for ourselves and wondering just how in hell we would to make it back to the ship in time for Quarters. Behind us, on Magsaysay Boulevard, a sinuous snake of jeepneys and tricycles scrabbled to and fro carrying loads of forlorn sailors in mass migration to Shit River Bridge. We continued nursing our beers, holding out for the last minute. Bob looked over his shoulder at the chaos and back at me, made a grand gesture that took it all in. "None of this shit matters. Truth is we're all going to die pretty fucking soon and pretty fucking brutally and none of this shit's going to count for anything."

I knew what he meant. Knew with exactness how death comes, sometimes singular, sometimes in bunches like those of our tribe aboard USS Forrestal who were turned back to star dust when her flight deck erupted like a monstrous roman fucking candle. And yes indeed, we were tribal.

Time passed, I grew tired of sitting, so I left them, walked back to my rack, undressed, climbed in, did my best to relax. When I found sleep, it came in hurky-jerky fits and spurts filled with quirky dreams that caused twists and twitches. Just when deep sleep settled in, Flight Quarters sounded over the speakers of the 1MC and jerked me back to irritated consciousness feeling just a bit cheated.

* * * * *

I faced another day of déjà vu predictability, a tedium of dawn to dusk flying immersed in danger and boredom while surrounded by beauty that surpassed imagination, a relentless beauty of near endless water separated from sky by an almost imperceptible rim, of billowing clouds that showed only their tops over earth's edge and tricked the eye into believing them to be islands of land, of a thousand-thousand flying fish bursting forth from our wake in furious clusters, skittering across water's opalescent surface like giant squalls of fresh minted Spanish doubloons—to settle and rise again like the resurrected Christ till they skittered beyond sight, as our faithful small boys pitched their bows into gentle swells beyond.

I often went on deck after flying finished and the ship had darkened. In deep black water I watched writhing scintillations of trillions of microscopic plankton disturbed by our passage create flashes of seaborne lightning. Saw its recurrence along the distant horizon as flashes of airborne lightning. All of it combined with the power and beauty of the ship, her impossible bulk swimming through the water with stunning agility in the same surprising way a fat man sometimes moves with the unexpected grace of a dancer, her massive power during heavy seas of Pacific storms that drove her bow under a thousand tons of water only to rear up like a magnificent mare and meet the next massive swell, her whole being shimmying and quivering as though sexually excited. However, one had to remember her true nature, within her power and beauty lived a petulant bitch, a killing machine capable of cutting both ways, exampled one day when the Air Boss bellowed over the 5MC, "Hung ordnance in the groove. Stand well clear of the Foul Line." The Phantom on final carried a hung five-hundred-pound bomb on its centerline. Everything went serious, chancy. The plane trapped and hove to a stop. The bomb, armed after it snapped loose, skidded and twisted down the deck and off the Angle into the water. If the ship had pitched couple degrees, it might have redirected the bomb, causing it to slam into a pack of twenty or so aircraft on the bow being refueled. How big would the slaughter have been? The question didn't have to be answered that day, but that's how things were. After the incident, my memory flashed back to California where I learned to load onto aircraft what were dubbed Special Weapons, the sort of weapons that brought Japan to her knees. We were lectured for hours on each different type. Our instructor explained the theory and sequence of events that led to detonation. 'First this happens—then that—and so on and so forth, till the final picosecond, "Which," he said, "is followed by the rapid disassembly of this weapon."

We walked that fine line every hour of every day. No safe place existed. We were always looking over our shoulder—watching—waiting for that final picosecond followed by the rapid disassembly of everything around us—that being the true nature of our business.

* * * * *

Flying finished, my ass hung low, I climbed down a ladder to the O2 Level, walked the starboard passageway forward to the Tweet Shop, sat, watched Athens Georgia college boy Jim McQuinn diddle the knobs of the big radio Petty Officer First Class Billie K. Willson carried all the way from Covington Tennessee to the far South China Sea on the off chance there would be something interesting to hear. Because of his stint with higher education, McQuinn felt most qualified to twiddle things with lots of lights and dials. Soon as I sat, Freddy Flitter, a longtime friend of Billie, handed me a warm soda from the case he had smuggled aboard in the hellhole of his big Electronic Warfare aircraft. I listened to the obnoxious shrieks and motorboat chatters from Billie's radio expecting the usual noise, nothing more, but something came, something unexpected, a sound that made my crotch tingle, a female voice. McQuinn froze. "Holy shit."

"That's Hanoi Hannah," said Freddy. "I heard her when I was onboard the Ranger."

She spoke impeccable English in a sultry way. "American air pirates again failed in their effort to conquer the People's Republic of Vietnam. Many of your planes have been shot from the sky, your airmen captured. They are being treated with utmost kindness. Those injured are receiving excellent medical care. Some have already seen the error of their ways and confessed to the war crimes they have committed." After that, she doused us with American jazz music while whispering things that promised wet dreams, things that spoke to our squalid existence.

The Tweet Shop, a skuzzy space with sweaty bulkheads, filled to the gills with gray cruise boxes, yellow test equipment, a tiny two-drawer desk, and a chair with squealing casters, sat crammed under the forward finger of Elevator One. Billie K. Willson, a tall heavyset cracker with considerable management skills and little military bearing, ran the place. The rest of us, six in all, were a mixture of hankering insanities that somehow blended into a homogenous mix.

McQuinn's stint with higher education ended for want of money. He joined the Navy in the nick of time, beating the draft by only a few days. Stud-of-the-shop, he received perfumed letters virtually every Mail Call. Each time the bugle played it over the 1MC, he sang along to the staccato rhythm—*"I got a letter—I got a letter—You didn't get a fucking thing."*

Jim March, the five-foot-four inches of him, wore a dense Fuller Brush mustache. "Wanted to be a Mooorine. Joined up and got sent to Nam. My exceptional size got me volunteered as a Tunnel Rat. Got me a Bronze Star with a V device because of it. But my major claim to fame was getting shot in the ass. Happened while we were humping across rice paddies. When the shooting started, I busted ass running fast as I could—got hit anyway. It was like getting cracked hard with a baseball bat."

"What did you do then?"

"Fuckin' ran faster."

Thomas Lowery, a closed mouthed Floridian with bad complexion and one cheek pooched out by a golf ball sized wad of tobacco, carried a coffee cup stolen from the mess deck to spit in, kept pretty much to himself.

PJ Fry's charming country-fried face had rube written all over it. Innocent as the Lamb of God, he joined because his father told him that unlike the army there'd always be hot chow and clean sheets. "First new shoes I ever had were in bootcamp." When we found out he was still cherry, we chipped in to buy him his first piece of ass. Set it up to make him feel like a stud. Paid a hooker to grab him by the cock, lead him off to a short time hotel and fuck him down to parade rest. He came back with a smile so big it had to hurt.

Dirty Bob was the sixth.

* * * * *

First launch of the day, Number Two Cat; Gabitis, head BB Stacker, Mormon, beloved father of seven, and well liked by all, pulled the arming pin from a rocket pod. In a flash of searing heat a Zuni rocket torched off—streaked over the bow—flew hurky-jerky till it hit the water. The exhaust blast whacked him full in the face. He went down hard. Everybody thought him dead. Launches from the bow halted till Pecker-Checkers loaded him on a stretcher and carried him to the Emergency Aid Station. There, they found a pulse, covered his face with medicated gauze and waited for the Flight Surgeon who got him medevaced on the same launch cycle. After, Musselwhite, a chicken breasted Tennessean, disliked by most, but much loved by Gabitis, locked himself away in his cramped office. Those who passed by heard his sobs.

*****

The line period finished, we steamed to Subic, tied up to Layette Pier, swarmed down the after-brow with pockets full of money and crotches full of desire, shoe horned into waiting cattle cars for a jolting twenty-minute ride to the main gate. There, Marine guards scrutinized IDs and liberty cards of sailors desperate to cross Shit

River Bridge, find the woman of their dreams, and do the four-legged mambo.

I stood in line at the moneychangers not feeling right. Something needed doing. Something foreboding. Gabitis lay in the hospital a short walk away. I sighed, turned on a heel, started toward it. Outside, I paused to collect myself.

Musselwhite sat beside his bed. I looked down at Gabitis, no face—no eyes—no ears—nose—lips—no nothing. What remained was a mask of grotesque tissue that resembled blood smeared cellophane pulled tight around his skull. Fuck me to tears. He was talking to Musselwhite. Sounded like he was in goddamn good spirits. I couldn't understand how that could be. Were it me, I'd have said fuck it and croaked.

He sensed my presence. "Who's there?"

"Me."

"Goldie, how are you, man?"

I choked trying hard to swallow, felt tears well up, looked at Musselwhite with a what-the-fuck-do-I-do-now look. He said nothing.

Gabitis spoke. "Hey, hope you're not worried about me. I'm fine. Just fine. One of those things that happens, you know. Nobody's fault. Nobody to blame."

* * * * *

Outside the hospital, I wondered where to go—what to do. Remembered a no name shithole on Pagasa Street; just a tin shed standing on an uneven concrete slab, no electricity, no hookers, few customers. I'd go there, get drunk, forget the shit storm that composed my life. Rain fell as I walked back to the main gate and across the bridge that spanned a wide canal filled with torpid brown water that smelled of human waste and rotted animal flesh we called Shit River. Ambitious young Filipino boys swam in that poisonous water everyday begging money. Sailors delighted in tossing coins to watch them scramble like a school of minnows to fetch them. At the far side of the canal, sweet young girls wearing virginal white sat in fragile boncas; flashed big brown eyes extending small conical baskets fashioned of chicken wire begging their share.

At the beginning of town, illegal moneychangers formed a seething bickering mass flashing thick greasy wads of bills, bidding for business, beyond were bars, short time hotels, and small shops that sold carved salad bowls and pornographic statues. As I moved along, streetwalkers groped me. "I love you—no shit," they trilled.

I walked along the edge of Magsaysay, the main drag, unpaved, already turned into a morass by rain. Drunken sailors, freshly fucked, broke, weaved along in mud-ruined whites headed back to their ships. They chewed at sticks of barbequed monkey meat and bellowed profanities at everything that moved. I turned on to Pagasa, walked a hundred yards, soaked to the skin; opened the rickety screen door of the no name bar. Rain hammered its corrugated roof. In deep shadow sat the wizened momma-san looking very much like a chiaroscuro painting. She blessed me with a near toothless smile and handed me a San Miguel Beer from an ice filled cooler. I sat down on a skinny-legged chair at a wobbly table, drank. I started my forth beer, the screen door scraped open, Dirty Bob and Mac-The-Quack entered. Mama-san brought two beers.

"Thought we'd find you here sulking, you sorry fuck," said Bob.

Mac, tall, narrow assed, had ebony skin and short kinky hair that formed a widow's peak high on his forehead. Piebald scars crawled up from under his shirt and covered his throat on one side to the jaw line. He told me about the scars once when we were both in the depths of a proper drunk and conversational. "See this shit?" He pulled his shirt open revealing more mottled flesh. "That's what Willie-Peter does. Happened in Korea, back when you were still shitting yellow. My own boys fucked me up. Fucked me up good. Accidently put three rounds of it inside our perimeter. Used to be a pretty muthafucka, you know. Shit, no ladies going to lay pussy on me looking like this. Ain't that a bitch?"

He looked hard at me, challenged my self-proclaimed misery. "Know who Tiberius was? Course you don't. You're just an ignorant white fuck. He was a Roman emperor. Gave big goddamn parties all the time. Good ones with lots of food and wine and naked ladies to lie down with. Think I'd of had a good time knowing him." He nodded.

"Fuck me to tears," I said. "What're we supposed to do?"

Mac picked up his beer, polished it off in a single chug. "Not one fucking thing except get on with it."

Bob stood, pushed the screen door open with his toe. "Come on. Move your dumb ass. I'm not spending time in this shit hole." I tossed money on the table, we left, walked back to Magsaysay through rain and mud, past shit-kicker bars favored by Thomas Lowery and other big-in-the-hat-high-in-the-heel cowboys, past New Pauline's, an officer's hangout with its small fenced concrete pool where lay a somnolent six foot alligator. Baby ducks bought by squids were tossed in with the hope of seeing a little carnivorous action. They swam happily around gator's indifferent jaws.

Baby ducks were sold by business minded kids who knew Americans were stupid. They sold them for a peso or two, and later, after they served their purpose, fished them out of the gator's pond with homemade nets and sold them again. The cycle repeated itself till the ducks lost their fuzz and were taken home to raise, later to be had for chow—a thoroughly practical enterprise.

We came to the traffic circle where the street split two ways: left to The Jungle, a black only place, where hookers darkened their skin and kinked their hair and straying white boys learned a thing or two returning from their adventures there with cut lips and bruised egos. Right, where we headed, stood chockablock with rock and roll bars. Our destination, the Sierra Club, where hookers were sweet and the band imitated anybody on record so precisely you could close your eyes and dream yourself back to the real world.

Things were not yet cooking. Outside light, which poured in each time the door opened, painted the true shabbiness of the place. Missing too, the illusion of intimacy. It worked better in the dark with sailors a little fucked up and hookers made-up and warm with their friendly warbled 'I-love-you-no-shit' melodies. During the day, they sat slouched at tables playing cards, eating boiled peanuts and deep fried chicken feet, hair bound up in tin can sized rollers. A few schmoozed the place cadging cigarettes or trying to convince early drinkers it was time for bargains—that they could be sucked, fucked, and back in their chair before their beer got warm, but there were only serious drinkers that time of day, no takers.

At one table sat Billie and Freddy and an unhappy looking stranger with a bulbous nose that bore a raw, painful looking sore. He tossed down the last of his beer and left without words. A Cherry Girl brought three beers without us asking, took payment from a pile of Pesos that sat in the middle of the table.

Billie pointed. "See that guy just left? Know how his nose got fucked up?" He took a pull from his beer. "He was walking around last night fucked up as Hogan's Goat squeezing it between his fingers like a big assed seegar saying, 'Got light? Got a light?' Finally, some fuck stick torched it with his Zippo. Guy probably stopped thinking it was funny almost right away."

I spewed beer down the front of my shirt. My mind left Gabitis for a time. We sat that way drinking beer, bullshitting about the unimportant, laughing at the stupid.

A half hour passed. Horny Ernie, a member of Freddy's squadron, walked in, showed his wan, freshly fucked smile. Bob pulled a chair over from the next table. Right away the Cherry Girl brought him a beer along with a small rusted tin of tomato juice and a glass. Ernie mixed the two, drank it down like medicine to satisfy part of his superstitious nature. He believed the combination put lead back in his pencil, a necessary thing because of his persistent need for a wet dick.

So it went. Hours and days passed. Sooner than we wanted, the ship steamed past Grande Island and out to sea on its way back to the Tonkin Gulf.

* * * * *

Yellow Shirts taxied Mister Counts forward to the Number One Cat. Bob and I split up, one to each side of the aircraft. While the Cat Crew hooked up, we eyeballed every square millimeter of wings and fuselage, checked hydraulics and tires, found everything proper, scrambled out from under the aircraft. I ran to the centerline Checker's

Box, squatted, held my thumb high so Mister Counts and the Shooter could see it. At the Shooter's signal, Mister Counts cranked the engine to full power, gave his instruments a final check, flicked a salute. As the bow ended its downward pitch and began to climb, the Shooter threw his arm forward, a crewman hit a button on the deck edge control panel, hold back sheared, the plane trundled down the deck trailing an enormous cloud of steam, spewing a trail of JP-5 from its wingtips. In an instant, everything turned to shit. I sensed lethargy in the plane's motion, felt a problem through the soles of my feet. The shuttle slammed home at the end of the stroke, aircraft went tail heavy off the bow, dropped from sight, reappeared struggling— clawing the sky. Mister Counts punched off external stores to lighten it, but that proved futile as the plane settled more—drug its tail in the water, roared up a great salty rooster tail. Mister Counts ejected, seat rockets fired in a fleeing blaze of glory and salvation. He traveled up and up, but at the apex things went to shit again, the pyrotechnic squib in the seat failed, there was no separation. Strapped in tight, he rode over the top of a high parabola, down and down, smacking the water head first with horrible force. Bearing the weight of the seat, he sank under a thousand fathoms of water and died doing everything textbook perfect. I stood—dumbstruck, looked across the deck at Bob's bewildered face; it seemed the same for all who stood on deck. Air Boss called the launch to a stop as the ship passed by the spot. An Angel dropped behind to search, a second Angel launched, put swimmers in the water, but we all knew it was fruitless. The launch resumed. Mister Cotton, in the plane behind, folded his wings in protest.

The next twenty-four hours brought about much ado. Our planes were grounded, ejection seats pulled, torn apart, inspected in minute detail, the squibs in all the seats were found defective, as were all that were on hand. Musselwhite and Wajinski spent two days in their steamy cubbyhole doing the necessary to make Mister Counts officially dead.

* * * *

Wajinski wore a wig old and musty with two repaired lacerations that looked like infected scabs. Further, his hairline had continued its retreat since the wig's purchase causing band of pink scalp to show around its perimeter that he seemed unaware of. We others, much troubled, decided a solution had to be found, but disagreed on what it should be. Some argued that before we could find a solution there had to be a problem. Others argued we didn't need a problem if we already had the solution. Things stood that way till in a burst of bonhomie, as Wajinski sat enjoying a superb hand of cards, Musselwhite passed by, snatched the wig from his head, and ran hooting like a loon zigzagging through the berthing compartment, ricocheting off bunks like a hyperactive pinball, staying just out of Wajinski's reach till he ran smack dab into the tree trunk torso of Big Dan Smoot and came to an abrupt halt. Big Dan wrapped an oversized arm around Musselwhite and held him tight while Wajinski threw slaphappy punches and caught Musselwhite a good one on the snoot. Musselwhite couldn't stop laughing even while blood flowed down his chin and onto the white of his skivvy shirt. Wajinski continued to pummel. Musselwhite flung the wig into a distant corner. Wajinski, too embarrassed to retrieve it, went off to his cubbyhole, slammed the door, locked it, and spent the remainder of the night sulking. The wig lay for days like rotting road kill. Finally, a Coop Cleaner picked it up with the tip of his broom handle, and without ceremony, dropped it into a nearby shitcan. Later, the shitcan with the wig and its other contents found the waters of the Tonkin Gulf. With that, all our manly concerns were laid to rest.

* * * * *

A ship's evaporators broke; Captain imposed water hours with only water for drinking and cooking, and steam to power the Catapults. By the third day, the berthing compartment smelled like a week old corpse. I, and everybody living there, had no escape.

* * * * *

On deck an A-1 Spad boltered. At full throttle it roared off the angle deck, dropped from sight in abrupt, inexplicable silence. LSO waved off the next plane. The Spad lay in the water bleeding rainbow tendrils of AvGas—truncated—the engine somehow torn away from its firewall, pilot hung motionless in his straps, we gawked, helpless to do anything, Yellow Shirt started to jump from the deck to assist. Air Boss bellowed: "Stand fast." The plane grew tail heavy. Great quantities of air seethed from its fuselage and caused the nose to rise and the pilot's head to flop back. It sank amid a spume of air. A helo scrambled. Air Boss bellowed, "Plane in the grove. Clear the deck." We finished recovering fuel-starved planes while a helo loitered over the spot where the Spad went down hoping for some sign of life. None came forth. The day wore on. I began to think this might not be the life for me; that I didn't want to see shit like that anymore, that I had to find something else, tried hard to hate the place, but in my weakness, couldn't.

Amid the clamber of forks and spoons on tin trays, Bob talked. "You're like me, Goldie, you've got the knack. Not everybody does. When today is over and you're laying in your rack, try and remember everything you did. Think about every step, every move, every fucking breath you took. Imagine trying to tell somebody about it. How would you do that? What words would you use?" He paused, shook up two cigarettes, I took one, lit both with my Zippo. "Seriously, think they'd believe you? It's marvelous shit we do here. Don't ever forget that. That fucking pilot was doing exactly what he wanted to do. He wasn't ignorant. He knew the risk. He was doing marvelous shit and he fucking loved it."

We finished our smokes, set back to work under the influence of sweltering heat, breathed poisonous air, moved to the rhythm of the deck, escorted planes to the Catapults, crawled under wings and bellies, eyeballed everything, looked for the tiniest flaw while Cat Crews hooked up bridles and hold-back fittings and tensioned the Cat; with everything right, I gave thumbs up to pilot and Shooter, he made his throwing gesture and all hell broke loose. In the seeing of it, I realized what a remarkable goddamn place it was.

* * * * *

Freddy Flitter had a shiny sun browned scalp and narrow monk's fringe that circled half his skull. Claimed his hairline to be that way because he got such hellatious hard-ons the skin on his scalp stretched so tight it pushed his hair out by the roots. He lived an addiction of flying and fornication. "It's like joining the priesthood. Once you start, you want it to go on forever."

I shook my head, burped a soda burp, thought about the promises that slick fuck of a Chief made me way back when. "Man, that's all I ever wanted to do."

"Got the itch, huh?"

"Bet your ass I do."

"When you due for orders?"

"Filling out my dream sheet in a couple months."

"Put in for it."

"Got a snow ball's chance in hell. Once you get a tail hook shoved up your ass you never get rid of it."

He took a final swig of his soda, tossed the can over the side. "That's a dumb fucking thing to say. My plane's got a tail hook, or didn't you notice?"

* * * * *

Lieutenant Commander Shumaker got shot to shit by thirty-seven millimeter Triple-A as he strafed Chanh Hoa. He punched out feet-dry. Wingman saw the chute open low to the ground. No chance for a SAR pickup. We heard more on Billie's radio that night. Hanoi Hannah said, "The People's Army captured him immediately. He is undergoing excellent medical treatment for injuries he sustained ejecting from his crippled aircraft. He has expressed great remorse for his criminal acts." After that, he sank into oblivion as had all the others. The end.

* * * * *

Days continued to bruise and bend all. As time folded on itself, nattering of home and hearth began. The naming of our relief ship brought cheer for some, restless discord for others. For them, cross-decking to another ship became a hot topic. Bob and I sat with empty mess trays in front of us smoking a last cigarette before going back on deck. "You need to think about it," he said. "You won't be happy back in the real world. Not any more. This place spoiled you same as me."

During the launch cycle, Bob got trapped on the finger of Elevator One by an aircraft swinging onto the Cat. A tornado of jet blast twisted his body like a dirvisher and flung him off the deck and into the depths of the Tonkin Gulf. I stood in naked disbelief. A helo launched, put a swimmer in the water, but didn't find him. No time to mourn—no time for another one fucking thing, I got back to the business of slaughter. Fuck me to tears.

IV

You never know what the enemy's gonna do.

—James P. Musselwhite

Musselwhite called me to his cubbyhole. He sat massaging still tender gums with a fingertip, wiped the drool on his shirtfront. Brand-new false teeth sat on his desk atop a disorganized stack of papers. "*Phft* Y'all got orders." He pushed some papers in my general direction. "Gonna be a *fft* flyboy like y'all wanted, *ftt* asshole." He changed his expression into what might have been a smile. "*Phfftt,*" he said, signifying nothing.

I walked the passageway forward to the shop, wrapped myself into a corner, gathered my thoughts, said to McQuinn, "Got orders."

He sat Buddha style on a cruise box bent around a coverless paperback novel. A familiar pose—familiar as the grimy shop run by Billie K. Wilson.

"Asshole," he said without looking up. "Where you going?"

"Yeah," said PJ. "Where?"

"Japan."

Soon as I spoke it everything changed. I became separate—superfluous—things were already moving on as though I were never there. Two days later, I flew off the ship on a COD, landed at Cubi Point, rode a bus to Clark Air Force Base, spent a couple days whoring in the local ville, flew back to the real world.

* * * * *

123

Met a squid named Jim Hart on the Greyhound Bus traveling south to North Island where both of us were to learn the flying business. Spent twelve weeks there. At the end, we packed our trash, dressed in civvies and took a final choppy ride across San Diego Bay aboard the Nickel Snatcher to the foot of Broadway where we stopped at a ham and egg joint for breakfast.

"Think about going home, Goldie," said Jim. "Your place is just a ferry ride from me. We've got thirty days leave. Be a long time before you can see your folks again. Besides, we can raise some hell in Seattle."

I shook my head. "Nah. Got no desire to go. Nothing there for me but a trail of tears."

Waitress came by. "More coffee, boys?"

"Yep," said Jim. He studied his coffee as she poured, looked back at me. "Things change."

I scoffed. "I'm heading straight for Travis. Want to catch the first flight out I can. This whole fucking country can kiss my ass."

"Piss poor attitude."

"I suppose."

The waitress brought our food. We stopped talking and chowed down. When we finished, I shook two cigarettes from a fresh pack, Jim lit us both up with a snap, we smoked them down, paid the bill, hoisted our sea bags, left.

At the Greyhound Station, we parted company with a handshake. "See you in Atsugi," he said.

"You bet."

He climbed aboard the bus. It roared off leaving me in a fetid cloud of diesel fumes. I went to a restaurant that evening, ate a big steak thinking it might be a while before another came my way, slept the night at a YMCA, next day, caught a bus for Travis Air Force Base, waited almost a week for an open seat. On board the flight, I put away all my thoughts to armor myself against the load of dependent wives and their squalling rug rats. At Tachikawa, I stepped off the plane in my woolen dress blues in the middle of a Kanto Plains' semitropical June, searched for the military bus that would take me on the final four-hour ride to Naval Air Station, Atsugi.

* * * * *

Inside the duty office, the tall, rangy Leading Chief named Ring greeted me. "You go get checked into the barracks and get some sleep. We'll get you squared away in the morning." He called the Duty Driver. "Drop this fella off at the barracks and make a mail run." He looked back at me "See you tomorrow, Oh-Eight-Hundred sharp,"

Driver and I spoke only a few words on the drive to the barracks. In the MAA Shack a First Class Boatswain named D.C. Tony, introduced himself. A tiny TV sat on his desk. It showed Sumo wrestling. He issued blanket, linen, and pillow—showed me to the open bay dorm—assigned a bunk, returned to his office.

I unpacked. Stowed my gear, got naked, wrapped a towel around my waist, walked the length of the cavernous bay to the head, shaved, brushed my teeth till my gums bled, showered under tangy needle sprays of water so hot it turned my skin lobster red, crawled between clean sheets, slept through the rest of the day and through the night; woke to the hustle bustle of reveille.

* * * * *

At the mess hall, I ate a huge breakfast, drank coffee till I got the whips and jangles; smoked two cigarettes, walked the mile and a half to the hanger, arrived just as Colors sounded.

Master Chief Ring, a genuine North Dakota cowboy, wore his hair close cropped and his khakis with knife edged creases. Above the fruit salad he wore sat Combat Aircrew Wings from the Korean War. "Take a seat, son. You married?"

"No, Master Chief."

"Neither am I. Far as I'm concerned if the navy wanted me to have a wife they'd of issued one. Now—let me tell you a little about this place. First and foremost it's the most interesting duty a man could ask for. I'm on my fourth year. Don't want to go anyplace else. The missions we fly help our boys find targets, and at the same time, keeps them a little safer, so the sooner you get checked out the sooner we can assign you to a crew.

"Most aircrewmen can afford to live off base. With the Flight Skins and Hostile Fire Pay you'll be making it's easily affordable, but there are some things you need to know about the Japanese. They're outwardly friendly, but on a deep level they didn't like or trust us because we're gaijin. That's a dirty word that means foreigner. Far as they're concerned, we're hairy barbarians that smell bad. My advice? Avoid them.

"Hachioji is a little town up the road a few clicks. It's a dangerous place, so steer clear. During the war some captured American fliers were publicly beheaded there. Photographs of the executions showed up in newspapers and were seen by our boys. So they adopted the motto: Save one for Hachioji, and every mission they flew a stick of bombs were dropped there. Killed almost everyone. We've had a couple men near beat to death there since I've been Leading Chief. Don't go there, that's my word to the wise."

I craved a smoke; looked around for an ashtray; saw none. Guess the Master Chief read my mind. "Don't smoke, myself. Like my air fresh and tasty." He went on. "This facility was built by the Japanese Imperial Navy back in thirty-eight. In forty-four, when things were going bad, the Japs turned it into a kamikaze base. After the war, we came and started painting Kilroy Was Here on every damned thing that couldn't get out of the way. So, that's the long and short of it. Any questions for me?"

"Not at this time, Master Chief."

"If any come up, you know where to find me."

> **There we were... at five thousand feet...**
> **over the Tonkin Gulf... one engine out...**
> **The navigator screamed over the ICS... OH MY GOD...**
> **I FORGOT THE BOX LUNCHES**
>
> **—Thomas Goldman**

The sun, a blinding crystal of shapeless light, stood at its apex in cloudless sky radiating heat that pierced me to the bone and raised pearls of sweat on my exposed skin. The carrier barely moved over the oily waters of the Tonkin Gulf.

We had landed aboard the Shitty Kitty early that day with a busted wide band UHF, my problem to cure. I pulled it from its rack deep inside the plane's hellhole, carried it to the 03 Level for repair, sat relishing the comfort of air conditioning. Techs finished the repair, but I dallied. Crew Chief came looking, found me slouched in a chair. "What're you doing?"

"Getting the Wide Band fixed."

He tapped the radio next to me with his toe. "This it?"

I nodded.

"Still broke?"

"No, it's ready to go."

"Why the fuck are you still sitting here? Get your ass back on deck. Get that fucker installed and checked out. You know damn well we're down without it. We can't fly without encryption. You fucking well know that."

I shouldered the bulky radio, double-timed it up the ladder and across the deck, Chief Rowe harping at my back. "You don't get that fucker installed and working, everybody on this cycle will be flying without our cover." At the plane, he grabbed the front of my flight suit, twisted hard. "If we don't make this launch it's your fault, understand? Any planes shot down, any pilots killed; it's your fucking fault. People depend on us. Goddamn you. Goddamn you."

The pilot came to do his kick-the-tire-light-the-fire preflight. Crew Chief grabbed my fight suit again; hauled me in front of him. "I want this fuck stick off the crew right here, right now. I won't fly with him. None of the rest should have to. He's doing S-Band. We can damn well get along without it this cycle. Better to go with an empty seat than carry him."

The ARC-27 weighed heavy on my shoulder, I felt ruined. Earlier, I had walked around like the cock of the walk in my olive drab flight suit, butt of my side arm sticking out from its armpit holster, had the world by the short hairs. I had left the grubby confines of the flight deck and became closer to God because I flew at forty thousand feet. But now, crashed, burned to cinders, turned back into the incompetent punk Dad said I was. The nauseating thought of that brought the taste of vomit to my mouth. After an eternity of silence, the pilot said, "Let it go, Chief. It's his first time out." He turned, looked me square in the eye "Won't ever happen again will it?"

I scrambled to install the radio, checked it with the tower, flew the cycle attending the array of equipment in front of me while listening to all gears grinding and gnashing in my head. After we trapped and climbed down from the plane, Chief Rowe cornered me. He jabbed me hard in the chest with a forefinger to the beat of his words, "You broke dick motherfucker, don't ever pull that shit again. Not ever. If you do, I'll personally rip your head off and shit in your neck" He pivoted on a heel, walked away.

I fueled the plane with the help of Mike Colhouer. Finished, he said, "Come on Goldman, let's grab some chow."

Colhouer, senior by a stripe, looked quite average except for scars in his eyebrows and a bent prizefighter's nose. In the chaos of the mess deck, we sat at a table with two others unknown to us. They paid no attention as we shoveled down our food without tasting it. Done eating, Colhouer shook two cigarettes from a crumpled pack; I lit them with my Zippo. "Chief Rowe's a good guy," he said. "You might not think so right now, but he is. Because of him, nobody fucks with us. You flew a few SOJs before we came out to the ship. You did fine, but out here the game changes and you have to change with it. If you don't, he'll shitcan you in a heartbeat. Everybody feels cocky when they first start, but usually they're brought down to earth pretty fucking quick like you were." He took a long drag of smoke, crushed out the butt. "Got to quit these fuckers before they kill me." I got up. "Where you going?"

"To get more bug juice."

"Here." He handed me his glass.

I waited in line, filled the glasses, returned.

"Something I noticed is you got a lip," he said. "I've heard you mouth off a couple times. You're the new kid. You need keep your trap shut and your eyes and ears open. Christ, I've been doing this almost three years and still don't know everything. You settle down, learn your job, and Chief Rowe'll help you in more ways than you can count. He'll be the best friend you ever had. Believe me. It's true. But you have to do your part and you have to do it perfect. Put this shit behind you. Just wipe it off the map and get with the program."

"Yeah, but won't he be watching every move I make?"

"Fuck-an-a he will. Won't be just him. It'll be all of us. You're under the microscope. What else can you expect? Work your ass off and give it some time. In the end it'll be like it never happened. He'll treat you like a son. That's the way the chief is. And remember, we're dealing life and death shit out here. Every fucking day, it's life and death shit. If you haven't figured that out yet you're in the wrong fucking profession."

As we left the mess deck, I heaved a deep sigh thinking I still had a chance. It had all turned out to be a hell of a lot more than I bargained for, but deep inside, I knew I could do it. Things stood that way till our relief showed up and we flew back to the easy life of eight hour days and a relaxed schedule of hops every other day over the Sea of Japan to tickle the chins of the Red Chinese and the North Koreans while eating our daily grits in a decent chow hall.

* * * * *

At the end of the SOJ, I took my sweet time driving to the barracks in the crisp fall air, looking forward to the weekend. I intended going to Sagamiotsuka, to sit in one of the tiny, dim lit bars and drink Suntory Whiskey till break of dawn. In the barracks I stripped, grabbed a towel, headed for the showers. Found Jim basking in steamy water. "Man, where the hell you been? What took so damn long?"

"I fucked up, man. Thought I should do it proper and check into Treasure Island. They held me forever doing shit jobs. Finally went to Personnel, told them I wanted a message sent to my CO explaining why I wasn't where I was supposed to be. Seemed to light a fire under their ass. Couple days later they told me to pack my trash and catch the bus to Travis."

Showered and shaved, I drove us the three clicks to Sagamiotsuka in the smoke blowing Hino Renault I had bought from a Japanese translator on base for too much money. We wandered the narrow alleyways, ended up sitting on tiny, ass busting stools in the Bar Happy. Around midnight, Jim said, "Got to head back. Got an early wakeup for duty section muster."

"Want me to drive you?"

"No, you're too fucked up to drive. I'll catch a cab."

"Don't pay more than eighty Yen."

"I know."

I sat a while longer. Drank another beer, scanned the place hoping to find a night's worth of love, didn't see anything cozy, went to the car, curled up on the back seat, slept till woken by a tapping sound, opened my eyes, two Shore Patrol stood outside, I rolled down the window. "You okay, buddy?"

"Yeah."

"Too drunk to drive?"

I licked dry lips. "Yeah."

"Want a cab?"

"Nah. I'll just stay here."

"Okay, buddy. We'll look in on you now and then."

* * * * *

Jim and I spent the day looking for a place to rent. Found one just the other side of the train platform amid a clutch of farmhouses for ten thousand Yen a month. Soon after we moved in, Jim went downrange. Freddy came by. "Man, this ain't shit. You should see my place in Yokohama. Got an American style toilet and all the trimmings. You need to come up and have a look. Find something there and get the fuck out of this podunk ville."

I shook my head. "This place is fine for me."

"This place is for shit-kickers. You a shit-kicker?"

I scoffed.

"Didn't think so. You got to come up to China Town, hang out with me at the Stork Club, hear my girlfriend sing."

"China Town in Yokohama?"

"Yep. Bigger than the one in Frisco. Got great restaurants and nightclubs you won't believe. Nothing but class."

* * * * *

I stepped on the gas intending to meet Freddy in Yokohama, spent the next hours driving hopeless circles on unlit country roads, and with a near empty gas tank, ended up about where I started.

At the house, I lit a charcoal stove under the tub to heat the water, got a beer from the frig, turned on the TV, sat cross-legged on tatami mats and watched a slice-em-dice-em-samurai-shit-kicker. When the bathwater seethed, I bathed the Japanese way, laid down on my futon, slept.

Over time, I learned to greet my neighbors with a smile and proper bow. Shopped for small needs at businesses near the railroad platform, spent evenings reading the English language edition of the Mainichi Shinbun, learned a few Japanese words; used them whenever I could.

Next door lived a singular man of indeterminate age. Every night, late into the night, I heard him chant guttural prayers punctuated by the ring of a brass chime. Though he carried an unapproachable air when we passed on the dirt pathway, it felt as if he were evaluating me, that I had become a curiosity. On a balmy evening I walked past his open door; he called to me in impeccable English, beckoned me come in. I kicked off my zoris; stepped up onto the tatami mats inside, saw bookcases holding books in different European languages. "My name is Sekimoto Kumahachi," he said. "Please sit. Kumahachi is the name given me by my paternal great grandfather. It means Eight Bear. Though I was the youngest, he favored me. He and my grandfather served as a midlevel court officials during the Meiji and Taisho eras when Japan moved toward modernization. I invited you in because of your efforts to become part of the community. Do you drink whiskey?"

"A little."

He sat a glass in front of me, poured in a generous amount. "As a child my great grandfather saw two samurai meet on the beach of Inoshima near the end of their era. They faced each other just above the incoming tide with swords drawn and held high. For long minutes they stood motionless. The incoming tide began to wash around their feet. They paid it no attention. Suddenly, as if by some unspoken command, they charged, slashing with their swords. As they passed, one crumpled with a fatal wound. The other stopped, sword held high. Minutes passed. Slowly, he too sank to his knees and rolled onto his side in the bloody foam that edged the water. It was my great grandfather's first experience seeing death. An old man standing beside him smiled. He too smiled. It was a poetic moment."

* * * * *

On my second try at driving to China town I succeeded. Inside, Freddy sat at the bar behind which a quartet played background for the singer, a fireplug-sized woman with platinum hair and eyebrows to match, who sang in a thick-throated way and whanged out vocals like an Asian Ella Fitzgerald. She wore black lipstick and a long sequined gown that dragged the floor and scintillated as she moved through the lights. She smiled at Freddy showing deep and forever love.

We sat drinking Mai Thais from carved wooden cups. She finished her piece, gestured to Freddy; he stood, took the microphone, and to my surprise began to croon against the background in a sad, rusty-piped voice that made me want to lean into his words.

* * * * *

"As a recruit I was taught to respect brutality," said Kumahachi. "With the others I was routinely beaten and mentally abused. It was to toughen us up. To imbue us with fighting spirit. Each morning while standing in formation we had to recite our fighting code the Gunjin Chokuyu from memory. It was written during the Meiji era and told us we did not own our lives. That dying for the Emperor was our duty and obligation. If anyone faltered during the recitation we were all punished. Some were beaten so badly they had to be hospitalized. Some never returned to the unit either rendered unfit or perhaps dying from their injuries. We were told we had to lose our inhibitions. We had to lose our squeamishness so we could give and receive death. We also had to live up to the expectations of our superiors and the veterans who went before us. We were turned into meat machines."

Kumahachi refilled my cup with hot sake. As drunk as I had ever been, my head nodded. I had to focus hard to follow his words.

"Upon completion of the training I and my comrades were sent to China. There, we were each given five bullets. Four for fighting the enemy; the fifth for killing ourselves. I had been a daigaku student weeks before and the first thing I was taught on the battlefield was how to commit suicide.

"One day seven or eight Chinese men from a nearby village were blindfolded and tied to trees. They were being punished because they would not reveal the location of the Chinese Army. We recruits were ordered to execute them with bayonets. I was afraid to kill at first. Finally, I tried to pierce one man's heart but was unable because he kept squirming to avoid being stabbed. Eventually I bayoneted him in the stomach and shoulders. After the first killing I could not eat, but eventually justified my actions by arguing that I had no choice because I was a soldier at war. I still cannot forget their blood spraying. There was no beauty in their deaths.

"We were constantly on the move. Those seriously wounded left behind with the means to commit suicide. We tried to make it as easy for them by leaving a sharp blade or a razor edged piece of bamboo. They were told it was not necessary to cut their belly. They could simply open the vein in the front of their neck in the manner of a woman. There would no shame in it. That is how important dying was.

"There were times we had to cremate our dead comrades. It took several hours and it was horrifying to think that I myself might be turned to ashes one day soon.

"We grew to despise the Chinese. In our thoughts they were cowards, less than animals, but the bastards kept fighting, kept killing us. I lost many comrades in battle. Everyone's thoughts turned to revenge as we approached one city. By then, we were given the freedom to do as we pleased against them. It was the beginning of a terror campaign. Our demand for their absolute submission. The first problem was Chinese soldiers. They deserted in high numbers as we advanced. Many masqueraded as civilians, hid their weapons during the day, then retrieved them in the dark of night. Assassins. We executed anyone appearing to be a soldier. We looked for any evidence. Any markings. Even hand calluses. Anything suspicious and they were shot."

He offered up more sake. I waved him off. He chuckled, poured another cup for himself. "We went wild looting, raping. Common soldiers felt a new power over women. Some with cameras forced women to expose themselves for photographs. I did not understand any of it because there were comfort women available for our pleasure. We called them Jugun-ianfu. Most were Chinese, but some were brought from Korea. There were even paid prostitutes brought from Japan for the officers. They were all treated with brutality. It didn't matter whether they lived or died.

"Many of our officers came from Samurai stock. They carried swords that were very old and of great value that had belonged to their families for generations. The swords were deadly works of art, their killing power legendary. Sometimes they selected Chinese prisoners to test their mettle. We bound their hands, blindfold them, and forced them down upon their knees. Often the Chinese tried to protect themselves by hiding their necks. They would imitate a turtle and draw their heads back into their bodies. The officers would wait a while, but if too much time passed, they would smack them on the head with the side of their blade. Invariably the victims became curious and extended their necks as if to look around. Maybe they wondered what had happened. Maybe they thought it was over and that was what it was like to be dead. At that exact moment the officer would strike like a Cobra and the head would roll in a spume of corporal blood and peals of laughter. The Chinese faces always had a look of complete surprise. There has never been an apology for any of it.

"We were shocked when the war ended. It was beyond believing. All the propaganda told us we were winning. There was never bad news from the home front. Some commanders burned their unit flags. Some committed seppuku. Others simply put bullets in their heads. The shame was unbearable. We were lost. The Emperor ordered the surrender. We had to obey. It was said we were not dishonored. We were only obeying a sacred mandate sent down from the heavens, but we were returned to Japan anonymously. To the government we were considered dead. Still moving and breathing, but in reality, no different than those whose remains were sent home for burial. That was the way things ended for us.

"I returned to utter destruction. My family was gone, killed by phosphorous bombs dropped from B-29s. Cremated like so many thousands in fiery cyclones. The photographs you see on the wall are all that remain. Everything in the city was twisted and broken. Blackened as if touched by the vengeful hand of a hateful God. We lived in filth and rubble starving inch by inch, drinking and bathing out of buckets of water drawn from the few working faucets or from polluted canals. We dug holes in the ground to contain our excrement. Desperate for something to eat we hitched rides on freight trains to the countryside and traded old clothes or anything of value for sweet potatoes and vegetables. There was almost no rice. We Asians die without rice. Some were so desperate to eat they scavenged for grass and tree bark to survive.

"On the streets former soldiers like me begged for food. There were amputees on every corner. Many people had their growth stunted by malnutrition. Tuberculosis was rampant. Money worthless. Your Army was already in place. Early on our women worried about rape. Some went so far as to cut their hair to imitate the look of a man.

The most fearful carried cyanide tablets so they could commit suicide before being raped. Whorehouses flourished, opened officially by your Army in the hope it would prevent the spread of disease. Maybe it helped, I do not know. Destitute families, much like in medieval times, sold young girls to brothels through Japanese middlemen. They suffered you Americans in the same way the Jugun-ianfu suffered us. You share our guilt in the matter.

"Americans came to the city in big trucks throwing candy to children. They brought food. Much of it was looted and sold on the black market by newly formed gangs of Yakuza we called Gurentai. They were simply hoodlums. Low class scum swaggering about like samurai. They wore sunglasses and dark western style suits. Sported American crew cuts and talked from the side the side of their mouth in cheap imitation of Chicago gangsters portrayed in the cinema. They carried guns. The police were unarmed and could do nothing to protect us. We became victims of our own. And that is the way life was in this vanquished country for many years.

"I never married. How could one create a family under those circumstances? Anyway, that was my thought. Today, I have regrets about that decision but one cannot turn back the clock. Eventually, I found work as a painter. American money flowed in for reconstruction, and there was more work than workers. I painted everything, big or small. Houses, buildings, fuel storage tanks. I worked diligently and eventually formed my own small company A few years ago I retired to this place financially secure. Something I thought not possible at one time. So now, I have new work. To pray for the tormented souls of those I knew and for those I did not. My prayer is that they find peace and through their peace I find my own. I am busy with it."

And that is all I remember of it till I woke to my lonely house with a blinding headache.

This aircraft ain't nothing but a bunch a fuckin' spare parts flyin' in close formation.

—Mike Colhouer

I returned to Cubi Point from time aboard a carrier cruising Yankee Station stinking of hydraulic fluid, JP-5 and sweat. Back from four weeks of bad chow, bad sleep, and a struggle to keep the plane together while flying two double cycles each day shoehorned in its claustrophobic belly with absolute concentration on the equipment in front of me, while in the back of my mind, imagining the magical SAM that sneaks through all our clever defenses and all our gut wrenching hurky-jerky maneuvers to plant itself deep in our belly and eviscerate us—done for now. I stood in the shower soaping and resoaping my body head to toe under the scalding spray desperate to feel clean, to be rid of grime and foul shipboard smells. Finished, I dressed in civvies, and though early in the day, left the barracks looking forward to two days of crew's rest.

Under broken clouds I flagged a Blaylock Taxi Cab, told the Filipino driver to head for the main gate. He rolled the meter on and took off over the hill, past the Sky Club; past enlisted family housing, through dense forest peopled by chattering monkeys. A line from an old song started singing in my head. *Oh, the monkeys have no tails in Zamboanga... Oh, the monkeys have no tails in Zamboanga...* One line, all I remembered, went round and round; I couldn't shake it.

We crossed from the air station into Subic Naval Station, passed piers and warehouses and dry docks, ended up in the parking lot near the official money changer's booth guarded by two Filipinos with shortened twelve gauge shot guns slung from their shoulders. *Oh, the monkeys have no tails in Zamboanga...* I got out, walked to the main gate, a Jarhead microscopically inspected my ID; satisfied, he waved me through. I crossed the bridge, walked past streetwalkers and beggars onto Magsaysay for a click or so to a little bar called Alamo Club sitting across from New Pauline's with its concrete pool and sleepy alligator.

The Alamo Club, nothing special, just tables, bar, jukebox, and a half round stage where nightly a combo with a cute male singer whanged out melodies—the early watering hole of somebody I hoped to find. Before my eyes adjusted to the dimness, I heard his voice. "Hey you good looking motherfucker—don't you ever die."

When my eyes started working, I saw Freddy, saw too, somebody else. "Oh man, what the fuck are you doing with him?"

"Come on Goldie, you know you can't choose your shipmates."

Across from him sat I-Know O'Neal with an SOP smile on his smug mug. I-Know flew missions, feet wet, up and down the entire Vietnam coast onboard a four-engined Super Connie with its oh-so-powerful Big-Look APS-20 radar. The missions they flew were long and tedious. There was a galley for cooking chow and bunks for necessary snoozing while they screwed through the air. One time, well into Indian country, the radar operator ID'd a MIG coming after them. Utterly defenseless, the pilot ordered everybody aft to shift the plane's CG in hopes of picking up a few more knots of airspeed and hauled ass south. For unknown reasons, the MIG broke off and everybody came home with good stories to tell.

I didn't get on well with I-Know, a self-appointed expert on everything under the sun. He responded in an instant to anything said in his presence with: *I know*. It gurgled out of his mouth like a moist fart. Fat enough to have breasts that bounced and shimmied, he could have been an effeminate male or a slightly masculine female. The sparse mustache he cultivated only added to the androgyny.

In a dissatisfied way, I sat. One of the professional ladies held up a finger, I nodded, she brought the beer, sat it in front of me, took money from the pile on the table to pay. "My name is Rosa." She extended her hand.

I shook it formally. "Goldie. Have a seat."

"What ship you from?"

"No ship."

"You station sailor?"

"Nah. I'm in the same squadron as these guys."

She smiled pearls, sat down beside me. I sipped the perfect beer. She leaned toward me, crooned pure gold into my ear. "You got cigarette?"

I took an unopened pack from my breast pocket, tossed it on the table. "Help yourself." She opened the pack, tapped one out. I lit it with a snap, and watched as smoke curled around her face and vanished into darkness.

Freddy and I sat quiet. I-Know fumbled with something in his lap. A duckling. He put it on the table. It stood quite still as if trying to figure things out. Rosa reached out and stroked it with her finger. "Your duck?"

"I know," said O'Neal.

"You give it to me?"

He gave a chortle that fluffed his mustache. "What for? You'll take it home and cook it."

I felt indifferent to it all till the duck wandered aimlessly around the table, got too close to the edge and fell into my lap. I put it back on the table, got an ashtray from the next table, poured in a little beer, watched the duck eyeball it awhile. Satisfied with what he saw, he dipped its beak for a taste, jumped back, stood motionless, cocked its head side to side as if scrutinizing the situation from different angles, dipped its beak again and again taking in tiny nibbles. After drinking its fill, it took an uneven stroll, fell onto its side, went to sleep. I felt charmed. "Hey I-Know, how much for the duck?"

"Not for sale."

"Sure it is. Everything's for sale in this town."

"What're you keeping it for?" said Freddy.

I-Know looked around as if taking in the splendor of the place, his face formed a half smile. "Donno. Maybe I'll keep it to raise, or maybe feed it to the gator."

"Come on I-Know, what'd you pay for the little fuck? A peso? Two? Here, I'll give you ten. Good looking fucker like you can get laid for that."

"Nope."

"No? Not enough? I'll give you twenty. Think about it, twenty pesos."

"Nah. Six weeks in Danang, I got cash up the ass. Besides, what do you care? It's just a stupid duck."

Its importance doubled. I took a twenty-peso note from my pocket, tossed it on the table. "Consider it a done deal I-Know. Duck's mine."

He drank down his beer fast, got up with the duck to leave, bile rose in my throat. "I'm serious, I-Know. The duck stays."

He put it back on the table. For no good reason, I stood, struck him hard on the chest with an open palm. He flailed his arms, staggered back against the wall. Freddy got up, stood between us. "Hold it, Goldie. That's enough. You're done." I pushed against him; he pushed back. "Leave him be. He's harmless. Never hurt a fly."

I choked on my fury, said to I-Know, "We'll call it even." Sat down.

Freddy escorted him to the door, settled back at the table, gave me a hard look. "I'm disappointed in you, man. Didn't make you for such an asshole."

My face flushed. I felt grateful for the darkness. Without looking, I dug a handful of coins from my pocket, dumped them on the table. "Rosa, play some music." She sorted through the coins, took what she wanted, headed for the jukebox. After a minute something twangy started to play. Everything felt wrong, but the dumb rube in me didn't understand why. Best I could do; light a cigarette and pull the smoke deep into my lungs. It was finished; at least it seemed so. I took another drag from the cigarette. Dissatisfied, I stubbed it out. "God damn it. God damn it." I looked at Freddy for an answer.

He said nothing, but gave me one of his patented looks, the one that bored through my skull and watched my brain tick. What he saw must have amused him. "So Goldie, you've got a duck. What are you going to do with it?"

My mind had only one response: *Oh, the monkeys have no tails in Zamboanga...*

* * * * *

Tropical night, outside, stars stood close and bright, a new moon showed its edge. I sat at the desk inside the Quonset Hut we used for our Flight Crew Shack, deserted at that late hour except for the duck and me. I thought him asleep in his well-appointed box because I no longer heard scratching. Outside on the ramp where aircraft were parked, men worked with flashlights that flickered like amorous lightening bugs. Occasionally, I heard the muffled sound of their voices or the pure steel ring of a dropped wrench hitting concrete.

The hut was furnished with a stolen desk and a few chairs that bitched and moaned whenever they had to work. On the far wall, flight gear hung in coherent tangles from metal hooks set at eye level. The gear reminded me of pictures in old magazines of lynched Negroes hanging from tree branches. A song I remembered called them Strange Fruit.

In front of me sat a yellow pad and a pen. I intended to write a letter home if I could find words. Thinking long and hard, I honestly couldn't remember the last time I wrote. I began with the date and salutation: *Dear Mom and Dad…*

I froze, my mind withdrew into the zone it occupied most of the time, but there I sat, determined. Rain began. Fat drops rattled against the curve of the tin roof. In the corner, I heard the duck moving. Outside, men bitched. I continued to sit. Words came from some unknown place. I wrote about this thing and my involvement in it. Tried to make sense of it as I wrote. Painful work because it had come to define me. I hated myself for the exhilaration of sitting in a cramped space of a seventy thousand pound machine with six other souls waiting to be hurled into the air from the deck of a ship. Hated how abstract everything became and the dope-like rush of landing back onboard. But when we landed at Danang Airbase things were a different story. Half a click down the ramp from our temporary spaces, at the end of the runway, stood a sterile white Butler Hut; the sound of its heavy-duty air conditioning units whirred all hours. I could count the white aluminum boxes stacked beside it, containers for our own Strange Fruit.

I apologize, I wrote. *Didn't mean to be so morbid. Dad will understand.* And I wrote that because of his time in the Pacific as a Marine in his own war. I paused, remembered the first time I flew by Iwo Jima. The pilot called it over the intercom; I climbed three steps of the companionway, stood hunched over behind his seat—looking. It lay off our port wing. So small, it seemed; so insignificant as it gradually rose from the sea. I watched as a rugged peak grew at its southern end, the place where he almost lost his life. Flying so close, I could feel his presence; I could almost smell his blood. I finished with a lie saying how much I missed them, promised to write again soon, signed the letter, put it in an envelope, sealed it, addressed it, printed the word *FREE* on the upper right corner, placed it on the center of the desk where I knew Freddy would find it early next morning and carry it with him to post from Yankee Station.

I lit a cigarette, leaned back feeling the immense weight of years, not yet thirty, already growing old in this business. I finished the cigarette, stubbed it out, walked over to the box. The duck peered up; I snuggled into in my hands, still shy, it trembled. I held it softly against my chest, stroked its body with a finger. "Hey little guy, don't worry. I'm going to take good care of you. I promise."

I put it back in the box, stood a moment, breathed deep, left the shack, walked over to the building next door, opened the screen door of the Maintenance Control Shack. Along the length of one wall, hung status boards telling the condition and disposition of all our aircraft. Behind a counter that ran its width sat Chief J.B. Mello meditating deep into the mug of black coffee welded to his fist. He looked up at me. "What the hell are you doing here at this hour, Goldie?

"Looking for a ride up the hill."

"You're shit out of luck. Storekeeper's on a parts run."

"Guess I'll walk. Anybody goes up tell them to keep an eye out for me."

The rain had stopped; the sky became a patchwork of broken clouds with little light from the moon. Might make it up the hill before it started again. Five minutes into the walk, headlights painted my back. A pickup stopped. I climbed in next to the driver. "I'll get out at the stop sign by the barracks."

"No problem," said the driver.

* * * * *

I slept well. Woke, without remembered dreams to a near deserted barracks, showered, shaved, dressed in clean dungarees, walked across the street to the galley, ate breakfast, drank down two cups of coffee, wrapped my toast in a paper napkin; caught a bus to the flight line. Chief Mello stood outside the Maintenance Control shack waiting for his ride up the hill. He squinted through cigarette smoke. "Hey Goldie, what's the deal with the duck?"

"Don't know Chief. Just kind of a situation I got myself in."

He shook his head. "If it was anybody but you I'd be surprised." His voice trailed off as the duty driver came outside and climbed into the truck. He climbed in, gave me a last look and a shake of his head. The truck started to pull away but stopped next to me. "Seriously Goldie, what are you going to do with the duck?"

"I'd like to keep it a while, Chief. It's a cool duck."

"Cool duck." He rolled the words around inside his mouth as if tasting them. "Bad idea. Won't work. Flight line is no place for a duck or any pet for that matter. It'll get hurt—or worse, cause someone else to get hurt."

"Come on Chief. Let me give it a try. I'll keep it in the shack till I figure something out."

"Don't like it, but you can give it a shot. First problem, the duck's gone. Any officers complain, it's gone yesterday. Understood?" I nodded. He tapped the dashboard, driver gunned the engine; off they went.

The door to the flight crew shack stood open. The Willie crew peopled it. Some sat, others milled about smoking, yakking; all waiting to man up their plane, to resume their flight to Atsugi after the RON at Cubi to allow some to go to town and pick up custom furniture ordered on the way downrange. The duck wandered the floor checking things out. Animal Ed followed it like a sheep dog. He looked at me, said, "Cool duck."

For us, Ed's name was Animal Ed because of the Japanese woman he lived with, or rather because of the two monkeys left behind by her previous lover. The monkeys, a large aloof female and an undersized male, lived in a cage kept in the walled yard behind her house. The half-pint sized male spent his days trying to have his way with the girl, but his advances were always spurned. Sometimes he succeeded in climbing on her back, but she flung him off with disdain. He became a very unhappy monkey.

Ed thought long and hard about the situation. In a flash of humanitarian brilliance he taught the little guy to masturbate. Exactly how was a great mystery. In the end, tragedy struck. The little guy died. Near as Ed could figure, the poor creature had beaten itself to death.

"So," he said, "what are you going do with it?"

"Man, ain't that the question of the day."

Saw I-Know there too. He sat in a chair studying me.

An officer poked his head in. "Let's hit it." With a collective mummer of complaint everybody rounded up their gear and shuffled out in clusters. Animal Ed picked up the duck, kissed it on the bill, handed it to me. "Cool duck."

Cool duck, I thought. Maybe, but not worth making an enemy of I-Know. Paybacks can be a motherfucker.

I put the duck in his box. Somebody had diced an apple and put it there. Didn't know for sure who, but saw my letter gone, so I figured it to be Freddy. I broke up the dry toast, put it in. Sat a while in the still cool building; let my thoughts ramble.

* * * * *

Days folded into weeks, weeks into months. Pampered and coddled, the duck spent his off duty hours grazing the narrow grassy patch that lay between our buildings and the road dining on tender new shoots and various bugs. He grew corpulent and proud. Reaching the fullness of adulthood it wore spandy new khaki feathers. Our time at Cubi Point drew to an end. We were moving to our new facility at Danang. Days of cold San Miguel Beer and warm Filipinas would soon be distant memories.

"The duck's not going."

I squinted in the glare of sun.

Chief Mello watched the gears twist inside my head. "No room for discussion, Goldie. The duck stays behind. That's the way it has to be."

"Why Chief? He hasn't caused any trouble. Everybody likes him. He's part of the detachment."

"I knew this was going to happen. Goddamnit, Goldie, he's not part of the detachment. He's a duck. Do I make myself clear? A duck. Look it up in the dictionary. We're up to our asses in alligators with the shit that's going on. There's no time to fuck around. That's the end of it. No more discussion."

* * * * *

I climbed the thirty-nine steps to the Sierra Club. Jesus stood behind the bar; he flashed a solid gold smile, held up a finger. I nodded, sat at a table near the wall, drank down the beer, ordered another; drank it down too.

Horny Ernie's head appeared in the doorway. "Man," he said. "You look like you been shot at and missed, shit at and hit." He held up two fingers to the Cherry Girl, she brought his special ingredients and took payment from the pile of Pesos on the table. Ernie carefully mixed his witches brew. "I know exactly what you're thinking."

"Yeah. Been through it a dozen times in my head. There's no good answer. Chief Mello isn't having any of it. Leave him behind, he's duck soup."

Suffering his incurable itch, Ernie checked out the girls, flagged one, on the way out, said, "I'll be back. We'll talk." Sure you will, I thought.

I gave Jesus a hi-ho wave, started down the steps, checked myself as I descended, seemed pretty steady, Josie didn't like me well drunk. Outside the sun stood soon to set. I took my time walking amid the long shadows heading to her apartment. There, I gathered up her daughter and the three of us set out for Kong's Restaurant. Phoenix rested soft against my chest; delicate as a hummingbird, so light it felt as though I was levitating her, she looked up at me with the soulful eyes of her mother. I asked Josie once why she chose that name. "Was her father from Arizona?"

"No. I named her Phoenix after the mythical bird that raises itself from its own ashes."

The sun had set, the street crowded with a fury of hookers, pimps, thieves and sailors. Bars cast their greedy lights into the dark. Blaring music and the kaa-ching sound of money changing hands surrounded us as we passed the small concrete pool in front of New Pauline's. A fine young fleet sailor in spandy whites stared at the gator with deep fascination, a half dozen yellow ducklings swam around its sated jaws, kids swarmed the cherry, pulling at his sleeves—hollering at him from all directions—dancing—distracting, others picked his pockets. Fresh meat, I thought.

* * * * *

I first met Josie at Kong's Restaurant on a crowded day. She sat alone; I invited myself to share her table. We took our time eating while talking about this and that. I felt drawn to her, maybe the sound of her voice or her unapologetic manner. I don't know.

We had finished eating. She said, "I'm on my way to work now, but I'll stay the evening with you if you pay my bar fine."

We stepped out into dazzling sunlight, walked to her bar, paid the fine, which gave her the night off. She said, "Will you take me to the cinema?"

A barn sized tin shed held the cinema. It stood at the edge of Magsaysay, near the bridge. We walked into its shocking air-conditioned chill, found seats, and as the unremembered movie played, she permitted me to kiss her but resisted when I tried to touch her breasts. The movie ended, we walked to her apartment. "I'd like see you tomorrow," I said.

"Don't promise anything you don't intend to do. I don't tolerate liars."

* * * * *

There were some no-fly days, downtime while politicians wrangled about the conduct of the war. Jose and I woke early. In still darkness, we made our way to the bus station at the edge of town for a journey to her home province, a dusty hair raising ride of several hours while sitting on the wooden bench of an Ordinary Victory Liner shared by people and the things they carried. Animals squealed, clucked, complained. The din and smell of a poorly muffled diesel engine overpowered my thoughts. The driver flew over narrow mountain roads, slammed into tight hairpin turns at dangerous speeds while crashing gears and yakking over his shoulder with the conductor. He made tire skidding stops in places that were less than places where people waited to be picked up for the sole purpose of adding to the chaos. In small towns, vendors clustered around the bus competing to feed hungry travelers with dried squid, roasted bananas, and a dozen things I couldn't identify. Across the aisle sat a wizened old woman with lizard-like skin and sparse silver hair pulled back into a tight bun. Smoke dribbled from her nose. I couldn't see the source. Finally, she removed a stubby black cheroot from inside her mouth, hawked long strings of brown saliva out the window, put it back between her teeth and resumed dribbling smoke from her nose.

We got off the bus, walked a pathway through clusters of banana and mango trees to a farm where she lived as a child. Her mother greeted us, took Phoenix, disappeared into a small house built of gray cinder blocks. Nearby, a large hog slept, a few hens scratched out their living, and a scrawny, long necked rooster eyed me with suspicion.

"Come on," said Josie, "Let me show you where we'll sleep." She led me to a small nipa hut built on bamboo stilts at the edge of the clearing, mounted steps made from a single log cut with notches, beckoned me to follow. I made an awkward, self-conscious climb. "Christ, I must seem so clumsy to you."

She laughed, pulled my face to hers, kissed me. "My mother always complains that I don't bring Phoenix home often enough. She won't give her back until we're ready to leave." She moved me to the woven mats that covered the floor, removed my clothes, made love to me in the coolness of an afternoon breeze.

* * * * *

We took our last meal; walked the short distance to a lagoon, lay on a beach of pure black sand. Palm trees soared and curved in great arcs over the placid water inside the lagoon, while outside the reef's crenellated edge, violent waves slammed themselves in blazing glory. I watched them fade to invisibility as the sun dipped below the horizon

"I left home at sixteen. Traveled to Olongapo believing I could find success. In our barrio people told stories of relatives who went there and became quite wealthy. They said it was easy. Like picking money from trees. I heard those stories over and over, and believed I could do the same. When I arrived at the bus station in Olongapo, an elderly woman greeted me in my dialect as though she knew me—as if she were waiting for my arrival. She told me to call her Tita, which means aunt, and asked my purpose. When I explained, she said, 'I've helped many like you. If you wish, I'll help you too. You're welcome to stay in my home. There are two others like you living there now. There will be small expenses involved, but don't worry, you can repay them in the future. Trust me. You are in good hands'.

"I was overcome with gratitude. I believed God had put her in my path. I moved in with her and the others. Woken early each morning, we bathed, ate breakfast, and worked cleaning the house until late afternoon with a short break for lunch, everything done and redone until it met Tita's satisfaction."

She drew silent, leaned her head on my shoulder, breathed deep. In her silence, I listened to the loose sound of small, lapping waves.

"Over time I began to wonder. Nothing more was said about a job. One evening, I asked. She said, 'Don't worry, Daughter. I'm preparing a wonderful future for you.' It didn't feel right. I thought of running away but running away brought me to Olongapo in the first place. Where else could I go? I had no money, no friends, nothing.

"She explained that I could make big money working in a bar. 'I've helped others do that. The work is easy. Americans are stupid. That makes it possible to have a rich life in Olongapo City.' I was shocked. She said 'Everything will be explained and you won't have to compromise your morals.' The next day, she introduced me to a bar owner, a Chinese woman who wore expensive clothes and jewelry. I was told I would work as a Cherry Girl. Tita said, 'You don't have suitable clothes. We have to shop for new ones. 'I have no money,' I said. 'That's unimportant. You will repay me from your salary.' Later that day, I dressed under Tita's watchful eye and left the house unattended for the first time."

Josie paused. A fragment of moon rose. Stars began to appear. Far off, lightning illuminated clouds. I dug a handful of sand, let it slip between my fingers like quick silver, laid back, watched the slight movements of her silhouette against the sky, wished I could wipe away her sadness.

"It was simple work. I took orders from customers, delivered their drinks, collected payment. Some left tips on my tray. The owner put them in a big glass jar behind the bar. She said, 'This money will be divided among all of you at the end of each week'. When we were paid, she withheld most of mine saying, 'It's going to your Tita to repay your debt.'

"As I continued living with Tita, the debt grew. One day she said, 'I'm not satisfied. You have to earn more. If you don't I'll throw you out and there will never be future work here for you. There's more money to be made as a hostess. You're paid a commission on each drink a customer buys you. A hostess can earn a great deal of money if she works hard.' She was right, hostesses earned much more, but in the end most became prostitutes because their customers wanted more than drinking companions and were willing to pay. That's how one lived a rich life in Olongapo City."

I sat up. She brushed sand from my back.

"I agreed. I believed I could earn enough to live on my own, but it seemed the more I made, the more I owed. One night, a beautiful American sailor came into the bar. I fell madly in love with him. He was tall and slender and fair skinned with blue eyes, blond hair and a tall nose. I went to his table and sat beside him. He immediately said he wanted to go home with me. I told him, I didn't have a place of my own. He said we could go to a hotel. He paid my Bar Fine. We spent the next three nights at the Golden Hotel.

"I trusted him and told him of my problems. He promised to help. I was heartbroken the day he left. He gave me his address and what I thought was a lot of money and promised to come back to marry me."

She sighed. Shook her head.

"I returned to Tita's house, told her of my American and of our plans. She laughed at me. 'Don't be stupid. It's all nonsense. Every bar girl in Olongapo has heard the same promises many times. How much money did he leave? I showed her. She took most of it, said it was her portion. 'You see what I've been telling you? See how easy it is to become rich if you are willing?'

"With the money I had left I thought of going home, but was afraid if I left I might never see my American again. So I went back to work. It was fine because everything had changed.

"I wrote him long love letters. Then, my period didn't come. I was full of joy. I had become a real woman. I was going to give the man I loved a child. I wrote a letter describing everything knowing he would be a wonderful husband and father, that our child would be an American citizen. I waited and I waited. No answers came. I believed the letters were lost in the mail. I wrote again, but there was never an answer. I fell into despair. Morning sickness came. I tried to conceal it; to hide it from Tita's watchful eyes, but it wasn't possible to fool her.

"One morning she caught me vomiting. 'I suspected it. You'll have an abortion. It's a simple thing. I'll take you to a doctor I know.' I refused. She slapped my face. I could take no more. I slapped her back. She shrieked at me, 'You ingrate. I've been more than a mother to you. Everything you have is from me. What I have given I can take back. Get out of my house this instant. I never want to see your face again.'

"I left with the clothes on my back and the money in my purse. There was nowhere to go except to the bar, the only place I wasn't a stranger. Still morning, too early for customers, everyone sat around grooming or chatting. I sat, started crying. One hostess named Mona beckoned me. She was my friend, and like me, a simple girl from the province.

"I sat next to her. 'I am pregnant,' I said, 'and I have no place to live.' All talking stopped. Mona said, 'You're lucky to be free of that bitch cunt. I have room at my place for you to stay. Don't worry. You will be just fine. Do you have money?' 'Only a little.' I opened my purse to show her. Others started opening their purses, putting money in the center of the table. I was overwhelmed.

"My belly swelled in a way impossible to hide. I couldn't work as a sexy hostess any longer. The owner showed unexpected kindness and found other work for me to do. I began to find joy in my life. I was going to have a beautiful fair-skinned child.

"Several months after Phoenix was born I saw the sailor I loved so much walking on the opposite side of the street with a group of others. I ran to him and tried to talk. He pretended not to know me, and I realized Tita was right. I knew exactly what I was to him. Just another Little Brown Fucking Machine, no different from any other. That's how I came to understand you Americans."

The moon stood high. I stripped off my clothes, walked waist deep into the water, swam a slow measured pace toward the phosphorous flash of waves. Near the middle I stopped, floated on my back. Fragments of moonlight scattered across the water. In my mind, images flowed in silent loops. Looking up, I saw the bright, stable light of two planets and the dense cloud of stars that formed one arm of our galaxy. Looking deeper, I saw the faint smear of light that was Andromeda Galaxy as it drifted two and a half million light years away. I imagined beings there looking down on Earth that same instant—seeing not me, but my ancient ancestors breaking stones into tools for the first time. A physical connection existed. A constant river of massless photons created a tether turning distance into an illusion. Andromeda touched me. Its beings sang to me in polyphonic voices just beyond my hearing. There were other galaxies. Swarms of them, even swarms of swarms, all created as if God were an indifferent builder, as if he built things, set them in motion and lost interest like a bowler who rolled his ball, turned and walked away before the pins were struck. And time, fucking time—made my life not even the click of a cog. Fuck it. Fuck it all. I swam to shore. Josie lay sleeping in the sand. The realization I was in love with her hit me. I lay down spoonlike against her. Surroundings melted to nothingness.

28 MAY 1967 an EA-3B Skywarrior staging out of Cubi Point, Philippines encountered a typhoon. Four ECM crewmen bailed out. The flight crew successfully returned to base. One body was found on 31 May. Apparently he died 8 hours prior to recovery based upon forensic evidence. Two days later a Mae West was found with a note: "We are in the water and OK." There was nothing more.

—The Stars and Stripes

"Goldie, you're my friend. I've got to tell you something, and I'm scared shitless because I don't know what you'll do."

Jim and I sat in Kong's Restaurant drinking tall glasses of sweet iced tea.

"Spit it out, Jim. Can't be that bad."

"It's worse than you can imagine. I can't do this anymore, Goldie. None of it's what I hoped it would be. Seems like I've got no choice except to boogie. I'll head for Manila and try to get back to the world somehow."

"You're kidding, right?"

"I've never been more serious."

"Christ Jim, why don't you just quit flying if that's the problem? You can, you know."

"It's not flying, it's bigger." He paused, drew a breath. "I'm queer, Goldie. I can't pretend anymore. I've tried my ass off but I can't get rid of it."

I looked at him through disbelieving eyes.

"Goldie, I'm telling you because you're my friend. I hate it. I fucking hate it."

"Are you sure? I've seen you with women. Maybe you're wrong."

"No, I'm not wrong. I've known it since I was a kid."

"But what about the women?"

"I go with them because it's what everybody expects. When I get to their place, I pretend I'm too drunk to get it up. Truth is I'm in love with you. Have been since we first met."

We sat, avoiding each other's eyes. Jim lit a cigarette, seemed like something he didn't want, just something to keep busy.

"Look, I know you don't feel the same. I don't expect that. But I had to tell somebody. Thought you'd be the right one, so it's done. You can get up and walk away, or you can do any damn thing you want, because I don't give a shit anymore. Thought I'd feel better telling you. I don't."

I couldn't wrap my mind around it. Jim did everything different from the queer on the island. He kept his hair cut short, dressed in Levis. I tried to understand, but ignorance got in my way. I told him a shameful lie. "Far as I'm concerned, Jim, nothing's changed."

Over night he disappeared. Questions were asked of me. Our relationship scrutinized with microscopes. A few days later the OOD and the Master at Arms came to the barracks, cut his lock, inventoried his personal possessions, sealed them up in a pasteboard box and took them away.

* * * * *

Shocked, I knew the answer; so simple it embarrassed me. I had to find Ernie, knew he would understand, knew where he was at that hour, the Golden Hotel, his twilight roosting spot, the secure anchorage of his tempestuous life. The lobby circled the top of a creaky flight of steps. Charlie-the-Chinaman sat on a stool behind the counter half asleep. On the floor, houseboys slept off their night's work intermixed with several hookers who didn't find customers to share their beds.

"Ernie here?"

"Numba fifteen."

I held up two fingers. Charley nudged a houseboys with his toe, gestured. The bleary eyed Filipino rose, got two beers from the refrigerator. I carried them down the dark windowless hallway, past doors numbered crudely by hand, entered fifteen without knocking. Ernie laid sprawled, naked, ass high, in deep slumber. Startled by my entry, his guest, a regular Virgin Mary, pulled the sheet up to her chin. It made for a touching scene. I rubbed the bottom of Ernie's foot with an icy beer. He snapped awake. "I've got it," I said. "I know the answer."

"Fuck, you're slow on the draw. I figured it out last night. Got to make him an officer. Got to see Sergio first thing."

I knew the rightness of it. "Crazy fucker'll go for it big time. Come on, get your ass in gear." I picked his pants up from the floor, threw them at him.

He threw them back on the floor. "Fuck, you got to be kidding. Where you going to find him this time of morning? Besides, it's Sunday, motherfucker."

Yeah, good point, I thought. "Guess I'll just be on my way then."

In the lobby Charlie woke as I passed. "You go now? I got good girl for you. Horny girl. Almost cherry. Treat you right."

"No thanks. Got things to do."

He shrugged; his eyes slid shut as I started down the steps.

*****

I pushed my way into Sergio's tight, airless office, Ernie pushed in behind. "Hey Chief," I said, "you got to help us,"

"Yeah Chief, you got to help us," said Ernie.

Sergio, our Chief pencil pusher, spent his waking hours in the unappreciated job of keeping up with the Navy's flood of paperwork. A lovely cross between Sebastian Melmoth and Bozo the Clown, the kinky haired northern Italian from New York City and former truck driver with a rose tattooed above his left nipple possessed a high-pitched giggle and a strong preference for Eric Burden and the Animals. As usual, he sat behind his desk busting ass, his striker Revis, worked, clackity-clack on a big black IBM electric typewriter near the far wall.

Sergio looked up, leaned his chair back at a dangerous angle, clasped his hands behind his head, looked at us over the tops of low-slung glasses, a slur of sweat covered his forehead; dark, full moons stained the armpits of his shirt. "So, what's up kiddos?"

"Got a serious problem Chief," I said.

"Everybody's got a serious problem. I'm up to my ass in serious problems."

Rivas, the Mex-Am Personnel Striker with a James Dean fetish and a hankering for nose snow said, "Up to his ass" over the clackity-clack of his typewriter.

"Yeah, but this is life and death," Ernie said.

"Yeah, life and death," I said.

"You, and everybody," said Sergio.

Rivas shook his head. "You and everybody."

"This is different," I said, "Ernie and I have it all worked out."

"Yeah," said Ernie, "We just need a little help to make it happen."

"A little help," said Rivas.

"Yeah," said Ernie, "All you've got to do is make him an officer."

"Yeah," I said, "That'll solve the whole problem."

"Whole problem," said Rivas.

Sergio gave us a bewildered look. "What problem?"

"Otherwise he'll end up soup in some cooking pot," said Ernie.

"Cooking pot," said Rivas.

"Cooking pot?"

"The duck," I said, as if it were obvious, "The duck."

The clackity-clack stopped momentarily.

"Yeah," said Ernie, "Make him an officer and we can take him to Danang with us. Chief Mello wants to leave him here, but nobody'd leave a high ranking officer behind."

Sergio's mind grasped the situation. He gave a twisted giggle. "Ensign Duck?"

"Yeah," I said, "but that doesn't sound right."

"How bout Ensign Duckworth?" Ernie said.

Rivas' typewriter again stopped. "Ensign Donald Duckworth," he said, and resumed his clackity-clack.

"That's hot," said Sergio, "Needs some thought. Gimme a little time."

"Yeah," said Rivas, "Needs some thought."

* * * * *

Phoenix slept on a mat beside the bed; Josie lay curled against me, head resting on the crook of my arm, knee against my thigh. I didn't want to think about leaving, about how with everything, packed and stowed, stood in readiness to be loaded next day aboard C-130s and transported to Danang. Even the fact that Ensign Donald Duckworth would go with us failed to ease my mind. I listened to Josie breathe— the sound soft as a mother's whisper. I woke, not aware I had slept. Josie's small transistor radio played. Phoenix slept on. Josie pressed her warmth against me, melded her liquid skin to mine; drew me into her body… That's how I left her for the very last time.

IV

For most of the Vietnam War, EA-3Bs flew from Danang Air Base, providing continuous electronic warfare capability over the area, including the so-called Ho Chi Minh trail and all the way north to Haiphong harbor. The aircrew and ground support personnel were TAD from their home base in NAS Atsugi Japan.

—Los Angeles Times

* * * * *

Anybody who fucks a Vietnamese is just too lazy to masturbate

—Writings on the Shithouse Wall

The day hot, too hot for a smoke or for unnecessary movement. An ineffectual fan stuttered in a fitful way left and right, its blades whacked with impotence at the sluggish air inside the Avionics Trailer. I sat with my flight suit stripped down to the waist, feet up on a battered metal desk. Outside, the sun spangled and washed out all highlights. It took such effort to breathe that all of us, except the true loonies, hid away best we could. Even Ensign Duckworth floated inert, unmotivated to move within or without the comparative comfort of his water filled tub under the belly of the trailer.

Between Ernie and me, two M-16s leaned against the desk. They made us a dangerous pair. All of us at Danang were armed. We bristled with guns, pointy knives, frag grenades. All the things we carried terrified our neighbors; the 1st Marine Air Wing, who didn't like having a bunch of weapon bearing squids next door. Considering they defined a navy marching formation as two or more sailors moving in approximately the same direction at approximately the same time, they couldn't understand why persons such as we were allowed to possess lethal weapons. Their boss, Lt. Col. William Hurd, paid a visit and held a confab with our OinC, Commander

157

Bill Bull in the sober belief that he would act as a reasonable man. The confab may have gone something like this: 'I agree,' agreed Lt. Col. Hurd, 'this is a dangerous place, and I recognize the need to respond appropriately in the event of an emergency. Having said that, I think it's a fine thing that your squids have weapons. But perhaps for the sake of safety you should consider confiscating them as we do not wish to suffer casualties due to their ineptness.' Our OinC thought the matter through, and after a reasonable amount of thinking, may have sagaciously replied: 'I will be happy to consider confiscating their weapons if you and your officers of 1st MAW can figure a way of doing so without damaging their fragile and precious fighting spirit.' Lt. Col. Hurd thought it over, couldn't. That marked the end of the confab, and from that time forth, officers and men of 1st MAW, of indignant and self-imposed necessity, treaded their flight line with fear and loathing.

Ernie sat cross-legged on the deck deep in contemplation of some unknowable and acerbic spirit; the energy he put into contemplation raised rivulets of sweat at his hairline that coursed down, converged on the tip of his nose, and dripped like waterfall on an ever widening moist spot on the chest of his dun tee shirt. We were silent in our combined misery till Ernie broke his trance and moved his mouth. "Come on motherfucker, let's get some chow."

"Fuck you and the horse your rode in on. It's a mile walk and a hundred goddamn degrees." Even saying that tired me, but like Ernie, I was off the flight schedule for the next twenty-four hours and boredom sawed at my gut even more than the infernal heat; so I drug my sweaty ass up from the chair, pulled into the upper half of my flight suit and we set out walking through the greasy smell and smoke of the previous day's shit being burned in diesel fuel along the roadway.

At the chow hall, we stood outside in the line of a hundred or so and shuffled forward step-by-step in Alabama chain gang fashion. Nearby, five spit-and-polish grunt cherries sat on the grassless iron red ground next to their rucks.

The sixth, a staff sergeant with unshaven jowls and eyes that cast at a distance, spoke in the hoarse rattle of his marine voice as he set about disassembling and cleaning his weapon. "Listen up. Y'all need to understand this. They're godless heathens out there. Different from us. They don't know the milk of human kindness. They'll slit your fucking throat and smile while you bleed out. They got no respect for human life. And most important to remember—they're fucking good at what they do."

For a mysterious reason, his words brought a remembrance of myself as teenager walking up First Avenue near Pike Street on skid row one sleet cold November morning. Ahead of me, just past the Twenty-Five Cent Open All Nite Green Parrot Theater, five careworn men dressed in frayed at the elbow overcoats stood clustered in a tight fist around a smoldering shit can basking in its meager warmth. As I passed, one spoke with deep hurt in his voice. "I was up on Fourth Avenue yesterday. Asked this lady for a dime. She called me a wino. *A wino*. I'm no fuckin' wino. I'll drink anything." In hearing the marine speak his piece I got the queasy feeling that my First Avenue remembrance spoke to his future.

* * * * *

After chow, we returned to the ramp, stood in the scanty shade of the trailer, listened to the growing rumble of reciprocating engines from the far end of the runway. "Peter Rabbit Two-Two back from Karat," said Ernie. "Probably loaded to the gills with Thai goodies, and a couple cases of Thai Clap.

Mister Duckworth joined our conversation flapping his wings, sounding an approving series of quacks, figuring somebody onboard the Willie would be toting leftover chow to share with him. As the big plane lumbered up the taxiway, four men rolled out a boarding ladder. It arrived, swung ninety degrees, hit its mark, kowtowed to a stop. Engines shut down one by one till the last prop shuttered and freewheeled to a stop. The rear hatch swung open, crew filed off, officers first, each carrying a sausage shaped parachute bags full with necessaries they descended the ladder. At the bottom they climbed into the bed of a waiting pickup. With all aboard it whisked them away for debrief and on to the BOQ for chow and Happy Hour.

Down came the enlisted troopers carrying portable possessions, among them Animal Ed, discernible by his shaved head. He stepped out onto the ladder, tossed his parachute bag to the ramp, it landed with an apathetic plop, then reached back inside the plane and grabbed up two failed black boxes by the handles, carried them down the ladder's quivering steps. Out popped I-Know with his parachute bag in one hand, a small wire cage holding some weasel-like critter in the other.

Ernie and I stayed put in the shade, Mister Duckworth continued to drift about in his tub, but the bucolic scene disintegrated to horror as I-Know drew near. Duckworth sensed something bad in the air, grew silent, tense. When the animal detected him it hissed and spat and threw Duckworth into a panic. He left his tub, toddled at a double time the opposite way straining, flapping his clipped wings in a futile effort to become airborne, but only skipped and bounced his desperate haunches across ramp.

My heart thumped. "What the fuck you got, I-Know?"

"A pet. You don't have to worry though. I'll take care of it."

"Take care of it? Take care of it? You fucking barely take care of yourself. That thing's dangerous. You've got to get it out of here."

Animal Ed swaggered up bearing both weighty black boxes. "Give me a hand I-Know, you lazy fuck." He sat the boxes down. Looked at me. "Hellish goddamn flight. Aircon died six hours out. Couldn't keep the avionics cool. Had to shut down most of it. When these fuckers died, I was out of a job."

I-Know put the cage down, took up one of the black boxes, the two of them started toward the EW Trailer.

"Hold on a minute, I-Know," I said. "Take that fucker with you."

"I'll be back."

I looked around the area, saw Duckworth poke his head out the door of the duty office looking to me for the All Clear. Behind him stood Jessie wearing his wondrous big-as-all-outdoors Hawaiian smile. He shook his head. "Yeah Goldie, you're a hundred percent right. I-Know's fucked up as a goddamn soup sandwich. But you gotta roll with it, bro. You just gotta roll. Can't make it so fuckin' personal."

* * * * *

Sleep came hard, night air barely cooled, even under the net, starving mosquitoes feasted on my blood. Like most nights, I dozed in and out of sleep on a wrinkled, sweat soaked sheet till morning. When I woke, Freddy stood at the foot of my bed. "Hey man, Smitty's dead."

"Huh?"

"Yeah, deader than a doornail."

I swung my legs off the bed. "What the fuck?"

"Got his throat cut looking for pussy over in Dogpatch."

"Christ, what was he thinking?"

"Pussy. Shit, you know he was worse than Ernie."

I pulled on my flight suit, stepped into my boots. "He's a Willy Victor guy. I hardly knew him, but shit, nobodies dumb enough to look for pussy in Dogpatch."

Freddy scoffed. "Not that sorry fuckstick. Come on, let's get some chow."

On the way to the chow hall I thought about Ernie and how his cock regularly overruled his brain. He told me one time he'd fuck a porcupine if he could just figure out how.

* * * * *

House Mouses were in the barracks when we got back. They did all the titivating. Eight of them arrived on bicycles each morning wearing au dais and mollusk shaped straw hats cinched in place with bright colored sashes. Most were middle aged with gory betel nut stained teeth and lips, but a couple were young and pretty. They worked all morning. At lunchtime, they squatted low on their hams in a circular bundle and ate their fish heads and rice while chattering singsong. Some in the barracks tried to seduce the pretty ones with smooth talk and promised riches, but for naught. They had no interest in our bodies, they wanted only the opportunity to make up our bunks and wash our clothes in exchange for a little money or cans of Charms Candy and boxes of sanitary napkins that could be bought at Freedom Hill Exchange atop Hill-327.

The road up Hill-327, a narrow gulch of rough laid tarmac, passed through the shanty ville of Dogpatch where they lived, and where women smiled provocative smiles and beckoned us, but our orders were: *Do not stop along the road for anybody or anything. If necessary, run people over to keep the vehicle moving.*

Marine patrol found Smitty there, queball pale, half buried in the muck of a newly tilled rice paddy with his genitals in his mouth and a leering smile carved deep into the flesh beneath his chin. Won him a Purple Heart, for sure.

* * * *

We had a small Acey Ducey clubhouse built of naked pinewood salvaged from packing crates and other cumshawed material, an altogether tidy and classy place. Those who could mustered there elbow to elbow and drank to Smitty's health declaring his death to be an honorable one. At seventeen hundred on the button, 105's on the hill started sounding off, doing their daily H&I, so we drank to them. As time passed, we found many other things of concernment and drank to them all. When dark fell, those of us who still walk migrated to the flight line and in torrid night air sat, on the concrete ramp to watch a movie projected onto the side of the Duty Shack. That night we watched Richard Burton and Liz Taylor acting out their own war, the sky along our perimeter lit by illumination rounds whose fierce white magnesium light leached life from everything it touched. Sporadic red or green signal flares punctuated that light. At a distance, I heard the methodical krump of artillery fire and staccato bursts of small arms. A C-47 Spooky worked a hill so far away as to be an insubstantial shadow. It flew moth like, circle upon circle, orbiting some central object, spurting a continuous fountain of red flame, twenty mike-mike leaving the barrel at six thousand rounds per minute turning everything beneath it to mush. While that went on, I continued to watch Will Shakespeare's war of the spirit, and when came the slappity-slap interruption as a reel ended, booed and hissed along with the rest while it was changed, cheered when the projector whirred again, and pretended my life to be as important and dramatic.

* * * * *

I-Know cobbled together a commodious cage from pieces of this and that. Though not a work of art, I couldn't criticize it. The animal was fed and watered daily, and when away, he arranged for somebody else to care for its needs. He seemed to have real love for the beast. That tempered my mood.

* * * * *

I finished eating at the chow hall and walked back to the flight line, saw the door of the animal's cage ajar, the cage empty. Holy shit, where was Duckworth? I spotted him near the yellow gear, ran toward him, he bolted. I stumbled, fell on the concrete, ripped a knee of my flight suit, tore the flesh under, caught up with Duckworth, grabbed him ran for Maintenance Control, burst through the door causing Chief Mello to spill his sacramental coffee, handed Duckworth across the counter, he recoiled, Sproule, our Alpha Zulu, grasped the situation, took Duckworth from my hands.

On the ramp, I headed toward the Duty Office; Chief Sergio carried a fistful of papers. I shouted to him, "He's loose. He's loose."

"Who's loose?"

"The animal. I-Know's fucking animal."

"Don't think so."

"Yeah it is. The cage is empty."

Sergio looked perplexed. "Doesn't mean he's loose."

"What the fuck does it mean?"

He pointed with his free hand. "Look." Just beyond the corner of the supply shack strolled I-Know carrying the animal. "See? That's what I was trying to tell you. Much ado about nothing."

I felt a flush. "Sorry, Chief."

"It's okay."

I-Know walked up to us. "Look at this sweet guy, see how easy he is to handle. He's so tame. Wouldn't hurt a fly."

I inhaled, blew it out through my nose, looked at the animal. It looked back at me. I swear to God, it smiled.

* * * * *

Middle of the night—sirens screamed, snapped me upright from shallow sleep. I swung my legs off the bunk into my flight suit and boots, left the barracks, dogtrotted toward the bunker. Felt thumping explosions from incoming rounds. They didn't worry me. Charlie never walked them this far inside the perimeter, they always just did a few hit and run potshots.

From behind, a hand grabbed my shoulder, spun me around, found myself face to chest with Jessie. His paw covered my shoulder like a baseball glove. "Hey Goldie. Hey Goldie, this ain't shit. This ain't shit, man." He waved a whiskey bottle in front of my nose. "Lookie what I got. Ain't she a beauty? Come on." He pointed toward the barracks roof. "Come on man, let's climb up to the good seats and watch the show."

Freddy came down the steps. Jessie threw out an arm catching him full on the chest almost taking him to the ground, swung the bottle in front of his face. "Freddy. Freddy. Come on. You gotta come with us, man. You gotta, man. Come with us and watch the show. It's gonna be great. It's just gonna be so great."

We climbed steps to the second deck, up a nailed on ladder to the pitched roof and sprawled out. Jessie opened the bottle, threw the cap into the dark. I heard him swallow, chug-chug-chug while illumination flares hissed. At any one time ten or more were in the air, all casting dead white light, moving shadows side to side as they swayed below their parachutes. He tapped my elbow with it. I took it, downed a swallow that bit my throat. "Come on man. That won't do. That just won't do."

I put the bottle to my lips again. As I drank, he tilted it up from the bottom with a finger; I couldn't swallow fast enough and choked. Freddy snatched the bottle away.

I looked over my left shoulder. Saw Monkey Mountain catching shit too. Counted five explosions in less than a minute, moved my eyes to our flight line, two rounds dropped in there—whoomp-whoomp. A shock hit me. Duckworth. Rounds were landing where he lived.

I bolted for the ladder; Jessie grabbed me, pulled me down. "Hold it, man. Hold it. You can't go no place. Can't do nothin', man. Just gotta sit it out." I pulled free; he grabbed me again. "Come on, Goldie. Easy does it." Freddy said something I didn't hear, Jessie let go. I scrambled down the ladder. A searing hot flash hit my back when the fuel farm took hits and torched off. The ammo dump went up next causing a series of secondary explosions that sent up red-hot shards of shrapnel whining through the air. Two—no—three rounds hit the flight line while I sprinted. The fiery hell of the fuel farm lit everything brilliant. Everywhere looked like the epicenter of a violent earthquake, everything jarred, jumbled, knocked askew.

Two trailers sat upright, but unsquare, sheet metal sides lacerated and dimpled. Chief Mello stood next to a bunker gesturing to me. I could see a pained what-the-fuck look on his face. Concussion sprawled me to my side. I could only breathe in rattley gasps; everything appeared as though I were looking through the rippled glass of an old windowpane. I tried to move, couldn't. Rough hands pulled at me, Chief Mello's angry voice growled words that sounded like gibberish. He kept at me. I came to my feet, moved on my own. Inside the bunker, air stood fetid and hot from crowded bodies. I dropped to the floor, felt shadow hands pressed against me, pushed them away. "I'm not hurt, goddamnit. I'm not fucking hurt." Tried to stand, couldn't. "Leave me alone goddamnit. I'm not hurt." Found a tight corner, pressed myself into it, bit hard on my lower lip to control myself, tasted blood. False calm set in, more jarring concussions came. Everywhere trembled, two flashlights switched on, their crossed beams diffused to almost nothing by sand that filled the air. Nobody thought to bring a weapon because we were not trained to fight in that way, we were vulnerable to everything, a brand new feeling.

People were hurt, no doubt. I felt shamed because my thoughts were about Duckworth—motherfucking Duckworth. Time passed.

Tremors stopped. The All Clear sounded. Daylight seeped in through the bunker's entrance. Outside, startling, bright, everything helter-skelter like the thousand pieces of a picture puzzle dumped over the ground. I saw Duckworth in front of the duty office gobbling an open can of beanie weenies. Rivas saw me, gave his Golden Triangle grin. Duckworth saw me too, became torn between his chow and Goldman, made a choice, waddled across the ramp, stepped around debris, greeted me with his best Willie Nelson quack.

Hunks of shrapnel littered the ramp like confetti—some small as dime, some big as shit can lids—all jagged, chipped, obsidian sharp. The ammo dump burned hell-hole hot, rounds cooked off sounding like a major battle in progress, a couple hundred meters from it, the fuel farm shot up great orange tongues of flame and columns of dense black smoke, particulate choked the air. There was no breakfast to be had because the chow hall had been demolished, but that wasn't really in the front of my mind. The OinC and a couple khaki suits, walked the ramp. They circled the planes one by one holding a close inspection to see damage. From a distance most of the planes looked to be good, but close up, damage was considerable. One Whale sat canted on a collapsed main mount, two Willies showed heavy damage to their tails, Ed and Ernie huddled near the semi-intact EW Trailer; they waved me over. "Freddy got dinged," Ernie said.

"And Jessie," said Ed. "Sergio too."

"How bad?"

"Don't know," said Ed, "Don't think it was too bad."

"Yeah," said Ernie, "Only one really fucked up is Lipton. Got glass blown in his face. Think he lost an eye. Anyway, he's out for the season."

We walked around the trailer. Ernie kicked the rubble. "Fuck, the animal's gone."

"No shit?" I said. "You're not jerking my chain are you?"

"Take a look"

Sure enough the door was broken and open, the cage empty. My heart sank "Fuck me to tears. Maybe it's dead."

"Maybe," said Ernie.

I started kicking away rubble hoping to find its corpse. "We've got to find that fucker. Make sure."

Chief Mello stepped out of the duty office, shouted something I couldn't make out and gestured for all of us to circle up. "We've got a shitload of work in front of us. This place has to be cleaned up so we can resume flight ops ASAP." He designated a runner, sent him to the barracks to round up stragglers.

"Hey Chief," I said, "I-Know's animal is loose. We got to find it before it gets Duckworth."

"We don't have time for that shit, Goldie."

"But you don't understand Chief…"

"Goddamnit, Goldman, you don't understand. We're talking about people's lives."

"Come on Chief, we can…"

"Fuck that. You get your ass in gear. Round up the rest of your crew. Pack your trash and get ready to go. We have orders to get two plane shipboard soon as the runway is cleared."

He looked at me with granite eyes. Fuck. I pivoted on my heel, walked away. Thought, Just keep your mouth shut. Keep your fucking mouth shut. All the way to Yankee Station, I kept reminding myself to keep my goddamn mouth shut.

* * * * *

"He's dead," said a disembodied voice. "He's dead."

"Who's dead?"

"Come on Goldie, listen up." The voice sounded familiar—so familiar, but I couldn't place it. "Listen up, Goldie. He's dead." I tried to move away, but it followed me with persistence, turned into an image of the animal. It looked at me through intelligent eyes, its muzzle smeared with blood. For a second time, I saw it smile. "He's dead." I woke. Christ, I couldn't escape.

After six days of flying the weather turned foul; a perfect complement to my mood. The ship pitched and shuttered and met the seas head on. On deck, aircraft strained and groaned against tie down chains. Lousy food. Lousy sleep. Lousy dreams. All of us exhausted, half-cocked, red eyed, on our last flight from the ship. Even at altitude turbulence was sickening. Again and again, I slammed against the limits of my harness. We rendezvoused with an airborne tanker. In the cockpit, Chief Rowe sat in his aft facing seat, oxygen mask covering most of his face, I saw only his eyes, fixed, tired. Beyond him, in the left seat, Mister Hosey fought with yoke and throttles to ease the probe up and into the basket of the fuel hose that extended from the belly of a tanker, his fourth try. With quick hands, he jockeyed throttle and yoke to close the distance again. A jerk of turbulence, the tanker bounced out of sight. Heard Mister Hosey over the ICS. "We're approaching a low fuel state. We have enough for one pass at the ship. If we make it, we'll refuel and finish the cycle. If not, we'll bingo to Danang. It'll be tight, but we'll make it. Heads up. Stay alert." I rotated my seat aft for the landing, counted time by heartbeats. "Prepare to land," said Hosey. I grabbed my harness with both hands to keep Gs from flailing my arms when we caught the wire, pressed hard into the seat, engines screamed, moaned, and screamed again as he made continual throttle changes to stay in the groove. Wheels smashed onto the deck, Hosey slammed the throttles to full power, engines shrieked, LSO yelled through my headset. "Bolter. Bolter. Bolter." We rolled unimpeded down the deck. I breathed a harsh sigh. Mister Hosey climbed the plane, brought it around to the compass heading for Danang. What will I find there? I thought. Will Duckworth be alive?

We landed. I scrambled down the lower hatch, stepped into near ankle deep water. Everybody else piled out. Mister Hosey headed for Maintenance Control to write up gripes; the other two officers threw their gear in the back of the waiting pickup, crowded into the front seat with the driver, and headed off to their quarters. Duckworth splashed happily in a puddle in front of the duty office, saw me, let out a series of quacks, everything well in his world. Chief Rowe, me, and the others, headed for the flight crew shack to sort out our part of things.

Slogging through puddles, I noticed still visible damage, but everything appeared cleaned up and back to working order. Duckworth caught up and began conversing with me in our secret language. Inside the shack, I set him on the desk, stripped off my harness, hung it with my helmet and sidearm on the hook labeled with my name, lit up a cigarette, inhaled deep, opened the tiny refrigerator hoping to find a tidbit for Duckworth or a beer somebody forgot. No luck, shrugged my shoulders. "Sorry."

Duckworth quacked disapproval.

"I know what you mean." Hungry, but sick to the teeth of being wet and uncomfortable, I decided fuck chow; I'd go straight to the barracks. I ground out the cigarette, left the trailer, walked to Maintenance Control. Duckworth went back to cavorting. Chief Mello and his coffee cup sat inside, he gave me a hard look.

I smiled. "Hi ya, Chief."

He answered with a nod, took pull from his coffee, his eyes told me to get the fuck out of there.

"Christ, Chief, you still pissed?"

He touched his chin with the edge of his hand. "I've had it up to here with you and that goddamn duck. Can't get shit done around here."

"Damn, Chief, I've been flying my ass off."

He fumbled in his shirt pocket, retrieved a rumpled pack of cigarettes, shook one free, tossed the pack to me, lit his, extended the lighted match toward me. "It started with that duck, then came O'Neal's animal. There's been nothing but trouble since. I'll tell you seriously, Goldie, I need you and everybody to get their heads out of their asses and get back to what's important. I shouldn't have to tell you that. You've been around long enough to know the score."

"Did they find the animal?"

"Damnit, Goldie, didn't you hear what I said?" He took a drag from his cigarette, exhaled loudly through his teeth, shook his head. "No, they didn't."

Chief Rowe entered "You ready?"

I nodded. "I'm sorry about all this, Chief Mello."

"Bullshit. Get the hell out of here before I put you on today's schedule."

I stepped outside with Chief Rowe. Rain fell harder. As we walked the road, I hoped there would be hot water in the head.

* * * * *

I stripped off everything, left it in a soggy heap on the floor, wrapped a towel around my waist; lay down on my bunk, collected my thoughts. A House Mouse gathered up my things. "Wash-wash?" I nodded. She extended one hand, rubbed the tips of her fingers with her thumb, held up five. I held up three. She shook her head, held up four. Too much, but I didn't care. Slept like a dead man, woke at first light, kept my eyes shut and listened to other men's sleep, smelled the musty air, heard no rain, grinding hunger twisted at my stomach and drove me from the relative comfort of bed. I dressed, left the barracks, ahead walked Freddy, his back to me, probably headed for the same place, I ran a few steps to catch up.

He heard my footfalls, turned. "Hey, you good looking motherfucker."

"Hey motherfucker. How's it hanging?"

"Hell, you know the answer."

I started to feel comfort when I caught something at the corner of my eye. I looked—looked again. In some bushes the animal sat on its haunches, I pointed. "Freddy, look." It dropped to all fours, disappeared.

"What?"

"The animal. I-Know's fucking animal."

"Where?"

"It's gone now."

"You sure?"

"Fuck'n-a." My heart pounded, I pointed again. "It was right there." I peered hard into the bushes. "There's still something there." I hurried toward it. There lay Duckworth. "He's hurt, Freddy. He's hurt bad."

Duckworth moved as if trying to get up. That gave me hope. I dropped to my knees, picked up his mauled body, his eyes were glassy, he lifted his head, looked at me, I saw a spark of recognition, his body sagged, became inert, I stood, aware of nothing but the dead weight, swallowed by agony.

Freddy spoke, I heard only gibberish. He tried to take Duckworth from me, I held tight, walked back to the Aircrew Trailer carrying the lifeless bundle, laid him on the desk, paced the floor, furious, trying to contain myself. Corner to corner I went fighting back tears, pain in my throat, intense, made it impossible to swallow. I stopped, lit a cigarette, inhaled, the taste nauseated me, I threw it on the floor, ground it under my heel, became aware of Freddy, I had forgotten him. Go away. Go away from me. I tried to project the words telepathically, he didn't hear.

"Goldie, take it easy on yourself. It's not your fault."

"My fault? My fault? Hell no, it's not my fault. What was everybody doing while I was aboard ship? Did you try to find that goddamn animal? Did you even try?"

"Try? Hell, we were up to our asses in alligators. We did what we could."

I looked at him hard, tried to bore through his flesh with my eyes. "Fuck me to tears, it's I-Know I want. Things were fine till he brought that fucking animal." Duckworth was fine. I was fine. Everything was fine. It's I-Know I want. It's I-Know."

Freddy extended his hand, touched my shoulder, I jerked away, pivoted on my heel, took my side arm from its holster, the solid weight of it felt good. Just how crazy do I want to be? I turned, faced Freddy, slapped it down on the desk next to Duckworth. Freddy jumped.

"What're you going to do? What're you going to do?"

"I'm going to hurt that fucker. I'm going to hunt him down same way his animal hunted down Duckworth. Going to drag him into the bushes. Maul him. Bleed him. Drink his blood. That's what I'm going to do."

"That's crazy. That's plain crazy. It's just a duck, man. It's just a duck."

"Just a duck? How can you say that? You really don't care. Thought you were a friend. Thought you were a man, but you ain't shit."

"We're better friends than you know. Better than you could ever dream. What you're saying doesn't mean shit to me. And I'll tell you the fucking truth, we're not leaving this trailer till we get this straight."

"You don't know how close you are. You don't have a fucking clue."

"Close to what? I'm trembling in my boots. I'm all you got right now. I know who you are and what you are; so don't try that heavy shit on me. I'm not leaving."

I couldn't bring my eyes up to him; felt him the same way I felt with Dad's fulminating anger, his look, his posture. His words cut through my cardboard image, penetrated my gut, searched out my insides.

"Look at you," he said. "All puffed up and hard edged, thinking you're so goddamn tough. It's bullshit even if you believe it. You think you're suffering? Shit, you're not suffering. You got it made in here just like the rest of us. You want suffering? It's there soon as you step outside the perimeter of the nice tight little nest we have. People are dying every minute. Human beings. Every fucking minute. That's where the suffering is. All of it's just borrowed time, Goldie. You got to realize that. Borrowed fucking time. You. Me. I-Know. The duck. Nothing's sacred. Nothing's carved in stone. There are no guarantees. No promises. He was here, now he's gone. It's not your fault, not I-Know's fault, not anybody's fault. It's just the luck of the draw. Just one of those sad things that happens in this world. Doesn't make sense? Doesn't have to make sense."

I never before heard Freddy's speak that way. Listening, I remembered the two of us riding back from the Acey-Deucy Club in Tiensha to Danang on a military bus, drunk as lords. The bus moved at a crawl as it crossed a bridge. On the other side lay bodies—a hundred or so shoulder-to-shoulder along the edge of the road. At first, they looked like bundles of bloody rags. They were old and young, male, female. American GIs were arranging them under the close supervision of an army lieutenant who appeared to be setting up scenery for some kind of macabre county faire photo-shoot, like something he hoped would win the blue ribbon. This here… That there… Sometimes he pushed at one with a booted foot till satisfied. A GI stood by with a 4x5 Graphlex ready to shoot. And on we went… My thoughts were interrupted by I-Know as he came through the door.

"This is a bad place for you, I-Know," said Freddy.

"I know what happened," he said. "I've got to be here."

I studied his face; saw something different, something like never before. "I think you need get out, Freddy. I-Know and I have business to take care of." Freddy started to say something. I cut him off. "It's private."

"Yeah," said I-know, "Private."

Freddy gave an unhappy look, left.

"I so sorry, Goldman," said I-Know.

"Too late. Doesn't help."

"I know."

"Doesn't help me. Doesn't help you. Doesn't help anything."

"Don't know how I could've been so stupid, Goldman, so I tried to make up for it." I felt myself leaning towards him, noticed he carried something that pulled up me short. "He's dead, Goldman. My pet is dead. I killed him. See? I killed him. Smashed him with a rock. Never hurt anything before in my life, Goldman, but I killed him. He trusted me. Didn't move an inch. I smashed his head with a rock."

He extended the bundle towards me like a religious offering, I recoiled, exhaled a breath that took forever, sensed his pain. He cried, his body heaved; I wanted to calm him, afraid he would never stop. I reached out; he flinched as my hand cupped the back of his head. I pulled him toward me till our foreheads touched, took a breath. "Call me Goldie. Please, I-Know, just call me Goldie."

* * * * *

Commander Bull found me on the ramp. "Goldman, we've received a message from the Red Cross. I'm sorry to inform you of your mother's passing. Sergio is cutting your travel orders. You're authorized thirty days leave—more if needed. We've scheduled you on a C-130 for Clark later today. The ATO there will get you to the states onboard a MAC flight. So get packed and meet Sergio in the terminal at eleven hundred. You have my deepest sympathies."

Without talking to anybody, I walked the dusty road that led to our clubhouse; found the padlock unsnapped. Inside, I poured a double-double shot of scotch, sat, let my mind wander as I sipped, left a dollar of Japanese MPC on the bar, went to the barracks, packed.

Sergio sat on a bench close to a whooshing fan, orders in hand. "Sorry Goldie. I don't know what else to say. When you return, it'll be to Japan. Give you a chance for a little breather." He sat with me till time came to load up.

I climbed the loading ramp of the C-130, found a cubbyhole amidst the jumble of cargo, curled into a ball on the aluminum deck, tried to sleep; must have because I dreamt of patricide. Inside the dream, I walked down First Avenue, passed familiar sights of peep shows, and flophouse hotels, passed under the garish neon flapping wing marquee of the Green Parrot Theater. Rain fell. Wet to the skin, I entered a pawnshop, bought a handgun and ammunition, but before anymore happened, turbulence jarred me awake, booze had left my mind and that caused a new a flood of thoughts. I wondered if things might become different between Dad and me now that he was alone in the world. Wondered, too, if the problems between us were due to the lack of a blood connection, but knew better. The problem lay with me from the time he swept me away from all I had and all I knew and made me rootless. Because of that I seethed against him. In the end, I got away. Now, I was returning. That rattled around inside my noggin till the C130 landed at Clark in the Philippines where I mustered with the ATO, and after, drank and whored in Angeles City till my dick stood at parade rest, and finally loaded my broken ass aboard a contract flight for fourteen hours of confinement with chatty military wives and snot-nosed rug rats. From Travis I caught a Greyhound to the airport. Outside the main gate, some raggedy-assed hobo looking fucks stood holding a bed sheet banner bearing the words: WELCOME HOME BABY KILLERS.

Twenty years a cowboy and never stepped in horseshit

—Stosh

Mom sat roasted and toasted and packaged in a shiny black box on the kitchen table next to a whiskey bottle. It seemed impossible for her life to be contained in such a way, or that I knew as much about her as I would ever know. Maybe in the end that's the way it is for all of us. Maybe. We scattered her among the season's fading roses in the small, finicky garden she kept. After, Dad got another glass from the cupboard, filled it half full with whiskey. I drank it down in searing gulps. He poured another. As I drank, a slight blitheness came to my mind. "Is there any food in the house?"

"Check the refrigerator. Don't cook for me though. I got no appetite."

"Don't eat you're going to die."

"Maybe so."

That night, I found my familiar bed, watched shadows play out their stories out on the wall, thought about the child who lived here so long ago, grew restless, went downstairs. Dad still sat in his chair, head rested on a forearm, asleep. Went outside, sat on the porch railing, shivered in the chill of night air. Went back inside at first light, started the kitchen fire, boiled coffee in the old blackened pot, cooked breakfast. Dad woke to the coffee smell. I poured him a cup. He rose, got a fresh bottle of whiskey from the cabinet, poured a slug into his coffee, sipped at the hot brew.

We ate; talked about a few banal things, easy stuff, stuff with no controversy attached. I washed up when we finished. He got out the dominos. We played as if on autopilot. I felt like an organ grinder's monkey dancing to a tune it didn't like.

After an hour, he said, "This is boring as hell. You can spend another night, but plan to hit the road tomorrow."

"That'll be fine."

"I'll drive you to the ferry."

"Won't be necessary. I'll hitch a ride."

"Better still."

I left in the darkness of morning while he slept, felt it to be the end of everything between us. After a mile walking, I hooked a ride all the way to the north end, took the ferry to Seattle, remembered a story Dad liked to tell about a hobo.

He stood in the middle of a park desperate to take a dump, looked around, didn't see anybody, dropped to his haunches, did his business. Just as he was hitching up his trousers, he noticed a cop headed in his way. Thinking fast, he knelt down, put his hat over the waste.

The cop approached. "What's going on here?"

The hobo looked him straight in the eye. "Sir, I've just captured a rare and valuable bird. I need help to notify the city zoo so they can come get it. Would you be so kind as to hold my hat in place whilst I find a phone to make the call?"

"Sure. I'll be happy to help."

The cop knelt down, took a firm hold on the hat. Off went the hobo. Time passed. A crowd gathered. Somebody asked what was going on. The cop explained. More time passed. He began to get uncomfortable kneeling on the sidewalk. Somebody suggested he lift the edge of the hat and grab hold of the bird so he could stand up. With care, he raised the edge of the hat with one hand, reached under with the other, grabbed for the bird.

"Did you get it?"

"Yes, I did. But I think I broke every bone in its body."

It made sense. Dad only wanted one thing in this world, to disappear—to slip away from the pile of shit he believed his life to be. I had the same wish. In that way, we were much alike.

I stood on the bow while deckhands tied up to the dock. A car honked, flashed its headlights. I hefted my parachute bag, loaded it into the car, got in. The driver said he knew me from the past. I didn't recognize him. He yacked on and on about this and that as if I should remember, didn't seem to care that I said nothing, decided it would be better to catch a city bus, asked him to stop, let me out.

* * * * *

From Travis, I flew to Japan, hoped to find Jim at the house, hoped somehow he had figured things out and returned holding his secret intact. Found instead a lifeless shell bearing only remnants he left behind. Emptiness settled on my shoulders, I heated the bath water, soaked and soaked, tried to clear my mind, tried to attach my thoughts to the rising steam, to let them float off into nothingness.

Freddy came on the second day. "Thought you might be here. Got any beer?"

I pointed to the refrigerator. He got one, popped its cap with a church key, sat opposite me. "I know you got some bad shit going in your life, "but you can't crawl up your own ass and die. I won't permit it. So, shit, shower and shave you, worthless fuck. We're off for Yokohama."

I did what he said. The car wouldn't start, so we rode a train to Yokohama Station, caught a taxi to China Town, within an hour at the Stork Club, I sat listening to Freddy's enchanted lyrics, at peace for the first time in a long while.

He traveled back with me on the last train of the night, guided me to my shack-by-the-track, bedded me down, left till the next afternoon when he showed up with two ice cold bottles of beer and a new deck of cards with the intention of playing rummy till our eyeballs fell out. It went on that way till time came to check in from leave and go back to work.

V

**Here lies a Hampshire Grenadier
Who caught his death
Drinking cold small beer
A good soldier is ne'er forgot
Whether he dieth by musket
Or by pot**

—Grave Stone Inscription At Westminster Abbey

Now to the heart of the matter...

Early morning, in spangled sunlight I wandered aimlessly down the Boulevard, past pawnshops, past the Mexican Teatro, in the direction of Five Points, pressure of the day already percolating inside me. I romanced the idea of a drink to ease the mood. No problem getting it. Money jingled in my pocket, liquor store across the street, but Abe and I wrote our contract with sobriety number one on its list. I lived in a small room at the back of his tire shop with all the comforts of home, bed, folding chair, table, hot plate, all things to be kept—as per the contract—neat and tidy as a barracks room. All this came about after the navy pushed me out the door and onto the street because they felt they were no longer getting enough bang for their buck. A terrifying prospect because I knew no other way to live.

Upon rising each morning, I filled a bucket with water in the Employee Rest Room, washed my body and shaved my face. Once a week, I went to the nearby navy base, presented my retired military I.D. card, and at the barbershop got my haircut high and tight.

Another part of the contract. When day's work finished, Abe locked up, went home to his sweet wife and three sons, I got busy. I cleaned the shop top to bottom. The hours between morning ablution and evening titivations were free to me. I filled them best I could. Easy to do, except when given to the cantankerous mood I felt that particular morning.

At a corner, waiting for the traffic light to change, I looked straight into the hustle bustle of work bound faces. Many averted their eyes as if afraid, perhaps, I would knock on their window and ask for something. Thought I ought to do just that to increase their discomfort, and maybe in the doing; I would get lucky and pick some fucker packing a weapon that would blow my stupid ass away, but the traffic light changed, everybody heaved a sigh and moved on.

Sartre or Camus or some other existential big shot said the first question we must answer for ourselves is: Do we want to live or do we want to die? He said till we answer that everything else is bullshit. To live or to die. "To be or not to be." Hell, Shakespeare wrestled with that four hundred years ago and probably stole it from something written a millennia before. I struggled to know the answer for myself. It seemed like a Chinese puzzle box, a vexation. Fuck me to tears.

Abe, built short and stocky, a retired Marine Corps Master Sergeant and sober drunkard involved in the program of Alcoholic Anonymous, which is where we met, and where Abe declared me his one and only *Pet Squid*, the greatest honor a Marine could bestow upon a U.S. Navy Sailor, and where we made our solemn deal, had become my great and good friend.

I walked and walked and as usual, found myself in the tiny 5th Street park, sat on an empty bench listening to **KFUCK TALK RADIO** broadcast its message of love and hope through huge loud speakers implanted inside my noggin while I passed time watching people go to and fro on their important missions to here and there. Some looked at me as though I were part of the scenery—a statue put there for their viewing pleasure. Rarely did I draw serious attention—but when I did, it usually turned out to be some armed and dangerous Jehovah's Witness full of information about their sure and certain path to salvation and desperate to help me become one of

God's elect so I could join them on their endless journey, but eternity was too damned long. When they promised to pray for me, I told them, "Short and sweet. Always pray for short and sweet."

There were others at that park. Some were raggedy assed fucks that shared my experiences one way or another. They hit me up for cigarettes because they knew me for an easy mark. I bought them tax free at the navy base, carried them in abundance, passed them out as part of my limited sense of social responsibility. When somebody cadged one, I gave two, one to smoke, one to tuck behind their ear for later, and I always offered a light because it gave me a chance to show off the Zippo lighter I had carried for two decades. Most were satisfied with the smokes, but some wanted to talk. I always put them off. Told them I was busy creating an empty mind. Fucking hard work, I told them— Harder than you can imagine. To do it I have to think of nothing forever.

* * * *

The town had a library an easy walk from the park filled chock-a-block with books, making it a dangerous place. I sat at a library table writing my ass off with no intention of ever being finished. I filled notebook after notebook with gobbledygook nobody would ever read. On that particular day, I wrote about the death of Freddy Flitter—a real no shitter.

A head cold did him in—my head cold. The flight surgeon grounded me for a plugged up shnoze, a serious thing that at altitude could fuck up my ears if the plane loses pressurization. Freddy being Freddy, volunteered to go in my place. He climbed into my seat, but never climbed out.

We broke for chow that day. His Last Supper. We didn't plan it that way—but that's how it was. We shoveled down our chow, smoked cigarettes end to end, talked about the merits of cold beer and warm pussy. Freddy, a city boy, lived with his tiny big-voiced girl friend on Yamate-Cho in a place that overlooked the old foreign cemetery and had a beautiful view of the night city. Good because they were so in love and couldn't stand being apart.

We stubbed out our final cigarettes and headed to the Ready Room so Freddy could suit up. I wanted to help with the launch to make up for staying behind, so after the plane was hooked up to a Waist Cat, and as the pilot brought the throttles to full power, I squatted under the starboard engine to check its bleed air. When it cut off, I ran to the Checker Box and gave thumbs up to the Shooter. A nanosecond after the holdback fitting sheared a catastrophic failure occurred, too quick for the eye, too quick for even the PLAT cameras to record.

The Cat's shuttle tore loose, ripped the nose mount off the plane, hit the water brake so hard it exploded and shredded the armored steel deck. The plane, an out-of-control-horror, dribbled down the deck at less than quarter speed, went nose heavy off the Angle Deck, dug its port wing into the water, flipped upside down, and quick as a wink, disappeared from sight to be gone forever. Dumbfounded, I stood rooted to the spot. Air Boss held the launch up while we cleared the deck of wreckage making it possible to receive planes. Helos searched, found nothing. Though not new to me, death that is, this one sent me into the screaming memmies. Freddy existed no more; he ceased to be along with everybody else aboard that plane. They were now nothing.

A blind guy explained 'nothing' to me once. He said most people didn't really understand blindness. They thought the blind saw black. "That isn't true. The blind see nothing. It's a hard concept for the sighted to understand." I understood. Blindness and death were near identical. The dead didn't feel black; they felt nothing, dreamed nothing, thought nothing. Things for them didn't just disappear— they ceased to be. Freddy didn't care because Freddy no longer was. All his troubles were over. Mine started, because at that moment, I realized death applied to everything in existence, even stars and galaxies—and sooner or later it would apply to me. Alone on the flight deck that dark night, I hollered a question to the Universe: "Is there a fucking point to any of this?"

The Universe answered with silence.

So having my answer, I stopped giving a shit about the things that had been so fucking important just hours before, all of it stolen in the worst possible way—a repeat of times before when somebody snatched me away from all my important things, from all the comfort I desperately needed.

So Freddy never made it to Yokohama. I did. Several times. Drove my smoky wreck to China Town, parked at the curb outside the Stork Club. Never went in. How could I? What would I tell her? What could I say about any of it? I just sat in the car burning tobacco—and watched raindrops accumulate on the windshield.

* * * * *

The Alano Club resided on the Boulevard a few blocks north of Five Points next to Ken's Market in a defunct furniture store with defunct furniture. A place that lived under a heavy pall of cigarette smoke where people met to talk about what it was like, what happened, and what it was like now.

For a long time, I couldn't make much sense of it—of how booze could be a problem, maybe *the* problem, because for me it had been the essential solution—the analgesic balm that limbered my joints and gave me the relief I sought. But the club, a friendly place with lots of hot joe, was a place where I could sit in the back, smoke, and listen without being bothered. I felt a sense of comfort there I didn't feel anywhere else. At least I did till Gus interrupted my soulful peace and quiet. He could have been just another of the many everyday handshakes that happened there, but upon grasping my hand he greeted me like a long lost friend. That peeved me. Figured him for a desperate old queer looking for love, so I gave him my well practiced hard look—the one that brought poor PJ Fry to tears when I felt mean, but it only brought a smile to his ruined face with its scarred eyebrows and flattened pip of a nose. "So kid, how ya doin'? Looks like you could use a little company. Somebody to chew the fat with. Am I right?" In saying that, he sat in the empty chair across from me. I hardened the Leave-Me-The-Fuck-Alone look, but it only caused his eyes to wrinkle with mirth. "So kid, you're a tough guy, huh?"

Yeah, I thought. I'm a tough guy, Fight fuck or go for your gun.

182

"I usually recognize one when I see him. It's easy because I'm a tough guy myself. Name's Gus. Pleased to meet you whoever you think you are." In the end, of course, he became a friend. How could that not happen?

He lived in a one room flat on the third floor of the Lemon Tree Hotel, a cancerous yellow building that ascended four stories from a garbage strewn alleyway behind Saul's Pawn Shop. Attached to the dinged sheet steel door that led into his room hung a sign that said: **Welcome to the Spiritual Saloon.**

On my first visit he told me, "I love this place. Love everything about it. Wouldn't want to live no place else."

Most residents of the hotel were drunkards or dopers who lived parasitic lives of scams and handouts and spent their days doing whatever they did. They were the kind of people Gus held closest to his heart. In fact, next door lived the full-blooded Sioux Indian who migrated down from Canada as a teenager. He wore his long graying hair in two thick braided pigtails kept laced up neat and tight in silver chased leather sheaths, wore a blue and white bandana as a headband, and a pair of wire framed glasses, bent and lopsided rode low on his wide nose. Since nobody knew his true name he was called Chief. All he ever wanted to talk about were super massive black holes he called singularities, the warping of space-time, and just what the hell *was* beyond the edge of the ever expanding universe. So down on his luck was he, he hoped every day would be his last on earth. Of all the beings that lived in the hotel, Gus loved him the best.

Everything in Gus' room, care-worn and threadbare, but kept immaculate. On one wall hung faded newspaper clippings and photographs growing brittle and yellowed by age that showed Gus back in his glory days as a prizefighter. "A legitimate contender. Even fought the great Sugar Ray ten rounds. Jesus…Jesus…Jesus… He hit me so hard I lost my senses. Kept my feet, though. Didn't know the damn fight was over until I was sittin' in the dressing room gettin' tape cut off my hands. My trainer said he stopped by to pay respects. Even shook me by the hand. Don't remember any of it, but Ray was a real gent so I wasn't surprised."

* * * * *

Some days were so good I wanted to frame them, to hang on the wall like a piece of fine art to admire forever. Late in the evening after finishing my work on one particular day, I attended the AA speaker meeting at Saint Anthony's Church on Saviors Road. The speaker, an elderly gent, told the story of himself in his younger days when he worked as a torpedo for a famous Chicago gangster. He told all the bad deeds he had committed and the prison time he served and how sobriety found him—and that over time his life changed in unbelievable ways. That now, he was a retired businessman, a husband, father, grandfather, soon to be great grandfather, and how others he remembered from the old days were long dead with nothing left behind but the misery they had served up. He loved who he had become, enjoyed the goodness of life that came from people in rooms like the one we were in, that he would not trade of the good or the bad of his life for anything. His talk penetrated my soul. Made me believe I could change as well.

Other days were a train wreck. Wondered hard if I could have made past things different; that maybe if I kept my mouth shut none of it would have happened the way it did. If I had just kept my mouth shut and continued to fly after Freddy's death things might have ended just fine. But it tore a hole in my gut and all the bile and gore spilled out. I shot off like the haywire Zuni that torched Gabitis' face. My new pilot took grim notice. "He's bad for moral. I don't want him flying with us anymore." In no time flat, the CO shit canned me to ground pounder. By that time, even Horny Ernie stood well clear.

Change of Station orders came. Again—I had again lost every worthwhile thing in my life. Returned to CONUS for shore duty, to settle among strangers, falling in the thrall of its passionless embrace with each month a carbon copy of the one before. After a year without scramble or dissonance, I knew what it was to be dead.

I sought escape at the bar of the Acey-Ducey Club, but even that turned out to be a miserable place where men with hash marks on their sleeves sang broken record blues of oppressive family obligations and whimpered the incantation: "My wife, she…" along with a million other bullshit things that had no fucking place in navy life.

I moved on. Found new madness, nurtured it, grew my insanity to a high point, and the navy snapped it to a wrenching halt. At the leading edge of that halt, a letter, readdressed, stamped in smeared block letters with the word **FORWARD,** found me on the 4th Floor Alcohol Ward of Long Beach Naval Hospital:

"Dear Thomas,

I been thinking about you lately. It's been a long time since I last heard from you. Time passes so quick it can get away. Like I said I been thinking about you. Remembering when you was a kid and some of the things we did together. We had some good times you and me. I remember the old homestead when your momma was here. Those memories are so sweet. Remember when we took the ride in that little seaplane? Boy that was a kick in the butt. You were so excited I thought you was going to pee your pants. Yeah we had some good times all right. I just wanted to let you know I been thinking about you. I know you must be pretty busy. I read about what's going on over there every day in the newspaper. Anyway I was hoping you could take a minute or two and write me a line. Don't have to be fancy. Just a little something to let me know you're doing o.k.

Dad."

* * * * *

The hospital was a clean, well-lighted place—a place devoid of comfort. Upon my arrival, a doctor explained that for the time being I no longer had the right to manage my own affairs, that my failure to deal with the problems I carried brought on behavior the navy would not tolerate, that I could not continue authorizing myself one raging drunk after another and continue in the service of my country, and if I had any desire to finish the career I started I better listen up because this was my one and only shot. I knew in my mind exactly what he meant because my last binge had been a real humdinger.

I woke curled up in a shivering ball under the sheltered entry of the Mexican Teatro, dirty, disheveled, no idea of the day, but with the clear understanding I had broken an important promise made to myself, and though only one of many, the one I most meant to honor. Beyond the sheltering roof, cold rain fell. Common sense said, get up, get the hell out of here—catch a cab back to the base—go to the barracks—sleep it off, but when I dug out my wallet it held no money for cab fare, and since my head hurt so bad, I told common sense to go fuck itself and lay back down, the extent of my memories till I woke in the back seat of a cop car, forehead pressed against the side window, a thin ribbon of drool connecting the corner of my mouth to the glass next to a smear of blood. As the cop drove, I recognized Pacific Coast Highway, knew where we were headed. The cop drove in silence. I heard occasional squawking messages on his radio, but nothing he answered, me being his only problem. Thought maybe I should ask to borrow the radio to talk with somebody about my situation, somebody important, a big shot who could get me off the hook again—maybe the President of the United States for starters—he should be able to help, but I remembered he had a lot to do so better not to distract him. I had a flash. I could call God, put the blame where it belonged, let that fucker deal with it, thought about that long and hard, believing it might just work, maybe God had the solution, but I couldn't remember his fucking call sign, so I gave up on the whole thing and slumped back against the seat.

I drifted into a dream—Mom worried while she cooked our small supper. She worried about Dad. I had heard her talk to somebody on the phone earlier that day. The shop had closed hours before; he didn't come home. On the phone she said, "God, I hope he isn't drinking again." We both knew that to be an empty chance. We knew him to be profoundly in love with a new mistress, that he didn't need us anymore; and that without him; we were nothing. He spent his time at the tavern, same tavern where his old man had been stabbed to death decades before, and he would not listen to her when she tried to talk about it. He would say, "For Christ sake it's nothing, just a few beers, I bust my ass for the two of you all goddamn week. Don't tell me I can't have a little pleasure of my own. Stop worrying about it." But she did worry; she seldom had money in the house, and when she suggested he might be an alcoholic he said, "Don't be ridiculous. I'm no alcoholic. I just love the taste of the stuff, that's all."

In my daze, I felt Dad's rough hands on me, he poked me, shook me, separated me from the dream.

"We're here," said the cop.

Christ, where the hell is here?

"Come on. Someone's waiting for you."

He helped me get out of the backseat to make sure I didn't bonk my precious noggin, gripped my upper arm with authority, walked me to the door of the Base Security Building—uncuffed me. Deep troubling fear set in. I started searching my mind for excuses. Two days later, I sat inside a navy van, my parachute bag a stuffed sausage full with clean uniforms, being driven down the coast to the hospital to search my soul; to put some order in my life in the hope I could finish my time.

Inside the ward, people who claimed to know more about me than I did myself held me under microscopic supervision, and after eight-and-a-half weeks of exploration, infused me with the answer, declared me a finished product to be cast loose upon the world. 'Go forth and multiply,' they said in their godlike way. Go forth and multiply? I knew a joke when I heard one. Hell, I didn't even know if my dick worked anymore. I returned to the tedium of Shore Duty life with its loose days and thin schedules away from the Oh-Six-Hundred runny egg breakfasts and Oh-Nine-Hundred group therapy, kept my nose clean for the years needed, stepped off into the deep dark waters of civilian life.

* * * * *

Went to Henri's Restaurant at 5 Points with a big appetite, finished, took an easy stroll back to the shop feeling the heavy pleasure of an overfull gut while misty rain washed grit from the air. When I arrived, Abe, unlocking and opening the rattley roll-up front door, said, "Come sit with me a minute. There's something important I need to tell you." We went into in his rude office while others came to work and made the shop ready for business.

"I got a call from the Fleet Reserve this morning. They said the Red Cross called them, that they had been trying to track you down for the past couple weeks. Your dad passed away. He was admitted to the Seattle VA hospital in a terminal condition. When they asked about his family he said he had none. Nurses didn't believe him." He shook his head. "Anyway… I'm sorry to tell you this. Just remember, easy does it. Think about what you want to do. Might be time to travel. You can talk to me day or night. You'll always be welcome here."

* * * * *

I sat in the library thinking. It led me back to the hospital and the memory of men who resided in the next ward with minds that had totally flown the coop. Their lives seemed free and easy with all bodily needs attended. They only had to lie around waiting to be rolled from one side to the other to avoid growing bedsores. Seemed an easy enough occupation with no serious consequences. Maybe the answer for me. Maybe if I dug in deep enough, I could find what they had and join them on their mystical voyage. I never saw any of them frown, nor did I see anger in their eyes. It seemed as if they were searching the limits of space-time, earnestly seeking infinity.

I had those thoughts while having ireful discussions with myself, writing about what it would be like to do everything over. My question became: *If from the beginning, I could choose anything and everything for myself, who and what would I be? Would I be anybody I knew? Anybody different?* My conclusion: *Nope.* That irritated me like the unscratchable itch of a mosquito bite.

Christ—I wanted to drink, wanted so much the sweet unknowing haze. Huge pressure built inside my head as though trying to squirt my brains out through my eye sockets. Yeah, I wanted to goddamn drink with all my heart and soul. I could almost feel the harsh liquid going down my throat, smacking my head like a baseball bat. But over time, odd changes had occurred within me. I knew other ways to

188

satisfy that gnawing. I packed up my notebook and pens in a plastic bag, walked to Gus' Spiritual Saloon; found Mike Graham there with his tape recorder cranking, Gus in the middle of his soliloquy: "Had that dream again this morning." He pointed at Mike with his chin. "Remember the one I told you about before where the cheers was bouncing round inside my head and I was young again. Young and pretty as can be. An' I was dripping sweat, moving on my toes like a ballet dancer holding both hands over my head, an' layin' on the canvas was my opponent, only thing movin' was his twitchy left foot, so the referee waved off the count at five an' it was over, I was the winner. I was young and full of fury. A bull. A destroyer, always wantin' more, never satisfied.

"Same night, my wife left me. She'd been threatenin' for a long time, but I never took it serious. That night she did. She was fed up. Fed up with the whole shebang, so she packed up everything she could carry and bundled up the kid and out the door they went. I remember my last words to her. "You'll come crawling back." It was the middle of winter. Weather was lousy and we was in New York City stayin' in a real swanky hotel. After she left, I sat there in that hotel with all that classy furniture and stayed drunk as a skunk for more days than I can count, drinkin' up classy booze, high-dollar hookers comin' and going all hours, thinkin' I don't give a good goddamn 'cause she needs me more than I need her.

"The parasites started comin' round, drinkin' up my booze, spendin' my money, glad handin' me, sayin' how great I was, how I was Mister Wunnerful, how none of it was my fault, an' I believed them. Every word they said I believed. Besides, it was too damn late to do anything about it 'cause my wife an' kid was long gone. Took time to sink through my skull but when it did I felt lousy. Lousier than I ever felt before. But hell, I was a tough guy so I sucked it up an' never talked to nobody that counted. When things got too lousy inside my head I drank it away. Worked just fine for me. Didn't know at the time, but that was when the end of everythin' started.

"My manager got hold of me. 'Life goes on,' he said. 'You gotta get your head outta your ass. We got work to do. Big things in the mill. Gotta get back in the gym. So I drug my ass back to the gym, but everything I did was half-assed. It was like my fire went out. Like I had another lover, an' by god I did. The bottle. My manager yapped at me the way a good manager's supposed to tellin' me to straighten out and fly right or get outta the damn business 'cause what I was doin' wasn't gonna work. Then I started coming to the gym half sauced thinkin' hell I don't follow no damn rules. I make the damn rules. I don't have to listen to no-goddamn-body 'cause I'm the moneymaker here.

"My manager hung around long as he could, but finally saw the light an' saw there wasn't nothin' he could do an' walked away. He had other fish to fry, an' if I wasn't gonna come round, his time was better spent elsewhere. He was right too 'cause I kept travelin' down that road I was on an' before I knew it I was back where I started in Jersey fightin' club house Palookas for ten bucks a pop. That was all she wrote for me. I was in the tank an' there was nothing more in the mill. No big money future. Nothing good down the road. No more nothing nowhere. I was headed for skid row. No place else for me to go, that was the end of the story. The last anybody ever heard of me, an' it all happened quicker than a blink of the eye. Christ it makes my head spin to think about it.

"For years I put the blame on somebody else. Weren't my fault. Couldn't be. I was betrayed just like some sweet baby Jesus. Nobody cared. Parasites took off soon's I was broke. All 'em with their thirty pieces of silver. I was nailed to the cross an' nobody come 'round to cry." Gus paused and surveyed the whole of the room with a cockeyed smile. "Now things have changed and I got all this." He swept his arms in a gesture that took it all in and took us in as well. "I'm satisfied as can be. Got enough. Everything I need. Je ne regretted rien. A Frenchie taught me that after I beat him in a decision. Means I got no regrets. None t'all."

* * * * *

Mike, a regular at the well-heeled Tuesday night meeting, had talked once about being in the middle of a creative writing frenzy where good ideas shot around his noggin so fast he couldn't keep up. A former Detroit cop, he had migrated to southern California to take a crack at writing Hollywood movies and found limited success. "Bust your ass in this town, live on stale bread and American Cheese sandwiches for ten years, one day you hit it lucky and people declare you an overnight success." His new best idea? Writing Gus' life story. I spent many mornings at Mike's place sucking up the black coffee he called *Truth Serum* while confessing my sins. My notebook scribbling's were the result of his interrogations.

He gave me a quote from Hemingway: *"Write hard and clear about what hurts most."*

"That's all you need to know," he said.

They finished. Mike turned off the recorder. Gus turned his attention to me. "So tough guy, what brings you here today?"

I pulled Dad's letter from my pocket. It resembled a medieval parchment by that time. Mike read it aloud.

"His liver blew up. He's dead. I've got to figure out what to do."

"How's your financial shape, kid?" said Gus.

"Checks come every month. Only cash them once in a while. Got a stack an inch high."

"Kid," said Gus, "here's my advice. Buy yourself a clunker, drive on up there and take care of it. If you don't you'll wish you had."

VI

All my works are fragments of a long confession

—Goethe

The harbor had changed. It bore a spit-and-polish air. Rich houses squatted the shoreline, each with a pleasure craft tied up to a private dock; working boats no longer rode at anchor. The machine shop too had changed, its comfortable shabbiness gone. Through clean windowpanes, I saw two men, unknown to me, working away at their craft. Even Inky's bungalow had a spandy new glow about it. I knocked apprehensively, wondering if he too might have changed. When the door opened, he showed a smile that nearly broke his face, pulled me into a great bear hug. "Goddamn, it's good to set eyes on you, kiddo. Come in. Come on in. Joe's hot."

We sat together inside his neat-as-a-pin kitchen, drank cups of black coffee in pensive ways, spoke only necessary words knowing much more would come later.

"Maybe better he passed before you got here. Easier you didn't see him. Things was pretty sorry in the end."

That night, I slept in the bedroom above the kitchen to the endless pantomime of shadows on the wall and sounds of wind swayed tree branches skittering the rooftop, all infinitely familiar. Waking at first light, I rose, dressed warm against the chill, went outside, chopped wood, started a blaze in the stove, brewed strong coffee, cooked breakfast from the things I carried, felt pangs of loneliness.

Drove to town in the afternoon. Visited Don Kellogg who still ran the semi-prosperous law office that had been there far back as I could remember.

"Business first," he said. "Everything's pretty straightforward. Go ahead, read through the will. If you have any questions, I'll answer them."

I looked at the date on the will. He wrote it after Mom died. In reading, I came to understand everything of his belonged to me. When I asked, Don confirmed it. "If you decide to sell, let me know. My wife can handle it. Property values are sky high right now."

As if on cue, the office door wheezed opened and Lois Kellogg entered. She stopped short, took a long look at me. "My god, I don't believe it. Is that really you, Thomas?"

"Yes ma'am, far as I know." I stood; she embraced me and I her.

When we stepped apart there were tears in her eyes. "I'm so sorry about your father."

"Thank you." I searched my mind for polite words. "We all have our time, I guess."

"Will you be staying?"

"Yeah, for a while. Got nothing else on my dance card."

"Well, come have dinner with us this evening."

"Will do."

"And if you decide to sell the property, let me know. I'll get you the best price."

"I'll do that too."

She made an impatient gesture. "Wish I could spend more time, but as usual I'm on the run. Just stopped by to see if Don needed anything. So good to see you again, Thomas." She gave Don a querying look. He shook his head; she kissed him and vanished into the thin air.

"Lunchtime," said Don.

We walked across the street to the Alibi, settled in the dim lit cocktail lounge at the rear. A waitress came to the table; pad in hand, looked at Don. "The usual?"

"Umm, yes."

As she wrote, she said aloud, "Virgin Mary—BLT with avocado—French fries" She turned to me. "How about you, sir?"

"Cheese burger, fries and coke."

"You look familiar. Do I know you?"

"Thomas Goldman," said Don.

"You're kidding."

"In the flesh," I said.

"Are you back for good?"

"For a while."

"Do you remember me? Donna Ingstrom. I was in the class behind you."

"A little I guess. Sorry, it's been a long time."

"That's okay. I understand." She left to place our orders.

Don returned to the business at hand. "When we get back to the office I have paperwork up the wazoo for you to sign. Also, I need you to sign a letter to the insurance company."

"Insurance company?"

"You don't know?"

"Don't know what?"

"He had a fifty-thousand dollar policy with you as beneficiary. The letter's all written. Just needs your signature. I'll get it in the mail soon as I receive the death certificate."

First goddamn thought to pop into my mind? *Kaa-ching*. The sound of a cash register. I hated myself for it. "Doesn't seem like something he'd do."

"He went through a lot of changes after your mother passed. He became lonely and regretful. Had lots of time on his hands to think things over. He and Inky worked together a few more years, then found a pair of young eager beavers to take it over."

"So, they sold it."

"No, they didn't."

I furled my brows. "Does that mean I own part now?"

"You will once everything gets run through the paper mill."

"Can I give my part to Inky so he has it free and clear?"

"I'll look into it, but you might want to think about it a while."

"Don't need to. I want Inky to have it. Can I hire you to do it?"

"I'm already at your disposal."

Chow came. We dug in.

I drove back to the house wondering if I knew Dad the way I thought I did. That maybe—just maybe, I didn't know squat about him.

* * * * *

Next morning, coffee in hand, I walked the perimeter of the fence line Dad and I spent so much time building, found scraps of barbed wire, corroded, brittle, cedar fence posts so rotted at the base an easy push toppled them, remembered beautiful white-faced steers that once roamed the place and how bright the future looked, came to the snarl of wire where the last steer tried to tear its way free after Russ' drunken misaimed shots.

The three of us, Russ, Dad, and I had set out on a harsh winter morning to butcher the steer after they polished off a bottle to fight the chill. Russ had carried his thirty-thirty. The steer, skittish, mistrustful, wouldn't allow itself to be teased to the gibbet, Russ shot at fifteen yards, the slug tore off a horn at the base, a half ton of enraged animal screamed, crashed down on its forelegs, come back up spewing blood, howling, berserk mad. It bolted across the field, tore into the fence desperate to free itself, to be far away from the agonizing pain. We followed as the animal, entangled in barbed wire, thrashed. At thirty yards Russ took a second shot, hit the animal's rear quarter further enraging it. Quick as a wink he levered off two more shots, the animal dropped to its side and thrashed its legs as Dad slit its throat, and in the doing, opened a gash across his palm that went unnoticed in all the gore and adrenaline till later when he washed it in a water bucket. "For Christ sakes," he said. "Will you look at that?"

While the steer bleed out, I ran to the barn to fetch wire cutters. With them, Dad cut the animal free, and the three of us worked like Volga River boatmen dragging the carcass to the gibbet to be hung and butchered. With the beef quartered, they cracked the seal of a fresh bottle and all of it evolved into fits of laughter. I saw nothing funny. The steer suffered, we lost good meat damaged by the errant shots, the fence went forever unmended, and never again did animals graze on the sweet grass and clover of that lush field.

I walked on a few more steps dumbstruck by the unfathomable thought that all of this belonged to me. Remembered myself as a rootless child, and as an adult who lived life possessing little more than the things he carried.

* * * * *

The phone rang. Don Kellogg's voice pushed through, "The funeral home has your dad's ashes. Shall I have them delivered?"

I thought a moment. "No thanks, Don. I'll drive up and get them."

After the to and fro, I knocked on Inky's door. He opened it. "You got him?

I nodded

"Where is he?"

"In the car."

"Don't leave him out there all by hisself."

I carried the boxed up ashes inside, sat them on the table, Inky poured a shot glass full of whiskey, sat it atop the box, snorted a laugh. "Good to have him back with us." It felt right to me. He filled two mugs with coffee. "Now, lets you and me sit and swap some sea stories."

"Your old man was a tough nut," he said. "Couldn't of made it in this world otherwise. Best damn friend I ever had. Loved him dearly. Told you afore, we was little kids when we met. Probably hit it off so quick because of the old country lingo. We was like blood brothers."

He paused, took a slurp of coffee, fanned his lips. "My folks had a nice place with peach trees in the front yard just up the hill from here. Long gone now. Bought and tore down and rebuilt into something else by one of them rich weekend warriors. There was four of us kids. My older brother drowned when a working boat capsized in a storm up north. My two sisters moved back to the old country after our folks passed. Don't know, may still be living. Lost contact years ago."

Inky snapped a stick match alive, lit a cigarette, took a drag, whistled it out through his teeth, tapped off the ash. "Yeah, he was a tough nut all right. Afraid of nothing. Threw fists at a heartbeat like his old man. Never saw him back down from man or beast. And living in that house? Gawd-a-mighty what a place it must of been, his folks fighting like two starving rats in a cage all the damn time." He took another drag from the cigarette. "He took off when his ma passed. Said nothing to nobody. Just up and disappeared like he dropped off the edge of the world. Nobody knowed nothing about him until the end of the war. He just showed up one day missing the arm, took up like he never left. I'd been home awhile working for Old Man Bohlen in the shop listening to him bitch and moan about how worn out and tired he was, wanting to quit. So me and your old man pooled our money and bought him out."

Inky refilled the cups, finished his cigarette, stubbed it out, lit another, focused his eyes inward as if searching for a specific memory. "At the end, he didn't want to go to the hospital. Told me just leave him be. Told him he was going, by God. He didn't have no damn choice because I'd pick him up and carry him if had to. Almost had a fistfight over it. He said, 'They can't fix me.' I said, 'I don't give a good goddamn. Maybe they can't, but they can sure as hell make you more comfortable.'"

I shook out a cigarette, leaned it into the match Inky lit, picked a shred of tobacco off my lip.

"At the hospital they put him to bed and shot him full of dope. He got fighting mad again. Didn't like being loopy. Kept drifting off to never-never land. Said 'Christ sake Inky, how in hell am I supposed to take care a business feeling like this? Need to talk about some stuff, so keep your yap shut and listen.' Spent the whole day telling stuff he wanted off his chest. Was a mouthful, believe me. Learned a bunch about him I didn't know. When he got done saying everything, it was time to go. He did it easy. Just gave up all graceful like. Closed his eyes, breathed out all the breath he was holding inside and he was gone. First time I ever seen him so peaceful. Didn't want to cry because I knowed it'd piss him off, but I couldn't hold it all back. I let out just a little, told him I loved him without getting sappy, said goodbye and left him to the tender mercies of them nurses knowing they'd handle him proper."

* * * * *

Drove to the Alibi in semi-darkness. Somebody had put coins in the jukebox, a song I knew from long ago crooned on about feelings of emptiness, my food came just as the mournful tune ended, I dug in, ate like a famished wolf, drove back to the house, went to bed, woke back to the night before's emptiness, busied myself, built a fire, cooked breakfast, sat, studied Dad's boxed up remains, sighed, smoked down a cigarette while the food grew cold, pushed the plate away, lit another butt, listened to the whirr click of the Kit Kat Klock, wondered what the hell to do, felt the presence of the house; a nagging push-pull created indecision within me, thought about Dad's last bottle sitting on a cabinet shelf an easy reach away. Fuck. Fuck. Fuck. I drank down the cold coffee, left the house, drove to town.

Don looked up from a pile of paperwork as I walked in. "Affairs of the heart," he said. "A divorce. My least favorite thing to do. Pour yourself a cup of coffee and sit down." He drew a sigh. "What's up?"

"No coffee for me, just a question."

"Shoot."

"Is there an AA meeting on the island?"

He raised his brows, put the papers he held on the desk. "This can wait. Talk to me."

"I'm confused."

He nodded. "You should be."

"Yeah, I suppose. I'm hoping somebody can help me sort it out."

He nodded. "First thing, you need to finish with your dad. You need to say goodbye and let him go. Until you do, he'll bog you down. He wouldn't want that and you don't need it. So make your plan and get it done. Second—yes, there is a meeting, but you may want to go to the mainland because the meeting here is only twice a week, and it's three days until the next one. I'll leave that up to you. Third, what are your future plans?"

"Don't have any. I think about this and that, but I end up like a dog chasing its tail."

"It's time to decide some things. Consider yourself lucky because you can pretty much do whatever you wish. My suggestion? Settle here a while. It's not a bad place, and you've been at loose ends a very long time. Dropping anchor will be a good change, and this is a good place to do it, trust me on that. Now—it's nearly noon; I'm starving. Let's get some chow."

We left the office, crossed the semi-busy street, walked into the lunchtime crowded restaurant, took the last two vacant side-by-side seats at the counter. As we sat midst the clamber and smells of it I felt the coil spring in my belly unwind by one click.

* * * * *

On a clear morning, Inky and I gave Dad back to the world. We each took a turn scattering his ashes. A light breeze carried him over sweet grass and clover, he disappeared to become a dusty memory, another of the tiny electrical storms I carried in my brain. We did it with laughter, the thing most lacking in his life, gave him that as a final gift before he left our hands.

* * * * *

I stirred coals to restart the kitchen fire, cooked coffee while Inky got Dad's last bottle from the cabinet and poured himself a generous slug. The coffee pot rattled. I put two mugs on the table, filled them to the brim. Inky took a slurp, burned his lip. "Goddamn. Goddamn. Just the way I like it, kiddo.

I sat, drew in a breath, thought about lighting a smoke, decided against it, sighed. "I remember Dad sitting in this chair almost every night with his nose buried in a book."

"That's how he learnt his stuff. Weren't no Rhodes Scholar for sure, but if he wanted to know something, by golly, he knowed where to find it. I was teaching him to weld when we first got the shop. End of the day, he went to the library, got a couple books on it. Few days later he showed me things I never seen before. That's how he was. Probably be president a some company somewhere if booze didn't take him." He shook his head. "Seems a pity, don't it?"

"Don't think he'd of wanted that. I remember him talking about educated idiots, about how if you didn't work in the trades you were nothing. He was a tough motherfucker. Don't think a suit and tie would have worked for him." I smiled, shook my head. "Think he wanted me to be a tough motherfucker, too. Maybe that's what all the fighting was about." I scoffed. "Maybe he succeeded. Seems my whole life has been nothing but fight, fuck, or go for your gun. Honestly, I don't know how I made it this far." I shook out a cigarette, offered the pack to Inky; he waved it away. I snapped my Zippo, lit it, watched smoke curl up and away. "I got a letter from him when I was in the hospital. Goddamn, Inky, it pissed me off so bad. It was all stuff he made up. Stuff he said he remembered us doing, but nothing we ever did."

"Yeah, I believe it. He started living in his imagination, dreaming up stuff he wished he did. Damn, kiddo, you can't imagine how sad he was."

I couldn't sit with the feelings, got up, refilled our cups, hoped to break the mood. "How'd you do it Inky? You had bad times too, but you're a happy guy. How'd you come out of it smelling like a rose?"

"I come back from the war full of problems same's most fellas. Lived day-by-day with them a long damn time feeling things was never going to get better. One morning I was down sitting on the old dock feeling pretty sorrowful. Watched the sun come up over the mountains, wind blowing hard gusts. Suited my mood perfect. Noticed the gulls. Watched them because of my love for flying. They was beautiful to watch, twisting and turning in the air, having a grand old time, just following the wind currents. Was almost effortless because they had true faith the currents was going to carry them where they wanted. Only took a tiny twitch of a wing to stay going that way. Picked up my spirits seeing their freedom. Seemed like it was all because they was willing to trust. Interesting too, because the same currents could crush them like an egg if they fought against it. Something clicked for me. Figured maybe them same currents was running through my life. If they could help them gulls have good times, they might could help me too. So little by little I started letting them winds carry me whichever way they wanted, and by golly it seemed to work. More I give in to them, the happier I become. Trusting them just like the gulls, pretty soon I was soaring, feeling like a happy kid. That was a lot of years ago. So far they ain't steered me wrong. That's best I can tell you." He looked up at the clock. "Well, day's passing. Need to get on back down the hill."

"I'll give you a lift."

"Nah. I'll walk it."

$$* * * * *$$

Rain fell. In the dark, with a broken windshield wiper, I splashed and rumbled down the hill. To my surprise, Donna Ingstrom stood at the backdoor of the church. "Welcome, it's good to see you." To my further surprise, Don Kellogg cooked coffee in a big electric pot while a baker's dozen sat at tables arranged in an open square, all strangers to me except a couple oldsters I felt I should know. I looked for an inconspicuous place to sit; a familiar faced Filipino gent gave me a knowing smile, extended his hand to be shaken. "Long time no see, Thomas."

"I'm sorry?"

"It's me, Eric. Have a seat next to me."

I remembered picking currents in his father's fields, took the offered hand, sat.

A gavel came down, the meeting commenced. It followed the routine of most with readings and things said by those needing to say them, and most all included a brief welcome to the stranger in the room and an invitation to keep coming back. After it finished, everybody milled about and chatted.

Don flicked the lights on and off. "Time to close up."

Donna approached me. "How 'bout you and me go for some coffee?"

"Cars not running right. Maybe another time."

* * * * *

Next morning, no rain, broken clouds, wet firewood, I decided to drive to the fu-fu coffee shack, an egalitarian place that catered to Prole and Patrician, and stood on the exact spot where old Toby slouched away his hours. With the morning crowd still in place, I had to search for an empty chair under the patriotic canvas awning, found one next to a wiry guy who sat rolling a smoke. He wore wispy Chinaman chin whiskers and styled his hair in a clotted mass of dreadnoughts. "Morning," I said. "Name's Goldie."

"Tucker." He extended a hand, shook mine in a semi-interested way. "You new to the island?"

"Yeah, for a second time."

"Interesting way to put it. Back from the wars, are you?"

"Yep. Lived here as a kid. My dad died last week, so I came back to take care of things."

A black man in bib overalls interrupted. "Somebody here got makin's?"

Tucker handed him a cloth bag of tobacco and papers.

"Who's this white fella? Don' recognize 'im."

"A newbie."

The man stuck out a callused hand to be shaken. "Call me Arthur. What do I call you?"

"Goldie."

"Goldie, huh. Well, ain't that precious. Whatcha do?"

"Nothing right now."

"If you can drive a nail, I got work."

Tucker pointed at him with his chin. "He's one of the finest carpenters on the island."

With the smoke made, Arthur said, "How 'bout a light? Anybody got a light?" With that satisfied, he got his coffee and went on his way.

Tucker turned his attention back to me. "Who was your dad?"

"Everybody called him Stosh."

"You're shittin' me. I knew him well. Drank beer at the tavern with him sometimes. So he died? I'm sorry to hear that. He was a hell of a guy."

"Yeah. That's what everybody tells me."

"I heard about you, too. Weren't you some kind of flyboy?"

"Kind of."

"Yeah, yeah, yeah. That was it. He talked about you all the time. Feel like I already know you a little. You come to stay?"

"For a while. At least till things get sorted out."

"Story of my life, man. Story of my life."

We sat a while sipping coffee. He broke silence. "So what do you do, Goldie?"

"Good question. Right now I don't have a clue."

"Understood. Well, don't worry. It'll come."

I finished the last of my coffee. "Got to go."

"Where you off to?"

"Town. Got to buy a couple things for my car."

"Can I hook a ride?"

"Sure."

He stood, picked up a sturdy bamboo cane I hadn't noticed, walked to the car with a limp. As I drove, our conversation ambled comfortably here and there. He got out at Center, a half click from the high school and across the road from where a sawmill once carved out lumber. I drove on to the auto parts store at the south end of town next to what my memory said was the Methodist Church which stood reincarnated as an antique store, bought what I needed, dropped in on Don Kellogg who sat at his desk sorting through the usual desperate heap of papers.

"Same filing system I use," I said.

"Oh, not to worry, I know right where everything is." He shuffled the heap left side to right, and back again. "Lois says I need a secretary, but as you can plainly see, I don't."

"Had coffee this morning with a guy named Tucker."

"Tucker? Oh yeah. Good guy. Straight shooter. Former Green Beret. Served a couple tours in Vietnam. Speaks the lingo along with a couple others the Army taught him."

"That where he got the game leg?"

"It's an artificial leg. Ask him. He'll tell you all about it. He's a painter. A gallery on the mainland handles his work. Pretty happy fellow, considering. By the way, I received your dad's death certificate yesterday. I put the insurance letter in the mail. You should be hearing from them soon."

I left his office, crossed the street, headed to the Alibi for a late breakfast.

* * * * *

The Kit-Kat-Klock Dad won on a tavern punchboard decades before hung from a nail high on the kitchen wall. It rolled its eyeballs left and right, while wagging its tail with the whir-click rhythm of time. Its sound reminded me of the clackity-clack rhythm of the small, one-lunged fishing boats that once populated the Sound. It also reminded me of the late hour. I had quit smoking a week before; heebie-jeebies still clung tight and pushed sleep away, so I sat at the table and scribbled away in the notebook I called *The Gospel According To Thomas*.

Earlier that night, I read part of a book in the small collection hidden away on a shelf in Dad's closet like cheap pornography titled, *On the Road*, written by a screwball named Kerouac. What a strange thing for Dad to have such a book.

In my own teen years, back when everybody wanted to be beboppers, one had to possess a copy of it, as well as sunglasses and a loose, lip-hanging cigarette to act out its vibe in the best possible way within the limited confines of rube island culture. I too tried to be cool, stole cigarettes from Dad's shirt pocket late at night, worked away reading a borrowed library copy though I didn't get beyond a few tens of pages because of the chore of it. Things were different this time. This time Kerouac grabbed me by the short hairs and pulled me along his trail of broken verbiage with the amazing way he flowed words and with how he crammed so many thoughts into a single breath. I imagined Dad sitting in this same chair, late night, reading it, the hot crackle-snap of synapses popping in intense electro-chemical storms inside his crania.

I first read pages he had dog-eared, searched for specific truths he found in its bebop rhythm, but couldn't. Started again at the beginning and read page by page. As I did, all the things of importance from the dog-eared pages were revealed. It brought to mind Dad before things became vile between us, when he told me of his hoboing days while we two worked building his particular brand of perfection into the cedar-post-four-strand-barbed-wire-fence that had surrounded the luscious pasture. In reading the book, I saw Dad all over it. Pictured him on dark-crescent-moon nights sitting cross-legged in front of the economical warmth of a fire built from twigs, spooning sizzling hot pork and beans from a tin can into his mouth with bare fingers while sucking air through his teeth to keep from burning his tongue, and in daylight hours, hitchhiking down near deserted two lane black top roads, sometimes scrubbing groddy pots and pans at the back of a greasy-spoon roadside restaurant for a sit-down meal. It reminded me of Franklin Freeman and the stories he told of peace found sleeping in open fields in the middle of nowhere to the ethereal sounds of far off barking dogs. I imagined Dad experiencing the same and realized how close they were without ever knowing. All those things came to mind as I read the book. And in the end, I realized what a perfect fit for Dad it was.

* * * * *

I sat with Tucker at the fu-fu coffee shack sucking down a big cup of their fine brew while he breathed in the smoke from a slightly bent cigarette. "Don't remember much of it," he said. "One minute I was there, next I wasn't. Woke up in the hospital at Kashini Barracks bandaged head to toe, hurting like a sonofabitch. While I was knocked out, surgeons trimmed up what was left of my leg and plucked a hundred or so pieces of shrapnel from my body. Kashini was a drab, god-awful place. Choked the life out of me with its spit-shine regular-army bullshit. Woke to nurses flirting here and there while they passed out meds. After morning chow, the docs made their rounds poking and prodding and scribbling notes on charts. When they examined me, I had to listen to the same daily bullshit about how lucky I was to still have a working knee. Finally told them to go fuck themselves, I'd trade places with them in a heartbeat. Thought about suicide, but the staff was wise to those ideas and kept us under close watch. Kept us busy making clay pots and leather purses. I grudgingly did a little, but I'm not a pot or purse kind of guy.

"One afternoon a Japanese National named Wada-San started coming in to teach painting classes. I thought what the hell, it's got to be better than what I was doing, so I sat around with four or five others slopping paint, secretly feeling foolish. But as time went on, a strange thing happened. I started feeling intention. The same kind of intention I felt before everything went down the rabbit hole. The feeling grew more and more intense until it took over my whole being. All thoughts of suicide disappeared."

He stopped talking to concentrate on crafting a new smoke. In the absence of words, I watched his fingers form shredded tobacco and paper into a workable cigarette while hoping we would become friends. He lit the smoke. "Well—time to go. Got things to do."

"You don't have a car?"

"Nope. Don't need the expense."

"How do you get around?"

"I depend on the kindness of strangers."

"Come on. I'll give you a lift."

At his direction, I drove to his place; a modest single story house that sat behind a fence built of bicycle frames, beyond which lay a deep yard littered with concrete sculptures of every size and shape that grew from the ground like mutated mushrooms, a Mad Hatter's wet dream. Tucker climbed from the car, gave me a silent nod, walked his careful way through the gate and to his house without a backward look.

My stomach groused about the acidic coffee I had poured down my throat. Took a rambling drive hoping to mitigate the problem. Driving up Morgan Hill, I remembered the stripped down hot rod bicycle I had as a kid, and how I used gravity to make screaming, death defying flights down its steep slope and through the hard left hander at the base, whooshing a thousand mile an hour. Wind howled in my ears, tears streamed from my eyes, I hooted at the rush of it. At the bottom, when I ran out of gravity, it all went away and I became mortal again.

I pulled off the road, turned off the engine, sat awhile-just breathing, collected a few thoughts to organize into some kind of coherence. Wondered if Don had the answer. Wondered if I should hang around and figure out what to do rather than avoid the whole damn mess by moving on. Started the car, made a U-turn, headed for Franklin's place; felt trepidation as I drove. Parked at the edge of the road, fought through a tangle of bushes. The shack tilted to one side like a drunken sailor, door and window missing. I went around back, found the pump head gone too. Inside, his books lay like moldering corpses on the floor, I sighed, remembered what he told me about not having anything you couldn't walk away from in thirty seconds, sat cross-legged on the floor, wondered if he still lived; hung my head, grieved. Time passed—didn't know how much, but enough I decided. Stretched cramped legs, lurched to my feet, felt pangs of hunger, pointed the car toward the Alibi, drove.

At the counter sat Donna decked out in her waitress uniform waiting to start her shift. She gave me a comfortable smile. I took the empty stool next to her.

"Good to see you again, Thomas."

"Good to be seen."

The waitress behind the counter came with her indifferent pen and pad, gave me a canned smile.

"Eggs over easy. Wheat toast. Coffee."

She scribbled it down, brought a cup, poured coffee, went on about her business tossing smiles here and there. Donna and I chatted till the minute hand on the electric Coca Cola clock sang out the hour.

"Gotta go," she said. "How 'bout you meet me here later and we can talk a while."

* * * * *

Sat opposite Tucker in the depths of his minimalist studio while he put finishing flourishes on the manufacture of a cigarette. "Stosh was one of my first friends here. I moved because there were too many distractions on the mainland and because I was becoming quite serious about my work. Serious enough to pack and leave a discontented wife. Fortunately, I was acquainted with a well-established painter here named Edmund Sawyer. I moved on his recommendation. He even took me in until I got my feet on the ground. He passed several years ago. His wife moved back east to where her family was. Later the house burned down. Sheriff thought it was vandalism. A pity. It had a wonderful studio.

"Met Stosh at the tavern uptown. Talk between us was easy because under the skin we were the same, a couple used-up soldiers trying our best to make sense of it. We talked about things we carried around inside our heads. Sometimes it was too much to bear, so we got snot slinging drunk. That's pretty much how things were." He pulled back a moment to build another smoke. "Stosh believed happiness was ephemeral, undependable. He craved settled things. Things carved in stone. That's why he loved booze so much. It worked the same way every time." He talked on more about Dad, took a final pull from his cigarette—squashed it out in an ashtray, squinted against the smoke as he exhaled.

* * * * *

I drove by Sawyer's place; time had erased most of its ruins. I remembered as a kid, finding a nest of baby quail in the woods, their mother dead, killed by some small predator. Took them to the house, showed Mom. She had said, "Take them to Mister Sawyer. He'll know what to do."

I carried them to his house in a small pasteboard box. He said he had never seen live baby quail before—that he always had to guess at their true colors in his paintings, now he could get them right. 'Don't worry,' he had said. 'They're in good hands. Come back in a couple days and I'll have something special for you."

When I had returned, he presented me with a beautiful little watercolor painting of a nested baby quail framed and signed.

"I never give away my work, but I'm making an exception because I'm so happy you brought me the babies."

After that, he had called me on the phone a couple times a year to come cut the ivy back around the foundation of his house when it grew too close, paid me well. One time a neighbor kid wanted me to ask him if he could work too. I did. Mister Sawyer said, "No, absolutely not. When you hire one boy, you get one boy. When you hire two boys, you get half a boy." I hoped the painting he gave me would still be somewhere in the house, promised myself to look for it one day.

*　*　*　*　*

I shed my rain soaked jacket, opened the stovetop, stirred embers, laid in kindling to bring them back to life. When the kindling flared, I added a wedge of fir, watched till orange and yellow flames snapped and cracked, closed back the iron lid. Donna sat at the table watching me put together makings for coffee. My movements caused Modigliani shadows to be cast on the wall by the bright pool of yellow light radiating from a kerosene lantern that sat on the table. Lightning strikes punctuated raging darkness. Electricity had failed during the AA meeting. Don called quits. Donna and I decided to spend the rest of the evening chewing the fat. I waited for the heat of the stove to rise, to bring the coffee to a boil so we could whittle away the night in easy comfort. We yacked back forth till near dawn when the need for sleep compelled us to say goodbye.

I continued to sit in the company of the Kit Kat Klock while drinking dregs of stagnant coffee; baffled, wondered if in her departure some mysterious opportunity had slipped through my fingers. Hell, what did I know of women? They were never much of my life except in a cash-and-carry sort of way. The need for sleep vanished. I fell into ruminations. My mind spewed forth in a stream of disjointed images. Tucker told me that sometimes he couldn't find colors deep or dense enough to express what he felt. I understood he meant. Fuck it. Fuck it all. I rose from the chair, fed the stove, cooked breakfast, when finished, went upstairs to sleep away most of the day.

*　*　*　*　*

"A couple generations back a shrink wrote about suicide. He didn't write about why we do it, but why, considering the pain of living, we don't do it more often. I wondered myself, considering how most in this country lived a tedious sparrow's fart existence while prancing around in the latest fashions while allowing an army of slick, klepto fucks who'd steal your ancestors given the chance define who and what they are. What makes life so precious for them? I can tell you for sure why it's fucking precious to me."

Tucker and I sat on stools at the bar amidst the clamor and murmur of shadowy masculine voices, punctuated now and again by the clink of a glass as in subtle darkness; those around us took their pleasure.

"I was part of an Alpha-Team. In our camp we had a hundred or so Montagnard and Nung mercenaries. We liked Ike and Ike liked us. Called us his more-bang-for-the-buck-boys because we could do big things with little or nothing. Kennedy thought we were the best things since parboiled rice. Considered us water-walkers. Authorized us to wear the Green Beret—*Beret, Man's, Wool, Rifle Green, Army Shade 297*, after the regular army had banned it. We didn't consider ourselves part of that army. We were members of the United States Special Forces, an elite group. We didn't have time for regular army bullshit. That rubbed a lot of fat assed generals the wrong way. None of them thought well of us. Hell, even Moscow Radio called us degenerates.

"We worked *Hearts and Minds* stuff. Hard core humanitarian work deep in the boonies with isolated tribes you've never heard of. Humped in what we needed on our backs. Prided ourselves in helping to protect them from NVA and VC attacks. They liked us. Mothers trusted us with their babies. Fathers fought at our side.

"I was a Medic. My job was to keep everybody healthy and happy. Things didn't always go that way. When someone got hurt and they were still breathing when I got to them, I did my best to keep them going, didn't always succeed. Tore my heart out. I was imperfect, and that can't be in those circumstances. Anyway… In the end, I was hauled out after a mortar round slathered me with shrapnel. The boys took good care of me in the hustle-bustle of the moment. So you see, I can't let them down by dying cheap. That's why I bust my ass doing what I do. Goddamnit Goldie, you have to get moving. You have to search your soul and find something worthwhile or you'll end up dying on the cheap. I see that in you. I see you as just another slow suicide like your old man." He tossed down the last of his beer. "Come on champ, let's blow this dump."

* * * * *

The sun shone as a mere brightening at the edge of a bleak overcast sky, early silence broken only by my footfalls and the shamble of rocks I kicked ahead. I walked a slow measured gait. Time to move on. Time to pack my trash and get out. Why not? A check for fifty-grand lay on the kitchen table. I could disappear. Nobody would be the wiser. Goddamn podunk place meant nothing to me.

Inky was dead. He died late the night before while I slept cozy. He telephoned for help, but it came too late. That ended things for me… Everybody gone… Every fucking important soul gone… Made me want to curl up in a ball and disappear, to buy a gun and blow my goddamn brains out. Dirty Bob said it right that morning at the scuzzy Hole in the Wall Bar when he said none of it mattered. It didn't matter. It absolutely did not.

Maybe I should take a walk and never stop—walk the whole perimeter of Earth, do it again and again till I tire, toss a rock, live where it lands, live naked, sleep on gravel, eat sand, drink salt water, wait for God-As-I-Understand-Him to send a message in a bottle telling me what to do next, and defy *Him* with gusto and big hallelujahs. Shout, *YOU* mean nothing to me… Away with *YOU*… I am sick of the diseased soul *YOU* inflicted on me… Sick of life full of nothing but sound and fury.

I left the road, found a small patch of bare loam hidden under a thick copse of alders, laid down. Rain began to fall in a heavy clatter that ricocheted through leaves and branches and spatted the ground like spent shrapnel. My eyes grew heavy; I slept, my mind wended through a treacherous dreamscape of curves and switchbacks that led to a chilled-to-the-bone waking. I rose to my feet, allowed rain to fall full on my face, to wash it clean, walked back to the road and on to the house, stripped, toweled life back into my body, felt pangs of hunger, stirred up the kitchen fire, cooked breakfast, ate it down, cleaned up the mess, slouched back in Dad's chair, rested my naked feet on the table, listened to the snap-crack of fire, hoped the sound would ease my mind.

Spent the day feeding the fire. As the room began to fall into darkness, I went outside to cut wood, thoughts of a hermit's life long gone. I no longer wanted to be alone. I wanted to escape to some bright place full of noise, of rank humanity, I carried the cut wood inside, stacked it on the floor, back outside, cranked up my sorry assed car, aimed it toward town. Its muffin sized engine sputtered and chugged along the way through a thin veil of fog without a murmur of complaint. In spite of my dark mind, a spark of gratitude for that faithful little machine lit me up. Caused me to think of other things in my life—small things, things that were spared little time or attention.

* * * * *

I fell into ruminations as I drove. When they occupied the full of my mind, I pulled to the side of the road, shut off the engine, became lost in my sparrow fart existence—and holy shit, how did that come to be that way? Headlights lit my rear view mirror, a spotlight blinded me to what sat behind, heard the crunch of footsteps, a metallic tap on the side window, a deputy sheriff put the beam of his flashlight on my face as I rolled it down.

"Is there a problem?"

I squinted up at the vague outline of his face. "No."

"Waiting for someone?"

"No."

He scrutinized me. "Been drinking?"

"Been thinking."

"Problems?"

"Death in the family."

"Sorry to hear that."

"Me too."

"Any open booze in the car?" He swung his bright beam around, searching the interior.

"No."

"I need you to move. It's a narrow unlighted road. Somebody's liable to rear end you."

"Yes, sir," I said, with military politeness.

"Have a good night." He returned to his car, drove on.

I sat in the wilderness another minute, stymied, forgetting what purpose I had started with. It struck me that when all else fails, hot chow is the answer, something Freddy preached the whole time I knew him. I cranked up the beast, drove to the highway, followed it to the Alibi, stood next to the garish jukebox while it cranked out some tepid fifty's June-Moon-Swoon rock-and-roll waiting for an open seat at the counter. Somebody left. I sat elbow to elbow with other human beings waiting for one of the harried waitress to free herself and take my order.

Two waitresses worked behind the counter, both dressed in spandy, starched white with greenhouse flowers pinned to their collars. They darted here and there, speaking their waitressing lingo with "*Hon*" this and "*Hon*" that, and in the ruckus, scribbled orders, carried thick crockery plates heavy laden with food, and cleared away the wreckage of the past while pocketing loose change tips. One sat a glass of water in front of me.

"Know what you want, *Hon*?"

I ordered, and while I waited, watched people come and go in hope of seeing somebody who smacked of familiarity, but all were strangers to my eye. Chow came. I dug in.

Meal finished, I thought how good a smoke would taste, gave the cigarette machine a long romantic look, but I had put that behind me, so I hoped. A feminine voice said my name. I turned, there stood Donna—her day's work done. She took the empty stool next to me, put a hand on my shoulder. "You look so lonely."

"Hard day."

"Whatcha doin' tonight?"

"Got no plans."

"Well, come with me. It's no good for you to be alone."

I followed her taillights to a proper little bungalow a couple clicks north of town. Inside, she turned on a lamp. Everything smacked of lace, fine smells, and softness. We sat a long while at her dining room table in dim light drinking coffee from small cups; spoke few words. When it became very late, she said, "You don't have to go…"

* * * * *

The stream of words that had flowed free onto the pages of the notebook came to a halt. Tried to find my way back into it. Couldn't. The only thing I remembered of what I wrote were the last words Grandpa spoke to me. "Love is the most important thing you have in life. Learnt that the hard way. Turned my back on your momma when she needed me most. Cruelest thing I ever did."

I wondered how the delusional twists of energy we call memory came to be. How a transient thought caused a conflagration that consumed everything in its path. Was it just scattered conjuring percolating down through the silt of a cluttered mind? My thoughts rambled with their own direction and purpose to the time I stood in front of the bathroom mirror holding a naked razor blade trying to work up courage to slash my face, to disfigure myself, to show in some visible way the invisible pain I felt. Disappointed because I couldn't, I put the blade aside and walked away from the mirror knowing myself to be a coward.

I flashed to a recurring dream of being submerged in pitch-black water with every molecule of breath snatched away, eyeballs squashed flat into my skull, desperate. Did insanity live in my mind? I grew frantic, got up, paced. Freddy Flitter's patented Goldie-You're-A-Dumb-Fuck laugh rang in my ears, so real it made hair on the back of my neck stand. I looked high and low for him, heard his mocking voice. "What weak-assed shit this is."

I spoke aloud. "I know. But it's the best I've got. It's just too fucking confusing."

He laughed again, switched to his loving father voice. "Settle down, Goldie. Go easy. You're just fine. It'll work itself out. Build a fire. Cook some chow. You never do well on an empty stomach. You know that."

I felt the room empty itself of him. After eating, I carried a cup of coffee outside to watch a fresh day's sunrise; waited to feel better knowing Freddy always to be right.

* * * * *

"Stop right there," said Tucker. "That's enough. I've heard all this before. Take it someplace else. I've got work to do. You need to be doing something with your time besides screwing Donna and moping down your trail of tears. Get to work; figure out your reason for existing on this planet. Go on. Get out of here. Come back when you've got something worthwhile to say."

I gnashed the car's gears, drove away thinking what the hell does he know. Sorry I bothered. Thought we were friends. Just needed a little understanding. Was that too much to ask? In the midst of that fine thinking a solution came. I drove a beeline, intending to snuggle into Donna's infinite depth and forget all the tiresome stuff.

* * * * *

We sat on the couch facing each other. "Look," she said. "We need to talk. This thing between us has been going on long enough without being defined. So here it is, I want a committed relationship. Unless that's what you want, we have to stop seeing each other."

I gnashed gears; drove to the house, slumped in Dad's chair, fulminated while fondling a fifty thousand dollar check, held it up to the light, studied the watermark, more than enough to take me away from this turmoil. After all, I had serious thoughts of leaving anyway, but not the foggiest idea where to go. I decided to give Tucker another try. He surprised me with a cordial greeting. "Come on, let's go. You're buying lunch."

"Lunch where?"

"The Alibi. Where else is there?"

"Not such a hot idea."

"Why not?"

"Donna's on the warpath. Pissed her off big time. She's looking for a hubby. Told her it wasn't me."

"Had to happen."

"Like, you knew?"

"It was a pretty easy guess. Actually, I'm surprised it took this long. She's a hard luck lady. Makes bad choices."

"So—I'm one of her bad choices?"

"Aren't you?"

That silenced me.

"Don't spend time worrying about it. She'll move on."

At the Alibi, we took our ease in a half round booth and waited for chow. Donna came through the door decked out for work. Passed by without seeing.

"See? She's already forgotten."

Food came, the waitress left, he said, "So now what?"

"Don't know. I was five minutes from packing my trash and getting out of here. Thought maybe I'd head back to California."

"Yeah? What made you change your mind?"

"Haven't."

"You're pretty good at that. Always considering this and considering that but never doing any of it. At least none I've seen. Thinking isn't doing. Trying isn't doing. Doing is doing. Seems like you want to continue to live life on the cheap. If that's the case, stop whining and do it. Go on back to California. But I can tell you, it's a bad idea. You won't find what you're looking for. You'll get there, and after some time passes, your friends'll get sick of listening to you whine, things'll stop being warm and fuzzy, and it'll be time to move again."

"Shit. Just what the hell should I do?"

"Stick here awhile. Stay off the hooch no matter how sweet its promises. Deal with what's in front of you. Christ, you know all that. Frankly, I'm about out of patience. You've become a huge pain in the ass."

"That's what Freddy used to say."

"Who's Freddy?"

"Somebody I knew."

"Sounds like a bright guy."

"The brightest. But he's long gone."

"Bothers you doesn't it? I hear it in your voice."

"Yeah…"

"Something you did?"

"Something I did."

* * * * *

The phone rang. I answered. Don Kellogg's voice said, "Where on earth have you been? Haven't seen you at meetings. Haven't seen you in town. Haven't seen you anywhere. I'm concerned. What's up?"

"It's a private thing, Don."

"Private? That's another word for secret. You don't have any room in your life for secrets. Come to dinner tonight. We'll talk. Lois wants to see you too, so we can kill two birds with one stone. Six o'clock. Be there."

* * * * *

When dinner finished, Don said, "So what's the deal? What's going on?"

"Donna gave me the boot. Figured I should steer clear a while."

"That's it? That's what's keeping you away? It's old news. Already been hashed and rehashed. This is a small community; remember? Very little escapes notice."

"Yeah, but I don't think I can sit through a meeting with her giving me the evil eye."

Lois laughed. "My god, Thomas, you're afraid of that frail little woman?"

"Nothing frail about her."

"She's not going to mug you after the meeting."

"Mostly, it's embarrassing."

"Yeah," said Don, "People dying in droves everyday from too much embarrassment. No one's dying from too much booze. Good thinking, Thomas. Show up tomorrow night. No guts, no glory."

"Will she be there?"

He scoffed. "You really think you're important enough to keep her away?"

* * * * *

I rejoined that cluster of people. My pulse jumped as Donna sent a chaste smile my way, crossed the room, kissed my cheek. "You can run, but you can't hide."

Eric came forward and shook my hand as the gavel sounded to start the meeting. As it passed, I felt relieved to be surrounded by necessary truths and people who lived them to the best of their ability. When the meeting finished, Eric clapped me on the shoulder. "Let's go get some coffee. There's something I want to talk to you about."

* * * * *

We sat at the counter, coffee in front of us. "My dad was in the navy when the war started. A Steward's Mate. Took care of officers. Wiped their asses, stuff like that. After the war he brought mom and me to live in Hawaii until he finished his time in the service. We moved here because good land was cheap. My brothers were born here. We still have a big family back in the Philippines. They're farmers too. I've been planning a trip to meet up with them. It's something that's become important to me. I was wondering if you'd consider coming along. It'll be a great time. I'm setting it up for next month."

"Philippines huh? Why me?"

"I'm a little nervous about it. You've been all over hell and back so you pretty much know the ropes."

"That's true I suppose. To a point, anyway. As far as the Philippines go, I've been to Manila and a couple provinces, but that was a long time ago. Really, I spent most of my time hanging around the bar town outside Subic. It wasn't anything but hucksters, hookers, and thieves. No place I'd take a friend. I can tell you, none of the Filipinos from the ship ever hung around there. They'd all put in for a few days leave, and soon as we tied up, they boogied down the after-brow with their diddy bags and we didn't see them again till it was time to pull out. If you're looking for a tour guide you're looking at the wrong guy."

"I'm not looking for a tour guide, Thomas. Family members will meet me at the airport. Everything's arranged."

"You should take your brothers."

"Neither one wants to go."

"So, you got to the bottom of your list of possibilities and there I was?"

"No. It's not like that at all. I was going to ask you even if my brothers wanted to go. I just think the trip will be better with you along. Honestly, it'll be a big help to me if you do. Think about it, please."

"Sure Eric, I'll give it some thought."

* * * * *

"Come on in," said Tucker, "Come watch me work. Not something I normally do, but I have a reason."

He sat on a backless stool in front of a blank canvas, started painting a seascape glowing with sunlight, paused a moment, went back to painting, with a few quick brush strokes he changed the entire character of the scene into a roiling storm, a few more strokes, back again to sunny. It mesmerized me as he moved the painting back and forth like time-laps photography. He did it over and over. With each evolution he brought subtle changes as if visiting it on different days or different years. "There's beauty in what I do. Can you see that?"

I nodded.

"There's beauty in the written word, too. I know you scribble all the time. Have you found any beauty in it? Have you even tried? I think it can bring you salvation in the way painting's brought mine.

219

That's no small thing. Bring something you've written. Bring me one of your notebooks."

"I don't write for anybody to read. Don't even read them myself. I just write till one's full, get a new one and start again."

"How many do you have?"

"A couple dozen."

"You can spare one."

"But they have no purpose. None of it's worth reading."

"Oh? Then why do you bother? Why do you put time and effort into the writing if it's worthless?"

"Don't know. Never thought about it."

"Think about it right now. Tell me why you write. I've told you why I paint. Told you how it started. You know about me. It's your turn in the barrel. Tell me, why do you write?"

I bit my lip.

"If you can't tell me why you write, tell me how you started."

"A friend got me started, but in a small way it started aboard ship. I was no good at card playing, so I read a lot. You have to do something to settle your mind before you sleep. Sometimes I got tired of reading, or ran out of books, so I'd write a little about what happened that day. Seemed to work. Also, there were people I wanted to remember, so I wrote about them. Then after I got out, I became friends with a writer. He pushed me to do more."

"What do you write about now?"

"Memories. At least things as I remember them. Don't know how accurate any of it is. It's just the way they come to mind. Sometimes it helps when I have the blues. Sometimes it soothes me like it did when I was aboard ship, especially now that I can't drink myself into a coma anymore. Feels like the only thing I've got left where telling lies doesn't matter. Somehow that keeps me hooked up with the real world. Sounds pretty stupid I know, but that's it in a nutshell."

"You're wrong if you think that sounds stupid. That's what any artist would say. We search for truth in what we see. Doesn't always match up with what the rest of the world sees. That doesn't matter because for us it's truth, and all of it, every bit of it, is good when done for the right reasons. People think Van Gogh painted the way he did because he was insane. They're mistaken. Painting was the way he stayed connected with what sanity he had. He was most sane when he painted and knew it. He painted the truth he saw. Look Goldie, there's really no difference in what we do. The process is the same. Painters… Dancers… Actors… Writers… We're all the same, all digging deep inside ourselves to find our version of truth. Studs Terkle was asked why he wrote about the seamy side of Chicago life. He said he was searching for roses in the garbage. Think about that Goldie, roses in the garbage. It's the only medicine that can move us through a life less ordinary. I've known you a while. It's time to cut the bullshit. I want to see your writing, and I want to see it soon."

* * * * *

I delivered a notebook like a hit-and-run driver, spent the rest of it ruminating about what he would say. Played his imaginary monologue on an endless loop inside my head, waited, waited. Time became a cyclone of torture. I concluded that I was a bullshit artist plain and simple, something Dirty Bob figured out long ago. So too had fucking Freddy Flitter. I wanted to call Tucker, tell him not to read a single goddamn word because the notebook held no art, not one speck or it, it just held rambled, scrambled bullshit, and not even good bullshit. Besides, he had no business reading my private stuff. I thought about all the other notebooks I had filled with gobbledygook. New to sobriety, I had been advised by a sponsor to burn them to ash. "It's the smart thing to do. Part of moving away from the past and turning over a new leaf." It shocked me. What a fucked up idea. The whole of my life lived in those goddamn notebooks. They were the only honest things about me. I was custodian, responsible for their care. How funny I would defend them in such a way. After that, I stopped writing—fell into despair for thinking I would even consider their destruction. They were the only proof I had of the magnificent human beings who had peopled my life. But fuck, I had to escape. Where would I go? Eric. Eric. Eric. Hell's Bells, none of it mattered anyway because I was going to PI and maybe never coming back.

I decided to call Tucker, tell him I was leaving forever, that he could keep the notebook as a memento of our phenomenal friendship. But goddamnit, that wasn't the answer either. Maybe I should call him, ask what the exact solution was. But no, no more questions for him. I needed to think it through on my own, wanted to go with answers instead of questions.

Anyway… Gawd-a-mighty… There I sat, writing out all the shit that was going through my noggin in minute detail to the electric rhythm of the Kit Kat Klock. I carved words hard into the paper as if with chisel and hammer. A river of ink curved and slanted and worried its way from the deepest parts of my mind. When the river worked its way to its end, I felt relief for accomplishing some finished thing as if there were meaning and purpose behind it… As if it were something meant to be done… I began to see what I had written as a single thread… A single strand in a woven whole… A fragment of truth seen through my own eyes.

* * * * *

A week passed without word from Tucker. I decided to hell with him. I rode the ferry to the mainland, found the number for a typewriter repair shop in the phone book, called, asked if they had any used ones for sale. "Yeah," said a woman's voice. Drove to the address, found it to be a tiny corner shop run by a woman dressed in mechanic's coveralls who repaired typewriters, sewing machines, and vacuum cleaners. Inside her shop shelves were heaped to saturation with bits and pieces of machinery.

When she caught me looking, she said, "It's not as disorganized as it appears. I can reach out and put my hand right on anything I need. You the one that called about the typewriter?"

"Uh-huh."

"Well, I've got a fine old IBM Electric in the back all tuned up and ready to go. Want to have a look?"

"Sure."

The machine rested on a high shelf, big as a slab of beef, just like the one Rivas whacked on *clackity-clack*. I loved it instantly.

"Want to try it?" I nodded. She hefted it down, carried it to the counter, plugged it in, ratcheted in a piece of paper.

Two fingered, I typed, *THe quick brown fix humps over the...*

"You type like Columbus," she said. "First you spot it, then you land on it."

"Yeah, it's going to take some getting used to."

"You'll get better. Want it?"

"Yeah."

I paid thirty dollars cash, she wrote a receipt. "I guarantee it working for sixty days long as you don't drop kick it across the room."

"Thanks a lot. I'll see how it goes."

She gave me a sweet smile. I left her shop. Lugged the machine to the car.

* * * * *

Laid cedar kindling and cut wood in the firebox of the stove, lit the underlying newspaper, watched till it caught well, replaced the iron lid, listened to the crackle. The room warmed. Wind swayed tree branches worried the roof. Rain fell. On the table sat the typewriter. When I hit the hair-trigger keys, it whacked letters onto paper with a hurky-jerky clackity-clack so erratic it had no beat—no underlying rhythm. Each time I hit the return key, the carriage slammed home so hard it jarred the table. It made for slow work, heavy laden with errors, sometimes enough to make the page near unreadable, but I sat, dogged, seeking the Philosopher's Stone, that single magic thing that would turn everything it touched precious. My mind rambled on and on, and in that fashion found its way to Inky and to all the grand warrior tales he told that now fell incomplete. I thought of my own generation, about how we were suckered into a war that turned out to be such a pathetic and myopic thing, eighty-seven thousand gone, poof, in a cloud of smoke. And now? Nobody cared. Yeah, for me that was the truth of it. Maybe for Inky too. I hated he had ceased to exist, that writing the unspoken parts of his stories would all be guesswork, but hoped with time I could dope it all out. Even so, I would never know for certain.

I pressed on till my brain hurt. At the end, with several pages laid to the side. I had figured out why so many writers drank heavy. Long before, I had read the kindest wish a Buddhist can have is that their loved ones die first because it is they who will suffer and mourn, not the loved ones. It made odd sense to me, but goddamnit, I had already mourned enough for two lifetimes. I thought there might be some justice served by my own death whenever that came. It felt as though I had already lived too long. I could see my death; I had visualized it so many times it had become like old furniture in a familiar room. I had lived it, so to speak. Looked down at the husk that was me. Watched carrion scrabble for it. Watched the remainder rot to dust. Wondered if there was anything to experience in it. Some claimed so. Something. Echoes. A freeing. But those who claimed that held nothing more than wispy beliefs. Buddhists said it wasn't the end, that you go round and round till you get it right. That meant I had a long road ahead. In the end, I hoped nobody missed me, that they just kept busy doing whatever they were doing.

*****

The phone rang. Don Kellogg said into my ear, "Thomas, I need you in my office ASAP. We have unfinished business." I got to town just in time to see him closing up for lunch. He pointed with his chin toward the restaurant. While we waited for our food he said, "Sometimes I feel you're running away from all of this. You haven't cashed the insurance check yet."

"Don't need it. I'm fine for money."

"Must be nice to be a rich millionaire."

"Quit smoking and you'll find out."

"Seriously, the insurance company is upset. Open an account at the bank. Get the check deposited. Have you given any thought to the future? Any thought at all?"

"Eric's asking me going to PI with him."

"There's a whole host of things to deal with here. The guys at the machine shop are feeling in limbo. They're interested in buying the place. Would you consider an offer?"

224

"Thought it belonged to Inky."

"The paperwork wasn't finished when he passed."

"I know nothing about running it. Be happy to give it away."

"Don't be foolish. Lois will be handle the deal for you."

"Never owned much more than a full sea bag before. Now I got all this fucking property. Thought it was supposed to be a blessing, but really it's a pain in the ass."

"It's called responsibility."

"Shit."

* * * * *

I sat at the bar nursing a coke. Tucker, on the other side of tipsy, sat next to me trying to build a cigarette. Things weren't going well. He looked to me for help; I shook my head. He gave up. "Story of my life, Goldie. Maybe I'm not the high and tight motherfucker I think I am."

I signaled the bartender. "Give him a pack of Camels."

Tucker opened them, shook one out, lit it, inhaled, greedy for smoke. "It's good shit you're writing, Goldie. Good shit. Don't stop. Don't let anything get in your way."

* * * * *

Eric and I sat at the counter eating French fries while a lone waitress migrated her way to the kitchen to sneak a smoke with the cook.

"So… You going to make the trip with me?"

"Yeah."

"You have a passport?"

"Got a passport."

"Good. I'm planning our departure for the fifteenth. That gives you two weeks to get ready."

"Kick the tire and light the fire, Eric. We can leave tonight if you want. Just let me know what the ticket costs."

"Don't worry about that, Goldie. It's on me."

"Oh no, no, no, Eric. Not going to happen. I'm not going to leach off you. I've got money. I'm paying my own way. That's how it has to be. I won't argue. Just let me know how much and I'll give you the cash."

"I'm sorry…"

"I'm not offended. Not at all. Your generosity touches me, but I've got to pay my own way in this world or I'll sink like a damn rock. It's just has to be that way."

"Yeah, I understand. We'll split the sheet."

"All of it."

"Cool. That'll work fine."

* * * * *

I caught the ferry to the mainland, drove to the typewriter shop. The woman looked up. "Trouble with the machine?"

"Oh no. Works like a charm. A real dream machine. Getting ready to travel. Need something I can carry with me."

"I'm taking a break right now. Been a hectic morning. Going next door for coffee. Come on. I'll buy."

A Cambodian woman looked up from her magazine, gave a big smile. "Hello," she said. "Who your friend?"

"Donno. He's a mysterious stranger. Never told me his name. You know how them mysterious strangers are." They both laughed.

I flushed. "Goldie. Most call me Goldie."

"Short for Goldman, I bet."

"Yeah, short for Goldman."

She turned to the woman and in a small squeaky voice said, "His name is Goldie. He's my best customer, so treat him right." She turned back to me. "Get what you like *Goldman*."

I flushed again. "Just a small coffee."

"Come on *Goldman*, go for it. Live dangerously for a change."

"Okay. Give me an apple fritter too."

"That's my man."

"Hell, I don't know your name either."

"Never thought of asking?"

"Huh-uh."

"Well, ask."

I scoffed. "What's your name?"

"Faye. My name is Faye." I extended my hand; she took it. "Were you in the service?"

"Yeah, Navy. Aviation."

"That's crazy, so was I. A tech. Fixed ARC-27s."

"Boy, this is crazy. I was a tech, too."

"Where were you stationed?"

"USS Neverdock mostly. I was a tailhook sailor."

"Med or Westpac?"

"Westpac."

"Ever get to Cubi Point?"

"Spent half my life there."

"That's where I was. Did my time and got out. Wasn't for me. Got real tired of being cruised by boys and *girls*. I look a little butch so a lot of assumptions get made."

I laughed. "That's funny because it was something that popped into my mind when I first saw you."

"Happens a lot. You said you were traveling. Where you going?"

"I've got a friend, Filipino-American. Wants to meet his family in PI. Asked me to tag along. Can't lug that big machine, so I was hoping you had something smaller."

"I have several on the shelf. Nicest one's an Olivetti. Almost brand new. Little expensive though. Don't know what your budget is, but if you can handle the price, it's the one I'd recommend."

"I can probably manage it."

"We'll have a look when we finish up here." She paused to sip her coffee. "So Goldie, what's your situation? You married, or what?"

I scoffed again. "Or what mostly. Never tried it. Never been settled enough."

"Yeah, I know the type. Is it anything you ever think about?"

"Nah, not really. Figure I've inflicted myself on enough women. Just doesn't seem to be in my blood."

"I'm of the same mind. Seems like a lot of work for a little pay off. Guess you could say I'm married to the shop."

The inside of her shop looked the same as before. She took down the small machine. "I have a hard case for it too. I'm asking seventy-five, but I'll knock off ten bucks and throw in a couple ribbons."

"That'll be fine."

"When you leaving."

"Middle of the month."

"Look me up when you get back. We can shoot the breeze again. You know my hours."

"Count on it."

She came outside with me. As I drove away, she waved and threw a kiss.

* * * * *

Inky once told me, "Make life too comfortable and you forget you're wearing it." I sat whamming the hair-trigger-keys of the IBM, searching for words to describe the world I knew…and waited… Waited to travel back to my beloved Asia. A phone ring interrupted my reverie. Don Kellogg talked into my ear. "Come to dinner tonight. Steak and green salad. I know you can't resist. Lois has the figures on the shop. You need to go over them and get the deal closed before you leave."

* * * * *

We ate by the light of six candles. The steaks were thick and blood rare, the salad fresh and crisp, the figures on the shop, enormous to my eyes. After things were discussed and settled we toasted life with sparkling cider in tall fluted glasses and hurrahed this and hurrahed that till our voices grew hoarse.

I left with Lois' words in my mind. "Beauty doesn't exist without us. It's not an intrinsic thing, but something we impart upon that which we love. It can even reside in dangerous things such as the finely honed edge of a polished steel blade. Once found, it must never be lost."

I drove home overwhelmed by the generosity of Dad and Inky and others who had peopled my life. Thought of another thing Inky said, "When they throw stones, throw bread in return."

For my whole goddamn lifetime I had carried bitter anger in my gut as though it were a badge of honor. How stupid and unnecessary. Thought again of standing in front of the mirror wanting to disfigure myself, remembered what brought it about. I stood, cornered by three classmates at school over some unforgivable faux pas I had committed. One stepped forward, I swung a fist, split the skin over his cheekbone open, created a bloody mess. There were angry phone calls, doctor's bills, harsh words from Dad.

And the day came when the risk to remain tight in a bud was more painful than the risk it took to blossom.

—Anais Nin

I putted down the hill, found Tucker slouched in a chair at the coffee shack sucking smoke from the nub of a cigarette. "Get yourself a cup. It's on me," he said.

"No, no, no, I'm paying my own way this morning."

"Don't give me any shit, I sold a painting yesterday. I'm flush with cash."

"Well you're about to get flusher because you're selling another one today." I laughed at the befuddled expression on his face.

He tugged his chin whiskers. "You know someone who wants to buy a painting?"

"Hell yes. I want to buy one of your damn paintings."

"Don't jerk my chain, fuckstick."

I pulled a wad of hundred dollar bills from my pocket, smacked it down on the table.

"Shit, you are serious."

"Like a fucking nightmare. Let's talk business."

He looked at me, took in a breath, exhaled. "Okay."

"Before we start haggling, I have to tell you, I'm so grateful for what you've given me,"

He scoffed. "What have I given you?"

"Understanding. Art, A new way of seeing things."

"You always had it. All I did was show you where it was hidden."

"It means everything to me."

"Then it was worth my time."

"I want one of your paintings hanging in my house. Want it there so I don't forget."

"Hell's bells, I'll give you a painting."

"No. Buying it is a way I can pay back a little bit of what I owe you. Please, let me do it that way."

"I understand."

VII

Buy the ticket, take the ride

—Hunter S. Thompson

Manila traffic, a rolling barrage of vehicles of all configurations and sizes, ran inches apart in a continuous undulating snake with no visible end, lane markers meaningless. As we drove, I watched kamikaze incursions of bicycles, pedestrians, and hucksters who strolled in casual haste through the morass hawking newspapers, bottled water and cigarettes. Eric sat in front next to his Aunt Tess yacking away in Tagalog. As he spoke, his Uncle Larry drove the way to their city place in San Mateo Rizal. I sat in the backseat getting uncomfortable looks from their two young daughters who were not accustomed to sitting next to a big ugly white guy. A cop flagged us down for some middling offence. Middling because every seasoned traveler knew traffic laws in Manila are vague and ill enforced. A bribe was haggled and we went our way.

Next morning, with hardly time to rub the sleep from my eyes, we were on our way and out of the city, driving the two-lane national highway, heading for Isabela Province. After several hours on the road we came to a small town. "This is Cauayan," said Tess. "It's the last town before Gamu and the barrio of Lenzon. We'll arrive within an hour."

Larry drove on. We passed a motorcycle attached to a sidecar carrying a boar hog with testicles the size of soccer balls, passed an army base, came to Gamu Rural High School, turned onto a narrow dirt swathe barely wide enough to accommodate the van. Low bushes scrapped its sides as we followed a slow moving wagon pulled by a caribou with a six-foot span of horns. Tess said, "This is the barrio of Lenzon." Toward us came a motorcycle with a sidecar carrying passengers, the Yellow Cab of the Philippines. Larry squeezed far to the side to let it pass. Ahead, land opened into rice paddies where men and women bent to their work. Caribou and Brahmas grazed. Chickens made suicidal dashes across the road. Beyond the fields sat a cluster of houses built from all manner of material.

Barking dogs heralded our arrival. In front of their house a crowd of expectant greeters waited. Small children, upon seeing me, shied away and clung to their mother's legs, an elderly woman stroked my cheek with gnarled fingers, teenage girls jabbered behind their hands. We passed through a gate into the courtyard, chairs were brought out; we sat in the shade wetting our whistles with ice-cold soda pops amid the hubbub. I felt uncomfortable with the focused attention, but as time wore on, the feeling diminished. They began to leave in ones and twos. Tiredness set in, but I didn't think the heat would permit sleep.

Upstairs Eric and I lay on mats with an oscillating electric at our feet. I drifted into dreamland; woke sometime after dark with mosquitoes thrumming my ears. Eric was gone. I rose, went down stairs, everybody sat at the dining table. I took the empty chair next to the daughters. The table held platters of pork adobo, roast chicken, pig ears cooked in sweet tangy sauce, green vegetables and rice, I chowed down like a starving animal. Later, Eric and I rolled out our mats again with intentions of sleep.

Jet lag kicked in. "Man," I said. "Haven't gone through this in a long damn time."

"First time for me."

Sweat burned my eyes. "Hotter than hell."

"Think you can sleep?"

A symphony of mosquitoes dined on my ears. "Don't know. How about you?"

"Don't think so."

The effort of talking took too much so we lay quiet avoiding unnecessary movement as air from the fan swept over us. Sleep did come, but seemed to last only minutes. I woke sprawled on my back, pools of sweat collected in my eye sockets. Eric woke too. Without words, we rolled up our mats and joined everybody breakfasting on coffee and sweet pandesal.

On the road that fronted the house, field workers walked to the rice fields carrying bolos with wicked curved blades. "When harvesting rice, they work for a share," said Larry, "At the end of the day you'll see them carrying their share home. To many, it's more important than money."

Lumbering wagons, with large wheels crafted of wood and pulled by placid Caribous, creaked their way past. A plethora of dollar-down-dollar-a-week motorbikes scatted gnat-like to and fro chased by woofing dogs with ambitious natures.

Sweat beaded on my forehead and trickled into my eyes. The daughters brought a small towel for my use. I watched the sun ascended its invisible Jacob's Ladder. Heat became intense. Memories came of how I had worked hard, dangerous hours on a carrier's flight deck under the rays of the same broiling sun. "You'll grow accustomed as time passes," said Tess. Yes, I will grow accustomed.

* * * * *

Work in the fields finished around noon. Tired men and women chatted amiably as they walked in clusters to their homes bearing their share of day's harvest in cloth bags balanced atop their heads. They bathed with cold well water, put on fresh clothes and prepared themselves for what followed. The smells of wood smoke and cooking came along with the clack of mahjong tiles, voices rose in conversation, children clambered for attention, men led caribou to the river for a cooling bath while others opened bags of rice along the edge of the road and spread their contents evenly over its hot surface to dry. Scraping sounds of long handled wood paddles sounded as they turned the rice over and over.

Eric and I walked with Tess and her two daughters across the road to visit a partially finished two-story house built of rough concrete blocks. "It's the house of my niece, Grecy. She's building it for her family. She works in the Middle East as a domestic servant to earn the money for it. She's coming home tomorrow with the money she earned to continue. Things are done here a little at a time and with great patience."

Evening, towering thunderheads gathered on the eastern horizon and moved westward. As light diminished, they flashed on and off like gigantic neon tubes with internal discharges of lightning, air cooled, mosquitoes came, nobody seemed to notice except Eric and me. By the time we went inside I had a dozen or more tormenting bites at my ankles. With time, the itching subsided and I could think of other things, like how tired my body felt, but how awake my mind was. I felt cranky, churlish. Next morning, we were going to mass. I was nervous because I had never been inside a church. A million thoughts, all directionless, intruded. I slept in fragments.

* * * * *

"What do I do?"

"Just be respectful," said Tess, "That's enough."

The mass took place in a four hundred year old Portuguese church built of a million naked bricks that was flanked by a graceful tower that could no longer tolerate the weight of bells. The mass felt convoluted, a confusing thing full of mysteries. "The priest is Belgian," said Tess. "He's been here for many years. He speaks Tagalog, our dialect of Ibanag and several others." He shook my hand and left. Outside, people crowded around. I again became an involuntary celebrity itching to be on my way.

* * * * *

Eric and I took a walk along the road that defined the perimeter of the barrio. At its farthest reach, we scrambled down a steep dirt footpath that led to the river, watched as men laved water over the giant humped backs of caribou. The river had ripples of current showing toward the middle and washed cool and pleasant over my feet. I waded toward the caribou. They sniffed the air, snorted their disgust, moved away. The men laughed, I shook my head, smiled.

Lunch had been set. The rest of the afternoon, we sat in the shade and relaxed. Clouds again billowed from the east. When it began to cool. I went upstairs, sat in a rattan chair in front of my sweet little Olivetti, whanged away trying to turn everything I saw and felt into a coherent memory.

* * * * *

Later that day, Tess' niece came home from the Middle East amid much ado. A crowd gathered at the unfinished house for talk, laughter, and food. Oh, so much food. A whole pig roasted on a spit, dishes of poultry, fish and vegetables, along with huge kettles of rice, sweet tropical fruits, and liquor for the men. Everybody ate with their fingers in the way of South East Asians.

She stood not five feet in height, ink black hair hung to her waist, her face oval shaped, smile dimpled. "So you are the Americano." She held my gaze till shyness forced me to turn away.

* * * * *

Rain thrummed the roof and cooled the night air. I lay restless to see her again, scared out of my wits, understanding none of it.

* * * * *

Next morning, Larry left to drive back to Manila. The following day, he would fly to Singapore to resume engineering duties aboard a merchant vessel. As we sat in the shade, Tess explained. "Few opportunities exist here in the barrio as in much of the country, even for the well educated. It is, as you see, a poor place. Because opportunities are so few, anyone with big dreams has to support them by doing menial labor in foreign countries and using their earned money to accomplish those dreams. My niece works overseas as a nanny because she dreams of building permanent house for her family. She's been away for two years. It is, of course, a great sacrifice, but it's such a loving thing for her to do."

It saddened me to be in a place where people worked so hard but had so little. I had a difficult time writing that night, it clashed with what I knew of the Philippines from before, so different from the squalid fast money shuffle of Olongapo City.

* * * * *

I saw construction had started. Men worked mixing concrete and adding to the height of the second story walls. Grecy walked my way, sat down beside me. One by one, everybody got up and made their way into the house.

She spoke, "Your name is Goldie?"

"Actually, it's Thomas."

"Thomas," she said. "Thomas. I like that name very much. I'm called Grecy."

"I know."

"I'm sorry. I don't mean to impose myself."

"I'm not used to being around ladies like you."

"Because you were a sailor?"

"You know about that?"

"Of course. My Uncle Larry is also a sailor."

"A different kind."

"In what way?"

"I was US Navy. We lived much cruder lives."

"Aunt Tess speaks well of you."

"She hasn't known me long."

"Have you done shameful things?"

"Yes."

"Are you doing shameful things today?"

"No."

"Then that's who you are today. Your past is your past."

I sighed. "Wish it were that simple."

"It is."

* * * * *

I got out the Olivetti. Typed a personal manifesto full of proud declarations I would never keep. Heard footfalls on the stairs. Grecy came, sat cross-legged on the floor beside me. "I don't care about your past, I only care about what you are today and tomorrow. When I look at you, I see a good heart. I see someone I'd like to know better. You don't have to tell me anything you don't want me to hear. Just think about it and remember what I'm telling you. If you'd like to know me better, come find me. I won't be hiding." She rose to her feet, kissed my cheek, left.

I wondered if it could be so simple. I must have sat a long time because Eric came looking for me. I pulled the paper from the typewriter, tore it to shreds. We went outside, walked the perimeter of the barrio.

I heaved a sigh. "Is there something wrong here?"

"Everything's fine. I think a good thing's happening. Don't screw it up."

I fought inside my head with the too good to be true situation. Those things didn't happen to me. As we walked, sweat beaded on my forehead. I wiped it away with the edge of my tee shirt, it beaded again, everything at that moment a frustration.

Eric put his hand on my shoulder. "You don't have to decide everything today. She'll be here tomorrow."

* * * * *

I lay thinking about it that night, woke Eric. "Sorry to bother you."

"It's okay."

"It's like a dream. I'm afraid it'll go away like a puff of smoke."

"Only if you want it to."

"God, I need a cigarette."

"Think it'll help?"

"No, but it'd give me something to do."

"Where you going to get one? No one in this house smokes."

"It's just something that sounds comfortable. Something besides laying here going nuts."

"Damn Thomas, you make it so complicated."

"It is—isn't it?"

"Nope."

I picked up a pencil stub that lay next to the typewriter, held it between my teeth like a cigarette.

"Does it help?"

"Hell no. Not one damn bit."

"Go to sleep. You need your strength for tomorrow."

"What's going to happen tomorrow?"

"How the hell should I know? I'm not a damn fortuneteller. Shut up and go to sleep."

* * * * *

I scrambled down the slope leading to the cornfields, the place we were to meet, saw Grecy with the morning sun at her back. She wore her hair drawn up off her neck, twice folded upon itself and held in place with a silver clasp. She greeted me with a smile, took my hand. We walked to the edge of the river, sat in wild grass, watched the water amble northward. She rose, walked out into a still pool, sat fully clothed in the shallow water. "Come. It's very pleasant." As we sat, she loosed her hair, leaned back, allowed the water to fan it out. "Do you swim?"

"Yes."

"Once, when I was young, we went here swimming. I was caught in a powerful current and dragged under. Father just managed to grab my arm. If he hadn't, I would've drowned. Since then I've been afraid to go into deep water, but I want to with you. Will you come with me? Will you stay beside me if I do?"

"Of course."

We waded out till the water lifted us from our feet; she swam fluid strokes beside me. I reached out, pulled her into an embrace. We kissed.

Our clothes dried as we climbed the path leading to the road. I felt as if it were a dream, as if none of it had really happened.

* * * * *

Days passed. Too soon our time finished. We were preparing for a nighttime bus trip to Manila. Before our goodbyes, Grecy said, "Mail here is slow and unreliable. When you write, send it to Aunt Tess's address in Manila. She'll be able to get it to me faster."

"I'll write every day."

"Don't be silly. You can't write every day."

"Often then."

"Don't say it unless you mean to do it."

"Often."

"Often is fine."

We parted with long kisses. I left the Olivetti in her keeping for my return. Two days passed in Manila. Erick and I climbed aboard the flight home. At altitude the sky sparkled, the ocean lay vast, near featureless. I remembered the thrilling newness of flying on my first TransPac aboard a combat aircraft long before it all went wrong. We lifted off from Atsugi amid the overpowering scream of engines and tooth rattling vibrations. The instant the gear clunked up and locked, Mount Fuji came to view as a solitary island nestled on an ocean of clouds. Soon, we were out over a seamless blue ocean broken only by the white wakes of lonely merchant vessels, all of it new, keen to my eyes, but now looking down upon it only brought loneliness. Eric's brothers met us at SeaTac. I sat quiet in one corner of the backseat while they yacked with him on the drive to the island. I returned to the empty house and to summerlike weather with no need for a fire in the stove.

* * * * *

With a cold iron stove, I drank my morning beverage at the coffee shack, filled time yacking artsy-fartsy stuff with Tucker, ate meals at the Alibi. Went to meetings. Eric, my new great and good friend, became too chatty with his continual 'Let's get coffee' mantra. I had to plan my escapes, to scoot before the final handholding prayer, crank up the car, get out of town so I could sit in the private of night with the whirr-click of the Kit Kat Klock and the clackity-clack of the IBM. I wrote more about my times in the Philippines back in the old days when I was a pup, and about my time with Grecy, attempting to rebuild memories the best way I knew. Though pages piled up, I felt no satisfaction. On impulse one morning, instead of going to the coffee shack, I drove to the ferry dock, rode to the mainland and drove on to the typewriter repair shop thinking it would be good to talk with Faye, feeling certain she would listen to everything without laughing and bring her wisdom to the matter. The place stood dark, locked up tight. I went next door to the donut shop--everything looked the same as before, kids played, the Cambodian woman read her magazine.

"Is Faye around?"

She looked up at me in a peculiar way. "Faye no more."

"What do you mean Faye no more?"

"Terrible. Terrible."

"What's terrible?"

"Terrible crash. She killed terrible crash. Drunk driver knock her down right there." She pointed out to the street in front of the shop. "Terrible. Terrible." Tears welled in her eyes, kids stopped playing, her husband came from the back, wiped his hands on a towel, stood blankly beside her. "Terrible. Terrible," she said, as if her English were reduced to that a single word.

My knees felt watery, I sat, the husband drew a cup of coffee, put it in front of me. Though knowing Faye only a little, I felt deep loss.

My god, what will become of her little shop with no one to cherish it? Will it pass into indifferent hands and all so precious to her become accumulated junk to be disposed of?

I sat while the coffee cooled, couldn't in politeness drink it as if doing so would finalize her death.

The only words I could say, "I'm so sorry. I'm so sorry."

Drove back to the ferry dock, returned to the island, to the vast emptiness of the house, wrote a long letter to Grecy writing:

'Please…Please be careful…Please don't take any unnecessary risks… Please stay well so I can be with you again…'

Went to the new concrete and chromium post office in town missing all that could be missed about the old one in the ville fronted with Doric columns, mailed the letter, drove to the Alibi hoping to find only strangers, put four quarters in the jukebox to hear Hank Williams croon a buck's worth of loneliness. So it was.

* * * * *

I marched time to the beat of an incompetent drummer counting days till something…something… Put manic energy into writing; wrote and rewrote till my fingers hurt and pages said exactly what I wanted them to say. It became my salvation—put rhyme and reason to everything. I fought a sleep filled with ghostly dreams of those lost to me, food became unimportant; over time I grew wan. Don worried about me as if I were his prized poodle. I insisted things were fine; I was in waiting, waiting for some sign of her… I spent three nights writing about Faye, about the uniqueness she bore, about her *art* and the void she left behind. I wrote too of a Navy Chief who tired of my bullshit once when I was still a kid and ordered me to fill a bucket to the brim with water and dip out a double handful. 'Look at the hole you left behind.' 'There is none,' I said. 'Yep. And that's the true measure of your importance in this world.'

I rambled about how the universe held only the illusion of stability and safety, how once realized and digested, much of what we possess becomes refuse to be cleared away because we have only room to carry necessary things, how I must live every day as if it were the Alpha and the Omega, that in death, everything disappeared because not even memories traveled to that side of infinity.

I told Tucker what I had discovered one morning as we sat at the coffee shack. "Goldie," he said. "You have a magnificent grasp for the obvious." I didn't tell him Dirty Bob had spoken the same words to me in the past.

In sleep, dreams pulled in eerie directions, confronted me with eyeless, waxen-faced beings. Hairless mole-like creatures that scrabbled at me from deep jagged crevasses, blinding me by dearth of light. To avoid the dreams, I slept little as possible, filled the hours with writing. Words became a snare that bound me to their needs. They came at me from unknowable places. At their end, they cast me aside as if I were of no further use. I sat like a stringless marionette, inert till the Kit Kat Klock brought me back to my own existence. Muscles ached. Eyeballs burned. I thought about the joy of smoking several king sized cigarettes.

* * * * *

I drank down the last dregs of coffee, remembered Bill's actions. How now they made perfect sense. Wrote about how he traveled back through time and space to reach out, to touch things tangible only to him, how his ears heard the overpowering mêlée of battle when he served in France as part of the segregated 15th Infantry Regiment, and fought one-hundred-ninety-one days straight of trench combat, the most of any US unit, that they were the most decorated and held in awe by the French who called them Hell Fighters. I imagined he was gone from this world. Imagined his tortured soul at peace. Maybe returning to the soil would be the only way any of us ever find that.

I opened a random notebook, found forgotten thoughts of Freddy Flitter and Dirty Bob put down when I lived in Abe's Tire Shop. Wrote the rest of the night about our war and the implacable sadness it carried.

* * * * *

I checked the mailbox. Found an envelope inked with my name in Grecy's neat hand, started to rip it open to get to the nugget, forced myself to slow down for fear of damaging the precious contents; read it standing in the middle of the road oblivious to traffic, read it a second time savoring her words:

Dearest Thomas,

First and foremost I send my love and affection and my strong wish for your happiness and good health. I'm fine and still feeling the joy of knowing you. I have some good news. There's work for me in Hong Kong. I signed a one-year contract with a Dutch family to care for their two young sons. I met with them in Manila. They're wonderful people. I'll be very happy working for them. It'll be a good thing for us too my dear, because they told me Hong Kong mail service is fast and reliable and we can even talk on the phone occasionally. When I get there I'll send you all the information you need to contact me. Please don't write until you receive my next letter. I miss you so much. Though we had only a little time together, I feel that I know you well. In spite of the thoughts you have about yourself, you are a good man, a man I hope to spend my lifetime knowing. Please take good care of yourself and wait for my letter from Hong Kong. With all my love, Grecy

Insanely hungry, desperate for company, I loaded aboard the car; drove to Tucker's place, pounded on his front door, there was no answer. Not satisfied, I pounded more.

Tucker opened it, peered out with a baleful look. "I might have known. Look… I'm in the middle of work. What do you want?"

"Sorry man. I got carried away. Got something to show you."

"Come back later." He closed the door.

Chastened, I drove to the Alibi. Found the place near empty. Don Kellogg sat in a booth eating while he shuffled through a stack of papers, a couple others sat at the counter. I slammed myself into the seat across from him. "Thank God you're here."

Epilogue

There's day and night, brother, both sweet things; sun, moon and stars, brother, all sweet things; there's likewise a wind on the heath. Life's very sweet, brother, who would wish to die?

—George Barrow

I lay awake listening to distant barking dogs, to voices of women chatting at the well behind the house while working the wheezy clickity-clack pump to draw water for their daily needs. When I first woke, I heard a man sing pure and sweet as he led his caribou to the field. Days begin early and finish when heat is full upon the land. Grecy lay next to me still in deep slumber, her belly great with child. Our third. I will hold yet another being while it learns to smile at the sight of my face. I am in the depths of love.

The dream visited again during the night. I didn't wake. Seems even my unconscious mind knows it for what it is. It involves boozing, something I did well for a long while. In the dream I felt the unbearable shame of some unremembered act, the kind that had become typical of me, and waited for consequences. I often thought of suicide during those times. There was only me, no one else to consider, but there didn't seem to be any guarantee of success, and no defense if botched. It would become another failure to add to the list. Perhaps the one most remembered, and I would be in some hospital ward permanently hooked up to beeping machines—kept alive for no good reason. I had reached my bottom, which meant one of two things: either I had lost everything, or was about to lose the only precious thing left. For me it was the later.

They hyped sobriety as a new beginning, something to be marked on the calendar with great fanfare. That seemed irrelevant for me; it seemed nothing more than a dry continuation of things as they were, a meaningless existence where hours and minutes ground through bone and marrow. The true beginning came after I became an older man. Some might say too old for the wonders given me. Maybe so. But it's not for them to decide, nor for me. So—confronted with a new day, I kiss Grecy's back, get out of the bed, dress, leave the room.

Downstairs, twin daughters await me, beautiful like their mother. Sweet Grecy carried both inside her tiny body and delivered them up into the world without complaint. Their skin is the color of Café-au-late, eyes near dark as their jet-black hair. They wait to sit with me while I drink my first coffee to be entertained by tales of being a child in America. Most days are spent with them on the front porch of the house Grecy and I built. Later, there will be more coffee together, and we will break our fast with bread and fruit while watching the children play. People will come throughout the day, some to ask if there is work to be had, or if we can do them a small favor. Others, just to yack about this or that. All are welcome.

Animals surround the house. They roam free. There are ducks, geese, turkeys and chickens of all shapes and sizes. I watch them with great interest; follow their exploits as some follow their favorite soap operas. There are mothers, fathers and children. Mothers march about proudly leading their broods. Fathers strut the sidelines talking sports and world events while hoping to find a good time at some point during the day. In one of the broods lived a tiny yellow chick with a withered leg. I watch its progress. It did just fine in the conga line formed up behind the mother and chugged along learning to earn its living on one foot. As time passed, it developed a comb and waddle and other features of a rooster. With that, things turned problematic. Like all males, he wanted that special something that comes with loss of innocence. Finding a willing hen, he wooed her and at the right moment, mounted, only to fall over. The disappointed hen shrieked her disapproval and scampered off leaving him alone and unfulfilled. He never gave up. Never. A revelation for me. Determination—the secret of a successful life. Eventually, he made a fine dinner.

A publisher liked the story I had whanged out and every month sends a check. I still whang on the Olivetti Faye sold me. Still miss her. The big IBM Electric Typewriter sits on the kitchen table sharing the old house on the island with the Kit Kat Klock. We visit sometimes. Don Kellogg has moved on to his final destination. Lois still lives. She misses him terribly. Grecy spends time with her when we are there. Lois treats her like the daughter she has become. Eric is farming his father's land. He continues to be my great and good friend and has visited the barrio twice. Donna has given up her search for Mister Right. A permanent sadness has settled over her. The twice a week meeting lives, the younger generation taking it over. That's the way it's supposed to be. I meet with Tucker at the fu-fu coffee shack. He still wears dreadnoughts and Chinaman chin whiskers. We yack on and on about the alleged importance of art and how it saved our lives. Grecy has many nieces. I suggest Tucker travel to our place and meet some of them. Perhaps he will one day. Perhaps. Everything I could possibly want, I have. But that doesn't make life all beer and skittles. I think about my daughters and wonder if at sometime in the unknowable future they will be misused, as was my generation. Inky said every generation pays the price for the untrammeled ambitions of those in power. And in the end, there is never an apology for any of it… Not one single one… I still mourn…

この道や

行く人なしに

秋のくれ

This road
No one walks along it
Dusk in autumn

—**Matsuo Basho**